WHISTLING IN THE DARK

WHISTLING IN THE DARK

lesley kagen

NAL Accent
Published by New American Library, a division of
Penguin Group (USA) Inc., 375 Hudson Street,
New York, New York 10014, USA
Penguin Group (Canada), 90 Eglinton Avenue East, Suite 700, Toronto,
Ontario M4P 2Y3, Canada (a division of Pearson Penguin Canada Inc.)
Penguin Books Ltd., 80 Strand, London WC2R 0RL, England
Penguin Ireland, 25 St. Stephen's Green, Dublin 2,
Ireland (a division of Penguin Books Ltd.)
Penguin Group (Australia), 250 Camberwell Road, Camberwell, Victoria 3124,
Australia (a division of Pearson Australia Group Pty. Ltd.)
Penguin Books India Pvt. Ltd., 11 Community Centre, Panchsheel Park,
New Delhi-110 017, India
Penguin Group (NZ), 67 Apollo Drive, Rosemont, North Shore,
Auckland 1311, New Zealand (a division of Pearson New Zealand Ltd.)
Penguin Books (South Africa) (Pty.) Ltd., 24 Sturdee Avenue,
Rosebank, Johannesburg 2196, South Africa

Penguin Books Ltd., Registered Offices:
80 Strand, London WC2R 0RL, England

First published by New American Library,
a division of Penguin Group (USA) Inc.

ISBN-13:978-0-7394-8483-8

Set in Janson Text
Designed by Spring Hoteling

Printed in the United States of America

For my sisters

ACKNOWLEDGMENTS

From the bottom of my heart, thanks a million to:
Ellen Edwards, Molly Boyle, and all the other talented folks at NAL.
Bill Reiss, my agent extraordinaire.
Generous early readers Eileen, Eileen, Hope, Emily, Angela,
Nancy, Stephanie and Donna.
The ever-supportive Backspacers.
The always delicious Restaurant Hama.
Wise and wonderful Dr. Mike Lebow.
Pete, one heck of a first reader and a darn good kisser.
Casey and Riley, the reason for it all.
Je t'adore.

PROLOGUE

I never heard exactly who it was that found Sara Heine-mann's dead body over at the lagoon. But it was Willie O'Hara who told us that she was lying neatly on the grass between those rotting red rowboats you could rent for a dollar if you wanted to do a little fishing. Sara's pink undies were wrapped around her neck like a bow and she was naked. And some of her blond hair had been cut off just like Junie Pias-kowski's had the summer before.

Something like that wasn't supposed to happen on Vliet Street. But like Daddy always said . . . things can happen when you least expect them. Things that can change your whole life. How right he was. Because after they found Sara's body, it seemed like our nightly games of red light, green light and the Fourth of July parade and even cooling off in the Honey Creek on days so hot they'd curl the hair on the back of your neck might become part of the good old days that Granny always talked about. Because one dead girl was one thing. But two dead girls . . . everybody started wondering who would be next. Except for me. I knew I was next.

It was the summer of 1959. The summer I was ten. That summer on Vliet Street everyone started locking their doors.

CHAPTER ONE

The morning Mother told us she was sick, Troo and me were just laying in the lime summer grass, smelling the bleach comin' off the wash that jitterbugged on the line and getting ready to play that name game with her.

"It's important for you to understand who you're dealing with so you can know what to expect from them," Mother said, pulling another sheet out of the laundry basket. "You've got to remember that people are different in the city."

How could we forget? She musta told us this over a gabillion times since we moved to the house on Vliet Street. We were a mother and her three girls. And I supposed I had to count Hall, because that would be the charitable thing to do. Hall was Mother's husband. Her *third* husband.

Troo and me, we liked our own daddy better than Hall, but he died two summers ago after a car crash. He was on his way back home to the farm after a Milwaukee Braves game. Our uncle Paulie, who was riding shotgun, went through the windshield and got his brain damaged when he hit a fire hydrant so he had to go live with my Granny over on Fifty-ninth Street. Some man at his funeral called our daddy, Donny O'Malley, lush. I didn't know what that meant so I looked it up the next day in that big dictionary they had over at the library. *Lush* is an adjective that means luxurious. That man was right. My daddy *was* lush. Stuffed with lushness. Like a chocolate cake with chocolate filling and chocolate frosting.

Mother shook out the wet white sheet and said, "And one of the ways you can know what to expect from somebody is by knowing what country they originally came from. Right? People's last names can tell you just about everything you'll ever need to know about them."

Troo and me groaned because the name game was gettin' kinda old and was about as much fun as a splinter under your thumbnail, but Mother, she loved this name game even better than Chinese checkers.

"I don't have all day." Mother gave us her do-you-smell-dog-poop look, so Troo called out "Latour?" real quick.

Troo was gorgeous-looking. Red wavy hair that stopped at her shoulders and freckles across her nose only. And she had the kind of blue eyes that looked like the sky when it just woke up in the morning and hadn't turned that blue jean color it got later on in the day. Troo was thin except at her lips, which were poofy and made her look a little pouty all the time, which was true some of the time. And she had long fingers, which were good for playing the secondhand piano we had in the living room. Mother thought pianos made a family look high-class. Granny told me that piano business was a little stuck-up of her daughter since Mother grew up in Milwaukee just a few streets down from where we lived now. Right across the street from the Feelin' Good Cookie Factory, which was known far and wide for its chocolate chip cookies. (What Granny really said, because she was always sayin' stuff like this, was, "Helen should know by now that she can't make a silk purse out of a sow's ear.")

Mother cupped her hand around her ear, so Troo yelled louder, "Latour?"

Helen and Troo. "Two peas in a pod," Granny also always said. "Just look at 'em."

I didn't look like Troo. Or Mother. My eyes weren't blue like theirs. Mine were green and they sat under eyebrows that were almost invisible to the naked eye but had some bulkiness to them. I was not as tall as Troo even though she was younger than me. I had long legs but small feet and hands because I was born a month early. And I had no freckles on my face. Not one. But I had been told once or twice that I had darling dimples and nice thick blonde hair that Mother and Nell got in an argument over every morning when they tried to put it into one fat braid that went down my back. Nell was my other sister. But only a half of one. Nell's father was Mother's *first* husband, who she told me died of smelling ammonia.

Mother answered, "Latour is French." She took a little whiff of her wrist that I knew would smell like Evening in Paris, her favorite. "The French speak the language of love."

Troo wasn't even paying attention. She was lookin' over at our next-door neighbor's house and wondering if the stories we'd been hearing about the place were true. Because we were sisters born only ten months apart, which made us practically twins, her and me could have the mental telepathy that lets you read somebody else's mind even if they don't want you to, so I pretty much always knew what Troo was thinking. "Kenfield?" she hollered out.

"Kenfield is English," Mother said. "They like to keep a stiff upper lip. That means they don't like to show what they're feeling." She bent down to take another sheet out of the basket, and when she did her hair came undone from the white ribbon. I was always surprised by how long it was. And when the sun shined on it, even though it was red, you could see the gold hiding in it. I thought she was more beautiful than the movie star Maureen O'Hara. And so must the men on the block because they set their beer bottles down when she walked by and sometimes, if those beer bottles were all drunk up, they gave her a low wolf whistle she pretended not to hear.

Troo nudged me with her elbow and started giggling. "O'Malley."

Mother shook her finger and said, "Troo O'Malley, being silly never got anybody anywhere in life." But the corners of her mouth went up just a smidge to let us know that we were better than everybody else and not just potato heads or micks, as the kids on the block who were Italian and Polish and German liked to call us. We called them wops (loud, but great cooks) and Polacks (not so smart) and bohunks (thick-ankled), so I figured it all came out in the wash.

Somebody down the block yelled, "Ollie, Ollie, oxen free," and Little Richard singing "Tutti Frutti" drifted by out of a car radio. That's how it was on Vliet Street. Something lively was always going on. Except for dead Junie Piaskowski, who everyone on the block said was murdered and molested. Sara Heinemann hadn't been murdered and molested yet when Mother fastened the last clothespin on the line and said, "O'Malley sisters, come over here. I have something to tell you."

Of course, I let Troo sit next to Mother on the stone bench near the pink peony flowers that were falling all over themselves because I made my daddy a couple of promises before he died. And if there is one thing you're gonna get to know about me, it's that I was a girl who wouldn't break a promise even if her life depended on it.

Right when the sun was going behind the trees, Daddy made everybody else go out of the hospital room and asked me to come lie down next to him in his bed that he could make go up and down whenever he wanted.

"Sally?" He had all these tubes coming out of him. And next to him was a machine that *ping ping pinged* just like the submarine in that movie Troo and me had seen at the Uptown Theater called *20,000 Leagues Under the Sea.*

"Yes, Daddy?" He didn't look so much like himself anymore. His face was swelled up and he had cuts around his mouth and bits of blood that didn't seem to wash off. Also he had a big purple circle bruise from the steering wheel going into his chest. Something had collapsed in there, the old nurse said.

"You need to take care of Troo," Daddy said ever so quietly. His usually fluffy red-as-a-pile-of-fall-leaves hair came into points on his forehead. "You need to promise me that."

I patted his hand that felt smooth because the old nurse had just put some cream on it. "I promise. I'll take care of Troo. Cross my heart. But I gotta tell you something really important, I'm—"

"You have to tell Troo for me that it's okay," Daddy interrupted. "Tell her the crash wasn't her fault."

Troo was in the hospital too, down the hall from Daddy,

because she was also in the car when it ran into that big elm tree on Holly Road. Since she was sitting in the backseat, she didn't get as hurt as Daddy or Uncle Paulie. She just got a broken arm that ached sometimes now before it was gonna rain.

Daddy took in a breath like it was the hardest thing he'd ever done, and when he let it out he said, "And tell your mother that I forgive her for what she did. Promise?" Then he started coughing some more and a little pink spit came up onto his lips. "I'll be watching, Sally. Remember . . . things can happen when you least expect them so you always gotta be prepared. And pay attention to the details. The devil is in the details." Then Daddy went to sleep for a minute but woke up again and said, "And Nell is not the worst big sister in the world. There are one or two that're worse."

The old nurse came back into the room then and said Daddy was either delirious or hilarious. I couldn't quite catch it because she had a funny way of talking.

Troo's fault that Daddy was in the hospital? How could all this be Troo's fault? Troo couldn't drive a car, she was only seven years old! Oh, Daddy. And I had no idea what he wanted to forgive Mother for and why he couldn't tell her himself, but maybe it was because she was crazy with grief like the doctor said.

Even though Daddy had fallen asleep, I whispered, "Roger, wilco and out." That's how we always said good-bye to each other. Just like Penny said good-bye to her uncle Sky King when he was up in the clear blue of the western sky in his plane the *Songbird*. Daddy and me just adored that TV show, watched it together every single Saturday morning because Daddy was a pilot, too.

And then the old nurse said, "Visiting hours are over."

"But I gotta . . . ," I tried to say, but she shook her head in a way that I knew there'd be no gettin' around. What I wanted to tell him would have to wait until tomorrow. I put my hand on his whiskery chin and turned his face toward mine so I could give him a butterfly kiss on his cheek, because that was his absolute favorite, and then an Eskimo kiss on his nose because that was my absolute favorite.

Daddy's funeral was three days after I made him those promises. I never did get to tell him I was sorry.

CHAPTER TWO

Mother took me to go see Dr. Sullivan last summer when I started having real bad dreams about *The Creature from the Black Lagoon*. In this movie that took place in the Amazon area there was this creature who lived deep down in the water but would come up to get people whenever it wanted to. After Daddy died, I started thinking all the time about how the Creature could come for me or Troo or Nell or Mother, and what would we do if it did? We weren't strong. We just were not. And after we moved from our farm way out in the country into the city, to make matters even worse, the Washington Park *lagoon* was just three blocks away from our house. That's where they found Junie Piaskowski's dead body our first summer on Vliet Street. They never found the person who left her there all alone next to those red rowboats you could rent. And I couldn't believe that not one person thought it coulda been the Creature that had murdered Junie because that Creature had a lot of stick-to-itiveness. Look how much he had wanted that actress Julie Adams!

But sitting there in the doctor's office that smelled like shots, I reconsidered about that for a while, and finally said

WHISTLING IN THE DARK

to Dr. Sullivan, "Okay, maybe it wasn't the Creature who murdered Junie."

The doctor smiled and nodded his head.

"Because of those pink undies being tied around Junie's neck," I explained. "The Creature doesn't have very nice fingers and you'd need very nice fingers to tie undies around a girl's neck, wouldn't you?"

Dr. Sullivan made me swallow some cod-liver oil and then put his face right up close to mine, so close that the pores in his nose looked like the insides of an empty egg carton. "Sally O'Malley, you have what is known as an overactive imagination." His breath was warm and putrid, just like I imagined the Amazon would be. "That's not good. In fact"—he looked over at Mother and shook his head—"it just goes to prove once again that an idle mind is the devil's workshop. Have you been attending mass regularly?"

Him saying that didn't give me a lot of faith in Dr. Sullivan. Because he was so wrong. My mind was never idle. Never ever.

The noon whistle blew over at the cookie factory and I heard Mother say from far off, "Sally? Sally! Did you hear me?" in that tone she got to let you know she had better things to do.

"Sorry." Thinking about the Creature and Daddy like that, that was what Dr. Sullivan called a flight of the imagination, which was something I musta inherited from my Sky King.

Mother sighed one of her big sighs and said, "I have to

go to the hospital tomorrow to have an operation. My gall-bladder has to come out." She placed her hand below her right ribs. "And while I'm gone"—she pointed her finger at Troo—"I want you to work on your charitable works, and you"—she pointed at me—"get control of that imagination of yours or I'll take you back to the doctor."

Then she looked down at her hands and twirled the wedding ring that Hall had given her, which seemed like it hurt because she had a pained look on her face. With the bad luck Mother was having with her husbands, Troo and me figured that one of the reasons she had married Hall so fast after Daddy died was because he didn't look like he'd decease anytime soon, with his muscles and wavy Swedish hair and that tattoo on the top part of his arm that said MOTHER. Nell said that tattoo must have impressed the hell right out of Helen. And maybe it had right after Daddy died. But now Mother was stuck with Hall because if you were a Catholic you couldn't get a divorce unless you wanted to go straight to hell and burn for all eternity. If you were a Catholic, Granny said, the only thing you could do if you didn't want to be married anymore was to pray really hard for a certain shoe-selling louse to get run over by a bus on his way to work.

Mother got up off the bench and said in her sternest voice, "While I'm gone, the O'Malley sisters better mind their p's and q's, because when I come home, if I hear you gave anybody any trouble at all, I'll give you a spanking that you'll never forget." And then she walked away like she'd just remembered what that better thing was that she had to do.

I waited until the screen door slammed behind her and then I said to Troo, "She's probably gonna die just like

Daddy, don't you think?" I didn't used to worry a lot, but I started up after Daddy died and now it was something that I did almost all the time. Because if you coulda seen my daddy. He was strong and brave with big hands and black hairy arms and wide shoulders. He was never even sick, my Sky King. So that just shows you what can happen when you least expect it.

Troo was holding a chubby blade of grass up to her mouth and trying to make it do that kazoo sound you can get out of it sometimes. "Nah," she said. "She's not gonna die. Helen's too ornery to die."

Troo never worried and had hardly cried when Daddy died, which I thought was a little weird. Because although Daddy loved me very, very much, so much that I'd never forget him in a million years, he loved Troo just a little bit more. That hurt my feelings for a while, but when you had a sister like Troo, well, you just had to expect these things.

Troo was also right as rain about Mother. She wasn't ornery when Daddy was alive, but nowadays she was and I knew whose fault that was. So that night I planned to say extra prayers that Hall would forget to look both ways before he ran across North Avenue on his way to Shuster's Shoes because that would give Mother another chance at marrying someone else who didn't talk with his mouth full. If she came back from the hospital. Which she probably wouldn't. Like I said, I didn't have a lot of faith in Dr. Sullivan. His breath, and I'm sorry to have to say this, his breath alone could just about kill you.

CHAPTER THREE

Hall and Mother getting married was another perfect example of what could happen when you least expected it.

A month after Daddy died, we went to Milwaukee and brought flowers from the farm to put on his grave up at Holy Cross Cemetery, where Daddy was buried next to his daddy. I laid down in the grass next to him and didn't want to leave, but Mother told me to get up and quit making a cryin' scene or she'd make me regret I was born. Later, we had ham sandwiches and Ovaltine at Granny's. Troo washed and I dried, Nell changed the sheets on the beds, and Mother laid a piece of shirt cardboard down on the wobbly kitchen table. She used Granny's laundry pen to write out—For Sale. 525-6788.

When Troo asked Mother, "Why you making that sign?" Granny answered, "No life insurance."

Mother made her mouth look like a minus sign and started looking in the mess drawer for Scotch tape. (I already knew we were just about out of money because Mother kept it in her sock drawer, and when I put her laundry away that morning I noticed that sock was pretty flat.)

Troo and me followed Mother outside and watched

while she stuck the sign to the back window of our Plymouth. When the edges were all smoothed down to her liking, Mother jiggled her car keys above our heads and said, "O'Malley sisters, I'm taking you over to Shuster's for new school shoes." Uncle Paulie walked past us on the way to his job up at Jerbak's Beer 'n Bowl, and Troo muttered under her breath, "Thank God for small favors," which meant she was happy Uncle Paulie was leaving. Mother thought Troo was being thankful for the new shoes or she woulda said something to Troo about bad manners, even though she herself could hardly bring herself to say "Pass the mashed potatoes" to her own brother. Was that why Troo didn't like Uncle Paulie? Because Mother didn't?

"No matter how poor we are," Mother said, backing into the parking space in front of Shuster's Shoes up on North Avenue, "we still need shoes." She winked at us. "They're important to our souls." Troo and me were bustin' a gut but stopped real fast when a Mr. Hall Gustafson met us at the shoe store door and said in an overly friendly way, "And what can I do for you beautiful young ladies today?" He was smiling at Mother like a rabid dog and just about drooling when he slipped a pair of pumps on her pretty feet. She didn't seem to mind one bit.

Mother and Hall went out that night to a movie called *Vertigo* that starred Jimmy Stewart. On the ride back out to the farm, Mother told us all about the movie and how Jimmy was afraid of heights and he would get an attack if he went up too high. I remember worrying that maybe Mother had caught vertigo. That's how dizzy she sounded when she went on and on about Hall buying her popcorn and Jujubes and wasn't he the nicest guy?

After that, Hall started coming out to the farm for supper almost every night. He'd tell us about his days as a sailor and how many shoes he sold that day, gobs of Mother's tuna noodle casserole peeking out of his mouth. And he always burped so loud when he was done with dessert that Troo's old dog, Butchy, growled at him like he was a thunderstorm.

"Hear ye . . . hear ye. I've got an announcement to make," Hall said two months after their first date. Oleo was dripping off his chin.

We all quieted down, except Butchy was still growling.

"I have asked your mother to marry me," Hall said, grinning at Mother. His teeth were the same color as the oleo.

Nell and I were struck dumber than dirt, but Troo jumped up out of her chair and asked Mother in her best disgusted voice, "You didn't say yes, did you?"

Mother told Troo to sit back down and Hall said, "We're getting hitched next week and then we're all moving into the city."

Troo and me shouted like Siamese twins, "No!" We could not leave Daddy's fields. Nell didn't say anything. She just looked choked up.

Going on in a bossy voice, Hall said, "I'm gonna be your new father and what I say goes. You're movin' into the city. I got a dependable job at Shuster's and I already got us a place to live." Then he drained his beer bottle and smacked it down on the kitchen table and bent down right into Troo's face. "Don't you know children should be seen and not heard? Quit complainin' before I give ya something to complain about." Then he straightened up and grinned yellowly at Mother, like he had just been joking around. But he wasn't.

And even though us sisters got down on our hands and knees and begged Mother that night, she didn't call Hall up on the telephone and tell him that we didn't want to move into the city. When she tucked Troo and me in, she told us, "Someday you'll understand." Her eyes started watering up and she swiped at them and said, "Damn hay fever," and left.

I suspected that a little part of Mother wanted to move to the city, too. Daddy not being there for the harvest, that had to have been as hard on her as it had been on me. And I also suspected Mother was looking forward to living closer to Daddy's grave and Granny and Uncle Paulie. Well, Daddy and Granny anyways.

So, on Halloween of '57, Hall and Mother got married at the white courthouse in Waukesha. After the ceremony, Nell whispered to me, "I think Mother might be letting herself in for more trick than treat, don't you?" The next week we moved to Vliet Street.

Out on the farm, me and Troo had mostly hung around with Jerry Amberson, who lived down at the end of our gravel road and peed on my leg once after we got done swimming in his pond in the woods. All the other kids we went to school with lived on farms just like ours that you could just about die of tiredness walking to. So if we wanted to play hide-and-seek or some other game like kick the can, where you had to have more than two kids, we were stuck with peeing Jerry Amberson, like it or not.

But on Vliet Street . . . well, for once in his life, Hall was right. There really was a shitload of kids. Somebody was always sittin' on their front steps waiting for you to ask them to jump in a pile of leaves or go sledding at Statue Hill or swimming at the pool in the park. That's because the neighborhood was chock-full of what Granny called "products of Catholic marriages." (Her eyes bulged out of her head when she said that because she had a condition called a thyroid, which was located in her leg somewhere.)

Besides there being a whole lot more of them, just like Mother said when we played the name game, people really *were* different in the city. Like Fast Susie Fazio, the kid on the block who always seemed to have news before everybody else did. She was the one who told Troo and me about Dottie Kenfield.

Our second summer in the city had just started up. After the streetlights popped on, the three of us were sitting on the O'Haras' front steps, waiting for the others to get there for our nightly game of red light, green light. Fast Susie was brushing her long, straight black hair that she had never cut since she was a baby and her skin got so tan in the summer she almost looked like an Egyptian in the movie *The Ten Commandments* that Troo and me had seen at the Uptown Theater, which we went to whenever we got a quarter. And because she was Italian—a people that Mother said matured faster than other people—Fast Susie was not only hairier than the rest of us, she had those bosoms. They'd even had to order a special Girl Scout uniform for her, one with more material in the chest.

"I heard that something bad happened to Dottie Kenfield," I said to her.

"Oh ya did, did ya?" Fast Susie never liked it if you heard a story that she hadn't told you. "Well, this time ya heard right, O'Malley. Month before last your next-door neighbor just up and disappeared. Just vanished one day." She put on a spooky voice and made her eyes look like venetian blinds. "Gone. Right into thin air. Poof!"

You had to pay close attention when Fast Susie told you a story because she liked to wave her arms all over the place, like all the Italians did. She even gave Willie O'Hara a black eye one time when she was acting out the Crucifixion.

"Yup, Dottie Kenfield is probably dead, just like Junie Piaskowski," Fast Susie said, back to brushin' her hair. "I bet they find her body soon. All dead and green and her eyes rotting out of her head and smellin' like Doc Sullivan's breath."

Last summer, Fast Susie said that Reese Latour had made her touch his weenie and told her that it could be used to make girls beg for mercy, and that when you got to be about thirteen blood would start coming out of you and that was when you could get a baby. See? Sometimes it was hard to know exactly when Fast Susie was telling the truth. Especially since I had every reason to believe that Dottie Kenfield wasn't dead.

"But what about that crying Troo and me hear comin' out of Dottie's room at night?" I asked.

Fast Susie jabbed me in the arm with her elbow and said in that trembly voice of hers, "Just watch your step, O'Malley sisters." She made a smile that was extra creepy because her eyeteeth were more pointed than they oughta been. "If you're hearin' crying coming out of that house, that can only mean one thing. The Kenfield place must be haaaunted."

That's exactly what she said. That all the crying next door was Dottie Kenfield's ghost.

And maybe Fast Susie Fazio was right this time after all, because that crying was the most horrible haunted sound you have ever heard. Poor Dottie!

Sometimes, after the crying stopped, I would go stand at my window and look into Dottie's bedroom because I was too afraid to do that when the crying was going on. A picture of a beautiful girl with brunette eyes and hair hung on a wall. I knew she was eighteen in this picture because she was in Nell's class. Dottie had on her mint-colored Senior Dance dress and her hair was swirled up on top of her head like a Carvel cone and there was a ruby going-steady ring around her neck. I remember the day she bought that dress downtown at Gimbel's. Right below her picture there was a small light that shone down from an aquarium hood into the water. And it had one of those deep-sea divers and little bubbles racing goldfish up to the surface.

Standing in the dark watching like that, I woulda bet anything that the Kenfields had not changed one thing about Dottie's bedroom even though she disappeared into thin air two months ago. Because maybe there was still the smell of her in that room. Like after Daddy died. In his closet I could breathe in his Aqua Velva. One day I sat in there next to his boots that still had some farm dirt on them and wouldn't come out. The day after that Mother gave away all his clothes to Goodwill Industries and shook me by the shoulders and yelled, "For godssake, Sally. He's gone and he's not coming back. It's time to let bygones be bygones."

But I hid one of Daddy's shirts . . . a blue one. To remember my Sky King. I kept it inside my pillow where Mother couldn't find it. Because at the end of the day, no matter what she said, I needed to lie my head down on Daddy, listening to Troo sucking on her two middle fingers, squeezing the life out of her baby doll, Annie, and not ever let bygones be bygones.

CHAPTER FOUR

Some nights, Troo and me could also hear crying coming out of Mother's bedroom, which was so hard to believe. That sound almost seemed like a mirage in the desert. Because during the day you never would hear something like that. During the day Mother was tough like beef jerky and would tell you that crying was for people who felt sorry for themselves. Granny told me that Mother really wasn't so tough, that she was just doing something called whistling in the dark. (Since I had not once ever heard Mother whistle, I knew right then that this granny was getting the hardening of the arteries the way the other gramma got.)

Troo was sitting on the soft stool in front of the dressing table that had a mirror and two drawers on each side. Another smaller mirror shaped like an ice skating rink sat on top of the table with her bottles of perfumes and lotions. I was holding the gold hairbrush with the swirls on the back that Daddy had given Mother for her birthday one year. We were watching Mother fold her blouses and put them into her round blue Samsonite bag between layers of tissue paper.

Mother snapped the luggage shut and brushed down the hem of her tan pleated skirt and said, "I have given Nell her instructions. She will do all the cooking and mind you during the day until Hall comes home from work at five thirty. You give either of them any guff and . . ." She took the hairbrush out of my hand, smacked it against her palm and then let it drop on the bed. "Hall took the car to Shuster's this morning, so I'm walking over to the hospital." She picked up her suitcase and slipped on her shiny black high heels with the bows. "I'll be back in a week or so."

"Can we come with you?" Troo said, which surprised me because she didn't usually act like she'd miss you if you went anywhere.

Mother said, "Don't be silly." And then she gave us her powdery cheek to kiss and we could hear her heels smacking against the wooden steps that led down to the front porch and then finally the door slamming shut.

We sat there for a while not saying anything, but I was feeling bad because we weren't ever supposed to be in Mother's room without her. Troo said suddenly, "Let's play dress-up."

She slid open the jewelry drawer and fingered the green glass beads and a silver medallion on a long chain and Daddy's old Timex, which I thought Mother'd given away to Goodwill Industries along with everything else. It made me so happy to see the watch that I slipped it on my wrist and held it up to my ear and it was still ticking. I wished I could wind it back so far that I would have a do-over of the day Daddy died. So I could say sorry. Troo lifted out the beads and put them around her neck. Then she pulled the cherry red lipstick out of the fancy golden tube and spread it on her pouty lips and rubbed them together like we'd seen Mother do. Troo was looking at herself in the mirror, turning her head from side to side.

"You look just like her," I said, staring at her reflection.

Troo smiled and got some of the lipstick on her teeth and said, "I know."

I pulled out another drawer and saw a picture of Daddy laying on top of Mother's white chiffon scarf. It was the picture from when he just got back from the Air Force and he had his uniform on and you could tell he was so happy to be home. Next to him, Mother was looking off into the distance like she hadn't even realized he was there.

"Let's go," I said, because I was starting to feel worried about Mother, and maybe if we went to the front window we could see her walking over to the hospital and we could yell something out to her like get well soon!

I let Daddy's watch slide off my wrist and set it back in the drawer. "You should wipe off that lipstick."

"No," Troo said, and plumped out her lips even more.

"Troo."

"I ain't takin' it off."

"Troo!" We weren't ever supposed to say *ain't*. That was something Mother told us the riffraff said.

Troo laughed and pulled on a pair of short white gloves she found in the drawer. So I walked to the living room by myself and stuck my head out the window. I could smell pink peonies mixed in with the chocolate chip cookie smell coming from the Feelin' Good Cookie Factory. Mother was small up on the corner of North Avenue. I was sure that would be the last time I'd ever see her again because look what happened to Daddy when he was in the same hospital. So I started to yell to her to please come back! But then she turned the corner and was gone. And she didn't come home in a week or so like she said.

CHAPTER FIVE

We were on our way to meet Mary Lane the next morning at one of our usual summer hangouts. Washington Park was 1,747 steps away from our front door and had everything a person could ever want or need. There was that lagoon that we skated on in the winter and fished in during the summer and where they'd found Junie. There was also a band shell that looked like a giant clam where we could go hear Music Under the Stars and a swimming pool that had a high dive. And best of all, on the far side of the park, there was my absolute favorite. The zoo!

We were almost to the park, right in front of Fitzpatrick's Drugstore, when Troo bent down to tie her shoe and said out of the blue, "I'm thinkin' about running away to France," and didn't say anything else.

I looked into the drugstore and wished I had a dime for a soda because even though it was still early morning, it was already so hot that my eyeballs were sweating. "France?"

I had no idea where she got this idea of France from. Probably out of a book at the Finney Library, where they were giving away these passes to the Uptown to the kid who read the most books. The librarian kept track of our names and how many books we'd read on this worm body that was called Billy the Bookworm and hung outside the boys' bathroom. Troo's most favorite thing was going to the movies, so she moved her name up the bookworm's body when the librarian, Mrs. Esther Kambowski (Polish—a real break for Troo) wasn't looking. Troo didn't give a damn if she cheated. I didn't feel that same way, but I almost never disagreed with her because of that promise I'd made to Daddy in the hospital. I still hadn't told Troo what he'd said about the car crash not being her fault, because she always got so mad when I brought it up and Troo, you didn't like to get her mad. Her mad was tall. And deep. Like a volcano, she could blow when you least expected it.

Mary Lane knew Troo was cheating on that bookworm ladder and had threatened to tell Mrs. Kambowski. Thank God it was Mary Lane because nobody woulda believed her anyway, because everybody knew that she told the biggest and fattest lies around.

One time she told us that her father's weenie did not look like a weenie at all but more like a bratwurst. Mary Lane said she knew that because she saw her mother and father having some of the sex on the bathroom floor, probably right after they had their baths. So not only was she a huge liar, Mary Lane was a peeper, which was a person who really, really, really liked to spy on people in their houses. She liked to light fires, too. Not because she liked fires but because she was just nuts about the fire trucks that showed up *after* she lit the fires. She was my and Troo's best friend. (We always called her Mary Lane because almost every family on the block had a kid named Mary so you had to find a way to tell them apart.) Mary Lane was also the skinniest person alive. I mean, you have never seen a person who was not a pagan baby living in Africa who was this skinny. Troo and me figured that's because she had six brothers who probably ate all the food in the house when her father went to work and her mother did the wash.

And even though Troo thought Mrs. Kambowski wouldn't believe lying Mary Lane if she really did rat her out about cheating on the Bookworm, Troo still came up with one of her famous plans. Just in case.

"We are having what is known as a *rendezvous*. That's the French word for meeting up with someone," Troo said. We'd climbed up onto different branches in our favorite zoo tree across from Sampson the gorilla's pit and were watching Mary Lane coming down that zoo path. Her wrinkled white shorts and dirty red-checkered shirt waving off her body made her look kinda like a flagpole. "I'm just gonna push her into Sampson's pit." Troo wiggled to the end of the branch. "I gotta win those movie passes."

I was pretty sure she was just talkin' big and wouldn't really push Mary Lane in. Pretty sure. Ever since Daddy's car crash I couldn't always tell what Troo would do. Sometimes I even thought my sister got a little brain damaged in that accident just like Uncle Paulie.

We hopped down from the tree and were leaning over the black iron railing just staring at Sampson, acting like we didn't know Mary Lane had arrived even though we knew she did because she always smelled like stale potato chips.

"Whatcha lookin' at?" Mary Lane asked, coming up next to us.

Sampson. I adored Sampson. *Really* adored him. Daddy used to bring me and Troo to this zoo after we'd drive in from the farm to pay a Sunday afternoon visit to Granny. Daddy adored Sampson as well and would sit and watch him and laugh right along. So I'd known Sampson practically since I was born. And now I always came to Sampson when I was feelin' out of sorts. I would imagine Daddy sitting next to me on my park bench and putting his arm around me and saying in his deep voice, "Sal, my gal, a lot of people say that the lion is the King of the Jungle. But I would have to disagree with those people." Then Daddy'd point at the gorilla and beat his chest and his voice would come out all stuttery. "I would have to say that Sampson is the King. Just look at him. He is magnificent!" I would look back at Sampson and nod my head like I was agreeing with him, but I was secretly thinking to myself that it was my daddy who was the King. Of the sky *and* the land. And he was magnificent!

Troo said loudly to Mary Lane, "Sampson's got something he wants to show you, but you gotta get closer. He's hidin' it behind his back. Just climb over the railing and lean over and you'll see it perfectly clearly."

Always ready for any kind of peeping, Mary Lane hopped right over and walked to the edge of the grass next to the pit. Troo turned and grinned at me and then climbed over the railing to join her. I didn't think that gorillas ate people, but the fall alone woulda killed skinny Mary Lane. Break her in half like a piece of cold gum.

Sampson was watching us carefully, foot tapping. I always thought he was singing to himself "Don't Get Around Much Anymore." That was one of Ethel Jenkins's favorite songs and she taught it to me. Ethel lived over on Fifty-second Street with Mrs. Galecki and was my and Troo's other best friend.

"Hey, Mary Lane, you know about that Bookworm ladder? You really aren't gonna tell Kambowski that I cheated, are you?" Troo asked this real sweetly, like she can when she wants something real bad. Granny calls it her dolly voice.

Mary Lane turned toward Troo. "Yeah, I am."

The lion roared and a couple of flamingos ran for cover.

Troo said, "Are you sure you want to do that? I'd feel real bad if you accidentally fell into the pit and they didn't find you until feeding time. Or if Sampson was hungry right this minute"—she lowered her voice—"they might never find anything but your bones."

So I guess gorillas did eat people but Sampson would be pretty disappointed if he ate Mary Lane, who had as much meat on her as a coat hanger.

Troo nudged Mary Lane a little closer until the tips of her half-undone high-top black tennis shoes, the ones she always had on, were half over the pit and half on the grass.

"You ain't gonna push me in, are you?" she asked. Troo was up close behind her so she couldn't escape.

"Thinkin' about it," Troo said, spitting her gum down toward the pit so Mary Lane would completely understand exactly how far she would fall. (I wouldn't have let Troo push her in, just so you know that about me.)

"Go ahead," Mary Lane said, and squished her eyes closed.

"Are you tellin' me you don't care if I push you in this pit and you'd probably die and go to purgatory for all eternity for the millions of lies you told?" Troo asked, amazed.

"I never been to a movie theater and I want them passes and the popcorn and soda." Mary Lane took a big breath and held it. "I'll die to defend them. And I never told a lie in my life, Troo O'Malley."

"That's your biggest lie ever," Troo said, and she looked at me and I looked at her and we both turned our heads back to Mary Lane, who was beginning to remind me very much of St. Joan of Arc.

"Okay, okay, I was just kiddin' around." Troo laughed and pulled Mary Lane away from the edge. "Go ahead, tell Kambowski." Right away, because of the mental telepathy, I knew that Troo was workin' on another one of her plans that would involve a librarian and an obituary.

Mary Lane stepped back and looked over at Troo like nothing at all had just happened. "You know who Sara Heinemann is?"

"Of course," Troo said, and then we went to sit down on the green park bench across from Sampson. Troo handed out pieces of Dubble Bubble that she always seemed to have.

Mary Lane stuck the gum in her mouth and said, "She's missing."

"Whatta ya mean?" I asked, trying to read the Pud comic that came in the gum.

"Just what I said. Sara's missing. Been gone for a couple of days now," Mary Lane said. "My dad told me not to talk to any strangers."

I closed my eyes, trying to picture the girl I thought might be Sara Heinemann. "She the third-grader with the blond ponytail that likes dodgeball so much?"

Mary Lane nodded. "She lives four houses down from me, right next to Judy Big Head. (Mary Lane was not being uncharitable. That really was Judy's last name. She was an Indian.) "Sara's probably been kidnapped just like I was."

Troo rolled her eyeballs at me. Last summer, Mary Lane had told us that she'd been kidnapped by Germans who wore hardly any clothing and they forced her to make potholders all day long and she only escaped by swimming across a huge lake full of slimy trout. What really happened is her parents sent her to camp up in Rhinelander. So this story about Sara Heinemann missing was just another one of her big fibs that you had to expect from her. For some reason I could never figure out, a lot of Mary Lane's lies were about kidnapping. And weenies.

"She'll probably turn up, she probably just got lost. That happens all the time," I said. But what I was really thinking was that if Mary Lane was right and Sara really did get kidnapped, they probably would never find her alive again. That's how it'd been with Junie. First she went missing and then they found her dead body over at the lagoon. I worried for a while after Junie's funeral that somebody would kidnap Troo. Granny took me home and made me cinnamon toast and told me not to be such a worrywart. That murders like that, like what happened to Junie Piaskowski, that was a once-in-a-lifetime experience. Granny was usually never wrong. Then again, like she always said, there's a first time for everything.

"You know what I'd like to do?" I said, looking at Sampson's sad eyes. "I'd like to kidnap him and take him back to his family."

Mary Lane laughed and said, "You know, O'Malley, that's a weird kid thing to say. Kidnapping a gorilla and taking him home. That's weird."

She should talk about weird.

"I think it's a good idea," Troo said. "And on the way there, we could stop in France."

Mary Lane started laughing again until Troo smacked her a good one and said, "What's so funny about France?"

"What the hell do you know about France?" Mary Lane asked, not rubbing her arm.

"As a matter of fact," Troo said, "I know quite a bit about France."

"Sure you do." Mary Lane slid off the bench, outta Troo's reach.

"France is where they speak the language of love," I said, staring at Sampson.

"*Oui*," Troo said quietly.

"We what?" Mary Lane said.

"Aw, shut up," Troo said, "before I change my mind about pushin' you in the pit." They were up on their feet now, toe to toe. Mary Lane shoved Troo and took off. I held Troo's arms behind her back so she couldn't go chase after her. She was madder than a hatter. When she finally broke loose, she spun around and got up real close to my face and yelled, "Sally O'Malley . . . your days are numbered."

As usual, my Troo genius was right.

CHAPTER SIX

"That tasted like crap," Hall hollered. He was sitting at the kitchen table, a cigarette hanging out of his mouth, the ash falling onto the nice white plates that Mother had saved S&H Green Stamps for a whole year to buy. Nell had tried to make us supper again, but the tuna noodle casserole with potato chips on top ended up very black and the peas in the can she had cooked on the stove had no water in them and even the applesauce didn't taste right.

Mother had been in the hospital for over two weeks and she'd always done all the talking to Hall, so the three of us didn't know what to say to him. Mostly, I just tried not to look at his white T-shirt that didn't have sleeves so you could see that MOTHER tattoo laying against the muscles in his arm. His wavy Swedish hair looked like it did right when he woke up in the morning. And the sweat in the silky hair under his arms smelled like all the beer he'd been drinking.

Hall had another puff of his cigarette and said to us like we were deaf, "You know, I don't hafta take care of the three of you. You're not even mine."

Nell said, "May I be excused?" and tried to stand up to clear the dishes, but Hall grabbed her arm and grumbled, "Sit your ass back down." But then he changed his mind and said, "Never mind, go get me a beer," and he shoved Nell so hard that she fell against the stove and her daisy sundress went up around her waist.

My eyes started to burn and Troo was looking down at the floor and licking her lips hard and fast, like she did when she got nervous. She musta been sneakin' into Mother's room because I could see a bit of that cherry red lipstick stuck in the corners of her mouth and I could smell Evening in Paris. Nell's face looked like she had a fever when she pulled her dress down and then got up and opened the refrigerator. There was nothing much in there so that Pabst Blue Ribbon was easy to find. Hall wasn't giving Nell hardly any grocery money. "It's not my fault," she'd shouted last night. Troo'd been getting so cranky about eating nothing but pigs in a blanket that she'd thrown one at Nell and gotten mustard all over her poodle skirt so it looked like it piddled.

Hall took a long drink from the bottle Nell handed him and then wiped his mouth on the back of his arm and said, "You know, your mother and me"—and then he burped extra loud—"we been havin' some problems for a while now and on toppa that, things aren't goin' so well over at the shoe store."

"Big surprise," Troo said in her sassiest voice.

Hall reached across the table so quick I didn't even see it coming, and neither did Troo. He slapped her on the back of her head. Hard. She just looked at him through her hair that had been knocked around her face and didn't say a word. So he did it again. Harder. Hall should've known that Troo would never cry, if that was what he was waitin' for. When he hauled his arm back again, he lost his balance and fell off the kitchen chair and just stayed there on the dirty tan linoleum and started crying out, "Helen . . . Helen . . . Helen."

We sisters looked at one another and got up and went out on the front porch and listened to the crickets and didn't say much. Because there was not much to say about something like that. About a man who you lived with but you hardly even knew, and didn't want to know, laying down on your kitchen floor crying out your almost dead mother's name. Later, when the streetlights came on, Troo, who hardly ever could stay quiet for long, said, "What a goddamn dickhead."

The next morning, Nell poured Wheaties and what little milk was left into our bowls. And then she started scraping last night's supper dishes under the running sink water because the smell of the crusty tuna was so bad. "Mother has something else wrong with her besides her gallbladder. I wanted to tell you last night, but then . . ."

Troo looked up from her bowl and said crabby-like, "What's she got wrong with her now?" and took another bite of cereal. As much as I loved Troo, I had to admit that she could be ornery like Mother if she didn't like you.

"Dr. Sullivan gave me this." Nell wiped her hands on her shorts and pulled the chair out next to me. We watched as she took a piece of paper out of her blouse pocket and ironed it down on the table.

Hepatitis.

"Isn't that when you got really bad breath?" Troo said. "That's what Willie told me. He said Dr. Sullivan has it and—"

"You nincompoop," Nell spat out. "That's called *halitosis*."

I was impressed with Nell knowing that. Or maybe she'd just made that up to make Troo and me feel stupid, which she could mostly do.

"Dr. Sullivan says hepatitis is a sickness in Mother's liver." Nell's voice suddenly got all wobbly. "It's not good." She ran into her bedroom and slammed the door. Nell had her own room and didn't have to share like me and Troo. If I had to list the order of like around here, I would say Nell was in first place, Troo a very close second and me—well, there was something about me that always made a sad look come onto Mother's face when I caught her staring at me. I had no idea what it was about me that made her look at me like that. Probably my imagination.

After that hepatitis talk, maybe a week later, Nell told us that things were getting even worse. Now Mother had something called a staph infection, which was a very bad sickness. Much worse than anybody could've ever imagined. Even me. Nell cried and cried until Troo went into her bedroom and slapped her and told her to shut the hell up.

Mother was at St. Joe's Hospital almost the whole month of June. And it looked like she might miss the Fourth of July, which was a darn shame because once I heard her tell her best friend, Mrs. Betty Callahan, that she should've named Troo Bottle Rocket—that's how much Mother loved the Fourth.

By then, Hall had pretty much stopped coming home for supper. He would wake us up later when he crashed into the living room furniture and started cursing a blue streak, sometimes in another language, which I took to be Swedish. And Nell had begun to get on Troo's nerves so much that Troo could barely look at Nell in her white blouse and saddle shoes, going on about Elvis . . . Elvis . . . Elvis. I thought Nell was okay. Not great. I always tried to keep in mind what Daddy had said about her being only the third worst big sister in the world. But Troo, who never liked Nell much in the first place, started getting so fed up with her that she would chase Nell around the house and hold a toothbrush up to her lips and sing "You ain't nuthin' but a hound dog" over and over real loud until Nell had had it up to here and smacked her a good one. Then I'd have to settle Troo down and give her something of mine, like my favorite steely marble, so she'd promise not to try and smother Nell in her sleep.

After Nell told us about that staph infection, I thought it would be a good idea to head up to church and do a little praying that morning, even though I thought God had some kind of deafness and wasn't listening to one darn thing I was tellin' Him. Nell didn't want to come with us because she was gonna go walk up to Fillard's Service Station and see her boyfriend, Eddie Callahan, who worked up there and was Mrs. Callahan's son. That was how Nell was spending her days. Going gaga over Eddie Callahan. When Mother came home, Nell would be in big trouble for minding Eddie Callahan instead of Troo and me, the way Mother had told her to. Troo already had her tattletale list with a capital *T* all figured out. She even wrote it down.

1. Nell says you didn't tell her she had to do me and Sally's wash so she isn't.
2. Nell broke the turn-on knob off the television and now Sally can't watch *Sky King* and that made her cry more than once. (I told her to take that

crying part out, because Mother would only get mad at me.)

3. Nell will not give us money to go to the Uptown so we had to miss a Sandra Dee and Troy Donahue movie.

And so on. The tattletale list was longer than Troo's Christmas list. And every day she grew more excited about showing it to Mother when she came home.

I mostly liked Mother of Good Hope church and school because they were only six blocks away and the O'Malley sisters could walk to them. The part I didn't care for was that we had to pass Greasy Al Molinari's house to get there. One of Troo's most favorite things to do in the whole world was to stand in front of the Molinaris' gray house and holler very loudly, "Greasy Al is such a little shit." She also called him other names like wophead and spaghetti for brains, and sometimes, when she was really out of sorts, she would sing that Harry Belafonte song "Day-O," but instead she would say, "Dago . . . da da daaago."

Troo was sure Greasy Al was the one that had stolen her bike last summer, and that's what she was so mad about. I could never stop her, even though God and Daddy know I tried, so we always ended up getting chased halfway to school by Greasy Al, who threatened to bronze our butts if he ever caught us, which he wouldn't, because his right leg was sort of withered up from polio. Greasy Al couldn't run exactly, but he *could* walk very fast in a hunched-up limpy kind of way if he wanted to go after you. I always said to Troo, "What are you gonna do if he ever catches you? He's got that switchblade, you know?"

Troo would laugh and laugh and this wild look would come into her eyes, like she didn't care if Greasy Al caught her. That bothered me. Almost every day I wished Daddy was here to calm her down because I didn't think Troo would be long for this world if she kept this sort of wild thing up.

That morning Troo was dawdling behind me, a little cranky because I'd told her I wasn't in the mood to get chased by Greasy Al, so like Mother said, she better mind her p's and q's. She was kicking a rock the way she liked to do when she was thinking and then she said real quietly, so that I almost didn't hear her, "She's gonna get better, right, Sal?"

I didn't turn around because if I did she'd get real mad. Troo hated it if I caught her being scared because she forgot to whistle in the dark. I figured out what that meant by paying attention to details. Granny wasn't getting the hardening of the arteries after all. Mother and Troo *were* two peas in the pod, both of 'em always pretending that things were okay when they weren't.

"Yeah, she'll be fine," I said over my shoulder, but wondered what would happen if she wasn't. Would Troo and me just go on living with Hall and Nell? Or maybe go stay with Granny and Uncle Paulie? Oh, Troo would just despise that. She avoided Uncle Paulie whenever she could. When I asked her why, she said, "Cooties." I suspected it was more than that, but never did ask her again since I did not wish to have Troo's volcano mad erupting all over me. Besides, Granny's house was too small, and she was in a bad way money-wise. Everybody in the neighborhood knew that.

"If she dies, what'll we do?" Troo kicked at the rock and it flew past me. "Do you think we'd have to go live at the orphanage?"

Every year around Christmas our Brownie troop would go to the orphanage up on Lisbon Street called St. Jude's, who was the patron saint of lost causes. That was a very mean thing to call your orphanage and musta made those poor orphans feel really hopeless. We would sing "What Child Is This?" and give them presents like holy cards wrapped in green tissue paper and red ribbons, and I hated it. I just couldn't stand looking at those kids who didn't have fathers or mothers or anybody else who gave one hoot about them. And that made me say, "No. We won't ever have to go live in that orphanage. I promise."

Troo had stopped in front of the Piaskowskis'. The yard was all weedy and the house looked like it was shedding and a concrete statue of Jesus was laying on its side next to the porch like it was taking a nap. Nobody ever saw much of Mr. or Mrs. Piaskowski after Junie's funeral.

"That would be just about one of the worst things that could ever happen to you, gettin' murdered like that," Troo said. We held our breaths when we walked past and didn't talk much for the rest of the way, but I was thinking that maybe there were some other things that could be worse.

After mass half the neighborhood was standing out on the church lawn and I heard Mrs. Callahan, who was still Mother's best friend and had been for a long time, say to Mrs. Latour in a very tired voice, "Helen is resting peacefully."

Mrs. Latour said back, "I heard that Hall has taken up with Rosie Ruggins."

And then Mrs. Callahan said back to her, "Helen should never have married him in the first place." It was rude to eavesdrop, but no one would tell me if Mother was getting better and I had to find out so I could get prepared if she wasn't. What Mrs. Callahan said, I took that to mean that Mother might be dying since she was Resting in Peace, which was what it said on Daddy's gravestone. And what Mrs. Latour said about Hall? That probably meant that Hall was gettin' some of the sex from Rosie Ruggins.

When Mrs. Callahan turned and saw us, she said in a surprised voice, "Well, O'Malley sisters, hello!"

I looked down at Mrs. Callahan's bare legs in front of that church. She had on a little gold ankle bracelet and she wore blouses sometimes too unbuttoned. Granny told me Mother and Mrs. Callahan were crazy little she-cats when they were young, when they lived in houses next door to each other across from the cookie factory.

Mrs. Callahan bent down and said, "Are you okay, Sally?"

I tried not to cry even though my eyes were blurry because Mrs. Callahan smelled so much like Mother and I bet she had made her kids sunny-side-up eggs for breakfast. "We're fine, Mrs. Callahan," I said. "Hall and Nell are taking very good care of us. Mother's gonna get better, isn't she?"

Mrs. Callahan said, "Well, my pa's been real sick up at the VA Hospital so I haven't been by to check up on Helen as much as I woulda liked, but I'm sure she'll . . ." Then she started to cry. And I just couldn't take that and neither could Troo because she pulled on my hand and we got lost in the crowd.

CHAPTER SEVEN

The reason I lied to Mrs. Callahan was just in case she went up to the hospital to visit, I didn't want her getting Mother all worked up. The truth was neither Hall nor Nell was taking very good care of us at all. Hall was drinking all the time up at Jerbak's. So Mrs. Latour was probably right when she said he'd taken up with Rosie Ruggins, who was a cocktail waitress there. And Nell was so busy with Eddie that she didn't want to cook for us, which was okay, because unfortunately I would really have to agree with Hall on that one thing and only that one thing—Nell's cooking *was* crap. She was also talking about going to beauty school, so she was spending a lot of time giving Toni perms in the kitchen, which had begun to smell worse than the bathroom up at the service station. Half the girls on the block now looked like they'd stuck forks into light sockets, thanks to Nell.

Because Troo and me were pretty hungry, Troo came up with another one of her famous plans. She said, "We should just start showing up at people's houses around suppertime." So last night we ate at the O'Haras', which wasn't that great because I really didn't like liver no matter how much bacon you put on it. But tonight, we were on our way over to Fast

Susie Fazio's house because they had the best food, and because even though they were Italians, the Fazios were okay Italians, not like the Molinaris. Troo told me that was because the Fazios were from someplace called Nice, Italy, not like the Molinaris, who were from another part of Italy that wasn't so nice.

There were ten Fazios plus Nana, so mostly I don't think anybody even noticed when Troo and me got plates out of the cupboard above the sink and pulled up chairs next to Fast Susie in the kitchen, which always smelled of that spice called garlic that Nana used on just about everything.

I was sitting across the table from Nana. I tried to smile at her even though I knew she wouldn't smile back because I had tried before and she never did. That was because she was a Strega Nana . . . a witch. Under no circumstances would you want to cross Nana. Other Italians came from all around the city and would bring her stuff and she would say some Italian words and wave her arms around to ward off the evil spirits and she always dressed like she was on her way to a funeral. Fast Susie told me, even though I didn't believe her, that Nana threw pee on somebody's new car once as some sort of blessing, so they would never get in a crash. I tried not to think about that when I reached around one of Fast Susie's older brothers for a piece of that nice skinny bread with butter.

"So how's your mother doin'?" Johnny Fazio asked right after I'd stuffed the bread in my mouth. He reminded me of this movie star called Earl Flynn who was in this movie Troo and me had seen and liked at Old Time Movie Matinee Day. It was called *Captain Blood* and Earl was a pirate. Johnny had a thin mustache like Earl's and his dark hair

WHISTLING IN THE DARK   43

grew up on his head like a big wave and he was a singer in a band called the Do Wops, which all the older girls thought was very hep.

"Eh . . . you." He poked me in the arm. "What's your name . . . I asked you how your mother was doin'."

"She's fine," Troo answered for me.

"Ain't she dyin' or somethin'?" Johnny asked.

His words hung in the air like skunk smell and made everybody stop eating. Then Nana Fazio's chair made a scraping sound when she pushed quickly back from the table. Her bosoms were so long she had to hold them to her waist with a belt and she didn't speak very good English, but Nana knew a wisecrack in any language. She had begun to undo her bosoms belt.

I pretended not to notice and reached for another delicious meatball in red sauce.

Then these words came shooting out of her little body—because really, Nana Fazio could almost be considered a midget—and she marched over to our side of the table and slapped Johnny across his shoulders with her belt. "You don' talk like that. Thas the little girl's mama, you don't say nuthin' about her mama dyin', *capisce*?" Nana shouted at Johnny in this voice you could never imagine would come out of someone so small. "You goombah!"

It went library quiet 'cept for the *drip drip* of the kitchen sink and a faraway lawn mower. And then from outta nowhere, Troo looked up from her plate and started singing, "Que sera, sera. Whatever will be will be. The future's not ours to see. Que sera sera."

All eyes went to Nana Fazio with the belt in her hand. They were all probably thinking like I was that Troo had just taken her life into her hands. Nana leaned down real close to Troo and I thought she was gonna put the hex on her or smack her like she had Johnny, but instead, she looked at Troo with her black olive eyes and said, "You, you kid, you lika Doris Day?"

Troo cleared her throat and said, "Actually, I think Doris Day is the best thing since sliced bread."

Nana slowly, slowly smiled. Now I knew where Fast Susie's pointed eyeteeth came from. "Me, too," she said. "I lika Doris Day, too. You and your *sorella* can eata here whenever you wanna, as much as you wanna." Nana reached across me and dug the big silver spoon into the white bowl and slapped three juicy meatballs onto my plate.

What a genius my sister was!

Troo wanted to sleep over in the Fazios' attic that night and I couldn't disagree with her. The last time we went home, the door was locked. Besides that, Troo and me both knew if Nell caught us she would force us to have one of those Toni perms that we both thought made you look like you just got off the boat.

Red light, green light was called off because it looked like it was gonna rain again, so we spent most of the night listening to Fast Susie tell us stories in the attic that had no light except for a dirty bare bulb way high up in the ceiling.

Fast Susie was sitting cross-legged on the stained gray mattress, facing me and Troo. "So then, after the grave robbers dig up those dead bodies, they take them over to Dr. Frankenstein's castle in a little three-wheeled wooden cart." She was using this voice she had that was husky. "And it begins to rain and the grave-robbin' men are ugly and skinny and cough all the time and are drunk with dirty hair."

Thunder rolled past the attic window and made it shake, and then a few seconds later there was pitchfork lightning that I could see perfectly, and it reminded me of our farm.

I looked over at Troo. She was rubbing the arm that had gotten broken in the crash and was hanging on to Fast Susie's every word.

"And then Dr. Frankenstein puts the body on this black table in his lavatory and he gets a saw to cut the bodies aaall up!"

The lightning flashed again and lit up the whole attic, which was full of boxes and suitcases and the thing I was keeping my eye on. This body that had no arms or legs and was standing over in the corner next to the window. Fast Susie said that Nana used it to make clothes on.

"And then"—Fast Susie made her voice drippy with creepy—"and then, Dr. Frankenstein sewed all these dead body pieces together and made this monster. . . ." She waved her arms around. "And Dr. Frankenstein put this monster down on this other table and hooked all these gadgets up to him and then lightning hit the castle and electricity came into the gadgets and went into the monster and Dr. Frankenstein yelled out, 'It's alive. It's alive!' " Fast Susie jumped up and started walking around with her arms stiff in front of her and chased me and Troo, who screamed, and I did, too, until somebody yelled up from downstairs, "Shut the hell up, we're tryin' to sleep down here."

After the Frankenstein story, Fast Susie showed us her bosoms and told us we would both get them too and, holy smoke, would the boys ever like us a lot! She said we could touch them if we wanted to. I didn't. Later Troo told me they felt like a water balloon but warmer.

When the rain started pelting the window, I tried to fall asleep, but that attic heat felt like a too-heavy blanket laying all over me and all I could think about was that Frankenstein monster murdering the three of us while he grunted, "Me . . . me . . . me . . . like you." Boy, that Fast Susie could make a story sound so real. I got the sweatiest I had ever gotten, hearing that monster's clunky shoes creaking on the attic steps. When I couldn't take it anymore, I rolled off that stinky old mattress and decided that even if Hall was snoring drunk, I needed to get home.

According to Fast Susie, Frankenstein couldn't run very fast because his legs belonged to two different people, so I figured I could outrun him because of my long legs. That was one thing Daddy always said, that I was really good at running. "You fly like the wind, Sal." That's what he said. *You fly like the wind.* I felt bad about leaving Troo behind, but if anyone could keep her safe it was Nana Fazio, who would take her belt to anybody for just about any reason, including Frankenstein. So I snuck down the Fazios' attic steps and out their back door into the alley, carrying my tennis shoes in my hand, being as sneaky as I could.

Music was almost always going on day or night on Vliet Street, no matter what. But that night, after the storm moved away, it was black and quiet except for the crickets and that dumb dog that belonged to the Moriaritys that always seemed to be barking two streets over. I went back through the Fazios' yard and past the Latours', who were their next-door neighbors. And just for a second I thought I saw something moving around in the Latours' yard. Something was over there. I looked away real quick and then back again real quick, but everything seemed okay. Just a swing on the play set getting pushed around by the wind. But behind me, the bushes that grew over the Spencers' back fence were rustling like something had gotten in there with them. Like Frankenstein. I got so scared to be alone in the dark without Troo that I started to walk faster. And then I thought of disappearing-into-thin-air Dottie Kenfield and dead Junie Piaskowski and what Mary Lane had said about Sara Heinemann being missing, and maybe it wasn't one of her big fat lies after all, so I walked even faster. There was a *hushing* sound in my ears that was so loud I could barely hear the footsteps that had come up behind me. But they were there all right. So was the shadow that the garage light made look long. And I shoulda turned around and seen who it was right then and there. Or I shoulda run back to the Fazios'. But I didn't. Because I got sorta frozen with fear like I always did on the high dive up at the pool because, like Troo always told me, when God handed out bravery I musta been in the bathroom.

I was pretty sure I knew who was following me. It was the guy that I secretly thought all along was the murderer of Junie Piaskowski. I'd thought it since the day they found Junie, but I didn't tell anybody because they would just cluck their tongues and say something about my imagination and so it just wasn't worth it. Everybody talked about how he especially liked little girls. That was who was coming for me. Officer Rasmussen.

I started to run and I could tell by how fast his feet were thumping that he was running, too. I got goin' so fast I almost fell over and I was almost home but I could tell by his breathing he could just reach out and grab me, but then I heard him stumble and say, "Shit." I ran through the Kenfields' gate and rolled beneath those pricker bushes they had next to their garage. He was right behind me. The gate creaked open, then slammed shut. I heard his footsteps, first on the path and then on the grass. He came right up to where I was hiding. If I wanted to I could've reached out and touched his argyle socks, pink-and-green ones that I could see in the Kenfields' back porch light. The socks were in thick black shoes with a spongy bottom that you could buy up at Shuster's. I could hear him breathing in and out, in and out. And finally, softly singing, "Come out, come out, wherever you are, Sally."

woke up underneath the Kenfields' bushes the next morning, kinda surprised I'd fallen asleep. My arms were covered in scratches and had bled a little so I licked my finger and cleaned them off and thought God would have done a better job if he had made blood taste like Three Musketeers bars. And then I remembered Rasmussen chasing me down the alley and my heart began beating like an Injun tom-tom right before they attacked the cowboys in all those western movies.

Mrs. Kenfield was up and about, hanging wash on her clothesline. Should I just roll out and say, "Why, good morning, Mrs. Kenfield. Need any help?" No. She might ask me, "What the heck are you doing under my bushes?" And since I wasn't a very good fibber, like Troo was, I would tell her about being chased by Rasmussen and then she would just shake her head at me and say in a voice that pained my heart, "Oh, Sally, not again." Just because last year, trying to be charitable, I told her I thought that her husband was a spy because he sure did act like one, all secretive and stern, sitting out on the porch swing every night smoking, which I figured had something to do with waiting for a sneaky spy package to be dropped off. So I knew that if I told Mrs. Kenfield about getting chased, she would run right over to the hospital and tell Mother I wasn't working on controlling my imagination. So I just laid there and said Hail Marys until she stuck her laundry basket under her arm and went inside the house.

Who *was* I supposed to tell about a guy named Rasmussen who liked to wave at you when you walked by his house and gave you this sweet smile that made him look like he'd lost something and was about to ask you if you'd help him find it? Who do you tell if that guy was also a cop? I was sure Rasmussen was a murderer. He just had that murderous look to him like all the bad guys do in the movies. Acting all nice and such but really not nice in their heart.

Should I tell Hall that Rasmussen had come after me? But I couldn't remember when I'd seen Hall for about the last week. Should I tell the other cop that hung around the neighborhood, Officer Riordan? He was a swell guy, but Willie O'Hara told me that Rasmussen was Officer Riordan's boss. No. I'd tell Troo. Being a Troo genius, she would know what to do.

I crawled out from under the bushes and walked to the front of the Kenfields' house and looked down the block. Ambulance lights were flashing like crazy in front of the Latours' and two men were wheeling somebody down the front steps. Mrs. Ruthie Latour was groaning and praying. Her husband, Bill, had his arm around her waist. A bunch of the Latour kids were just standing around watching like the rest of us. One of the littler ones was crying.

Troo was sitting on the sidewalk with Fast Susie, eating fritters that Nana musta made them for breakfast. Fast Susie tore off half of hers and gave it to me when I came up next to her out of breath.

"What's happening?" I asked, stuffing the puffed dough into my mouth. Ohhhh . . . that was good. Still warm. "Who is that?"

"It's Wendy," Troo said. "Where you been anyway? We gotta get goin'. It's Ethel day."

"Last night I got . . ." I started to tell her what'd happened with Rasmussen, but then I stopped because my breath was taken away. The sheet that was covering Wendy was streaked with blood.

I liked Wendy Latour even if she was a Mongoloid. She was so sweet with her straight black hair and that goofy smile and her funny way of talking, like she'd been adopted by the Latours from another country, probably Mongolia.

The whole neighborhood was quiet, until with a loud metal sound the ambulance men slid Wendy in and got ready to take her away to St. Joe's. I was about to ask those men if they had any news about Mother, but they peeled out and were already halfway down the block.

I pulled Troo up and we said bye to everyone and walked home and sat on our front steps. I was a little shaken up by the surprise of not only seeing an ambulance up close like that, but of seeing someone I knew inside it. I'd even forgotten about going to see Ethel over on Fifty-second Street.

"Do you know what I think?" I said.

"What?" Troo was laying back on the steps, looking up.

"I think it was Rasmussen who hurt Wendy."

Troo didn't say anything for a minute, but then pointed up to a cloud and said, "Look, Sally, it's a horse," and started laughing. She thought it was hilarious that I liked horses. I never told her it was because of Sky King and his Flying Crown Ranch.

"Knock it off, Troo," I said. "This is serious. I think Rasmussen did something to Wendy and I think—"

Troo sat up and cut me off. "You gotta stop thinkin' like that. Remember what Mother said about working on your imagination? Cops don't do stuff like that. They have to swear on the Bible not to do bad things."

"And it isn't only Wendy," I kept on. "Last summer, I saw Rasmussen with Junie Piaskowski at the Policemen's Picnic. They were flying a kite together. And then she got murdered."

"You are so queer. That's what everybody does at the Policemen's Picnic, hangs out with cops. Rasmussen was just being nice to Junie."

Too nice if you asked me. I'd watched the two of them together. Rasmussen smiled at Junie in a certain kind of way. And his hand was on her shoulder. Something was definitely up between 'em and it wasn't only the kite.

"He came after me last night," I said.

"Who?"

"Rasmussen."

"Your imagination," Troo said, fooling around with the string she kept in her shorts for when she got bored.

"And he had on pink-and-green argyle socks and he said my name and I had to fall asleep under the Kenfields' bushes and . . . that wasn't my imagination." I showed her my scratches and muddy butt. "It's not like when I thought the devil had gotten into Butchy's brain. And it's not like when I thought that Mr. Kenfield was a spy. It's not like that at all."

Troo looped the string around her fingers into a cat's

cradle and said like she had a bad taste in her mouth, "Is it like the Creature from the Black Lagoon?"

"Cut it out." I counted on Troo to believe me. But I swear, it seemed sometimes that I loved her a lot more than she loved me. I didn't bring up what Mother said to her about working on her charitable works and I could've. Maybe I should've. I darn well wanted to.

Troo breathed in deeply just like Mother did, like it was the last bit of air that was left on the planet Earth and she wanted it all for herself. "You know how Wendy wanders off sometimes and they find her at the zoo or down at the creek and that one time over on North Avenue at the record store dancing around?"

She was using her explaining voice, which wasn't one of my favorites.

"Well, that's all that happened," Troo said. "Wendy wandered off and maybe fell down and hit her head or something in the Spencers' root cellar."

I nodded, not because I was going along with this idea but because I didn't want to get in a fight with her.

"Remember that time Wendy came to our house and ate that stick of butter out of the refrigerator when Mother was in the bathtub?" Troo threw her head back and giggled.

I started to cry.

"Awww . . . c'mon." Troo swatted me on the arm. "Wendy's gonna be fine. Don't be so dang sensitive."

That's what Mother always said. That I was too dang sensitive, and that and a dime could buy me a cup of coffee, which was too bad for me since I couldn't stand coffee.

Troo held the cat's cradle up to my face. It was just this

white string she got off a bakery box, but by holding it around your fingers and moving it around it turned into something completely new and beautiful.

I pinched two of the string's edges and brought them into the middle.

"You'll see," Troo said. "Wendy'll be back home lickety-split, runnin' around without her clothes on again."

Wendy did that. Forgot to put her clothes on sometimes and then got out of the house when Mrs. Latour was looking after the other twelve kids, and there Wendy'd be on the playground swings sportin' her birthday suit. So one of us would take her home and Mrs. Latour would shake her head at her daughter and Wendy would say, "Thorry, Mama." And then she'd give her mama a big hug and not let go because Wendy *loved* to hug anything, but especially her mama, and for some reason . . . me, Thally O'Malley.

Troo took her turn on the cat's cradle, lifting it off my fingers into a diamond shape.

No matter what Troo said, I knew that Rasmussen had somehow hurt Wendy. There was just something about him that seemed so suspicious. Like how he was extra polite to everybody, not like any of the other fathers or brothers that lived in the neighborhood except for Mr. Fitzpatrick, who owned Fitzpatrick's Drugstore, who was also a very polite man. Seemed like all the other men on the block were always mad about something until they had a couple of beers in them, and then some of them got madder and some of them got nicer and would start singing "Danny Boy" or "Be Bop A Lula" and try to put their hands all over their wives' heinies.

So maybe last night Rasmussen got mad because I had hidden from him under the Kenfields' bushes and he ran

back down the alley and saw Wendy during one of her wanderings and pushed her down the Spencers' cellar stairs and
maybe even tried to murder and molest her. It would be all
my fault if sweet and silly Wendy Latour never wanted to
give anybody a hug again.

CHAPTER NINE

The next morning over our Breakfast of Champions, I tried again with Troo. "I'm telling you, Rasmussen was on a murderous rampage and when he couldn't murder me he tried to murder Wendy instead." The milk had gone clumpy so we ate the Wheaties dry. And the house, even Nell's room, smelled like something I couldn't quite put my finger on. Something like you'd smell over at the zoo.

Troo was trying to make her spoon stick to her nose the way Willie O'Hara could. "You know, you're beginning to remind me more and more of Virginia Cunningham in that *Snake Pit* movie."

That was so cruddy of Troo. She knew I worried sometimes that that was how I would end up because of my imagination. Looney people imagine things. Virginia Cunningham had and that's why they put her out in that mental hospital and the guys in the white coats made her take hot baths all day long even though she was plenty clean. Just for a second, I wanted to haul back and smack Troo just like Hall had. Knock that spoon right off her pretty little nose.

What a completely awful person I was to think such a thing. Thank goodness she beat me to it. She threw the spoon down and said, "C'mon, I wanna play tetherball. Last one there's a rotten egg."

The Vliet Street School was right across from our house. It was where the kids in the neighborhood that weren't Catholic went. But during the summer the city had this program on the playground that any kid could go to, no matter what country they'd originally come from or what religion they were.

There were swings and monkey bars and baseball diamonds. Four squares and hopscotches were painted right onto the asphalt in yellow paint. And you could play running games all day long, like red rover or dodgeball. Or standing games, like Captain May I and tetherball. And when you got worn out in the afternoon, you could sit down for a while on a green bench with a checkerboard painted right on it and watch everybody else get sweaty.

And there were these playground counselors that showed up year after year named Bobby Brophy and Barb Kircher who were not from Vliet Street. Bobby was the boss of the playground and Barb was his helper. Bobby was going to college to become a gym teacher so he loved to play tetherball and four square with us. Barb was going to college to be a cheerleader and meet somebody like Bobby, she said. Barb was extremely spunky. She was also the expert on lanyard making and had shown all us kids how to braid this long plastic stuff into a kind of necklace that you could attach keys to or anything you wanted, and wear it with any *ensemble*, which was what Troo had started calling her clothes. Troo and me had about fifty of these lanyards, that's how much we loved them. The luscious colors and especially the clean smell and how they felt. Slippery and cool to the touch. We could hardly stand it when Bobby would go into the shed behind the school that only the counselors were allowed in and after what seemed like a day or so he would come out with these colored plastics behind his back, telling us to choose one of his hands and not giving them to us until we had. That Bobby was a real card.

At the end of August, a King and Queen of the Playground would be crowned at a big summer block party with soda and food and music. Last summer, even though we'd only lived on Vliet Street for less than a year, Troo got to be the Queen. That's how outgoing she was. I was so jealous I didn't talk to her for a full week. (Sorry, Daddy.) I have a plan to be more outgoing this summer so I might be able to be the Queen as well.

Of course, I beat Troo over to the playground with my fly-like-the-wind speed and, of course, she never said anything about being a rotten egg.

I was already swaying on one of the swings when Troo came up and said, "I spy with my little eye . . ." She pointed over at the monkey bars.

Wendy Latour was laying flat on top of the bars, licking on a cherry Popsicle, a big gauze bandage half falling off her forehead.

"Big deal," I said. "Just because she's not dead doesn't mean that Rasmussen didn't *try* to murder her."

"Well, haven't seen the two of you in a while," Bobby the counselor said, appearing out of nowhere. He bounced one of those red rubber playground balls my way. "Fast Susie and Mary Lane have been lookin' for you. They wanna play four square."

Bobby Brophy was easy to look at, with his sandy crew-cut hair and blue eyes and a smile that showed teeth that were whiter than typing paper in his toast-colored face.

"Did you hear what happened to Wendy Latour?" I asked him. "Somebody pushed her down the Spencers' cellar stairs and she had to go to the hospital in an ambulance."

Troo snorted through her nose at me. "She *fell* down the Spencers' cellar stairs."

Bobby turned to look over at the monkey bars. "Like she doesn't have enough problems already."

I hadn't noticed her at first, probably because she was so darn skinny, but there was Mary Lane hanging right below Wendy. When she saw me, she jumped down and skipped over to Fast Susie, who was over near the bubbler waving her arms around at some older boy I didn't know. Mary Lane said something to Fast Susie and pointed at me and Troo.

"How about a game later, Sally?" Bobby asked.

He'd recently begun to teach me how to play chess, which was not at all like checkers even though it looked like it might be. I loved it when we played. How he'd bounce his legs up and down and rub his hands together like they were cold and he'd think so hard, like capturing my queen was so important that his forehead got papery lines in it.

I said, "Chess sounds great."

"It's a date." Bobby laughed, because he laughed almost all the time, that's how cheerful and full of energy he was, and then he walked off toward the baseball diamond where some kids were screaming at him to come over because it looked like they needed a pitcher. What a good egg Bobby was! So different from the other boys his age in the neighborhood. When I was grown up enough to go out on a real date, I was planning to take the bus over to the east side of town where Bobby was from. These west side boys, they could be trouble.

Mary Lane came up and knocked the red rubber ball out of my hand. "What was jerky Bobby talking to you about?"

Fast Susie was standing next to Mary Lane with her hands on her hips. Staring at Bobby's back, which was very long since he was pretty tall, Fast Susie whistled, *whoot woo*, and said, "I wouldn't throw that cat outta bed."

"When did you get a cat?" I asked.

Fast Susie looked back at me and shook her head and said, "Boy, you are such a square, O'Malley," and then she pulled me toward the yellow box. "Get it?" she said. "Square." She pointed down at the box. "Square." She pointed at me. "Get it?"

Fast Susie was always making fun of me like that because I didn't get half of her jokes. Troo said that was because Fast Susie was *très chic* and I was not at all *très chic*. I would have to agree with her because I didn't feel at all *très chic*, and I thought I would know if I did. I wondered where the heck Troo was coming up with all these new words. She was starting to sound an awful lot like a French librarian.

Fast Susie got into the server's box. "Did you hear that Sara Heinemann's mother sent her over to Delancey's for some milk, and guess what?" She smacked the red ball right at me, her long black hair going every which way, the sun sliding off it like a newly waxed car.

"What?" I asked, and smacked it right back at her.

"Sara disappeared into thin air. Poof!" Fast Susie caught the ball and threw it up high and waited for it to come down before she said, "Remind you of anybody?"

She meant Dottie Kenfield, but I didn't want to say that because then it made it seem true.

"When it got dark and Sara didn't come home," Fast Susie went on, "Mrs. Heinemann called the cops to start lookin'. They've been searching everywhere for her."

Mary Lane musta been eating something yellow, cuz when she stuck her tongue out at me it looked like that iguana's tongue up at the zoo. "Told ya," she said.

Fast Susie said, "And ya know what that means, right?" She dropped the ball and walked over to Mary Lane and put her hands around her neck and started choking her. They all laughed. Not me. I knew better than anyone that Fast Susie was probably right. Sara Heinemann was probably dead. And they might never find her, because I would bet my bottom dollar that one of the cops that Mrs. Heinemann had called to go looking for her daughter's choked body was Rasmussen. The murderer and molester himself.

After a long day of braiding lanyards with Barb, playing chess with Bobby and a wild all-playground game of red rover, we headed over to the Fazios' for some of Nana's excellent lasagna. During supper, Troo and Nana had a very big discussion about Doris Day movies and Nana got all silly over the actor Rock Hudson. After we'd helped Fast Susie dry the dishes, Troo and me left and didn't say much on the walk home because I thought we both regretted having to leave that nice Italian kitchen with good smells and arms waving all over the place like they were directing downtown traffic.

We found the door to our house wide open, but when I called up the stairs, "Hello? Anybody home?" there wasn't. Hall had definitely taken a long walk off a short pier. I figured it was because Mother was dying. But then that didn't seem right either because Hall and Mother were fighting and taking the Lord's name in vain all the time before she went into the hospital, so what did he care if she died.

Troo and me didn't bother washing up because the last time we'd tried, the water came out all warm and orange. We just took off our clothes and laid down in our bed and listened to the *creak creak creak* of our neighbors' porch swing. Mr. Kenfield sat out there by himself almost every summer night, just rocking and smoking. The sound and the smell always traveled up to our bedroom window and reminded me of loneliness. Especially that night, because me and Troo were all by ourselves and it felt so much like that was how it would be from now on.

Troo rolled onto her stomach and pulled up her T-shirt, letting me know she wanted me to rub her back, which was something I'd done every single night since I could remember. "Do you know why Fast Susie is called Fast Susie?" she asked.

I thought about that afternoon. "Because she is an excellent person to have on your team for red rover?"

"No," Troo said and laughed. "It's because she lets boys get some of the sex."

Fast Susie was three years older than me. Thirteen. A teenager. Different things happened when you got that old. Gettin' some of the sex must be one of them.

"Fast Susie goes to second base," Troo said.

What the heck was she talking about? Everybody knew that Fast Susie didn't like baseball and what did baseball have to do with the sex? "What do you mean Fast Susie goes to second base?"

For a minute, I got worried that talking about baseball like this would make Troo remember the day her and Daddy and Uncle Paulie didn't make it home after the game. Right after the crash I tried to ask her what happened. How come Daddy smashed into the elm tree? Wasn't he paying attention? But Troo wouldn't talk to anybody for a long time after the accident and now if I tried to bring it up she'd just get mad or pretend she didn't hear me.

"Going to second base is when you let a boy touch your titties, which is another word for bosoms," Troo said.

"Ohhh . . ." I tried not to act too disgusted. To be more *très chic.* "Is there a going to first base?"

Troo stretched out next to me, long and lean. "Frenchie kissing is going to first base. That's when a boy puts his tongue in your mouth."

I would never, ever let somebody touch my titties when I grew them or do Frenchie kissing to my mouth.

"And third base?" I asked. Eddie Mathews was the third baseman for the Braves and Daddy's absolute favorite. I really missed listening to the ball games on the radio with my Sky King. His beer in his hand, his gal Sal on his lap. I didn't really understand baseball but Daddy, he was an adorer of baseball. And I was an adorer of Daddy. The farm porch at night always smelled of his hard day in the field and the yellow light on the radio shined on his excited face when Hank Aaron would hit a home run and Daddy would jump up out of his chair and his gal Sal fell onto the floor. Especially the summer he died. Because that summer the Braves were gonna be in the World Series, he said, and we would go and eat salted peanuts and hot dogs with mustard and pickle relish. Which were my absolute favorites.

"Third base is when a boy touches you down there." Troo pointed to my undies.

I would never, ever let anybody touch me down there.

"So is a home run gettin' some?" I asked, finally catching on.

"Yup, a home run is gettin' some."

When hell froze over.

Troo asked, "You know that Junie was molested, right?" She rolled over and ran her fingers down my neck like it was a piano.

I hadn't known Junie like a friend. But I'd seen her at the playground sometimes and she seemed really nice and loved lanyard making as much as I did and was *very* good at it.

Troo said, "Do you even know what molested means?"

"No." I stuck my face into my pillow, until I reached the Aqua Velva smell.

"Fast Susie said that when a girl is molested it means that somebody touches her in her private parts and hurts her real bad. And then he gets some sex from her even though she doesn't want to give it."

I turned my head and looked out my window over to Dottie's bedroom. Her ghost had started crying.

"Sally?" Troo whispered, pulling the sheet up over our heads.

"Yeah?"

"You hear that?"

"It's Dottie's ghost."

Troo moved a few inches closer. "That would be a real bad thing."

I wasn't sure if she meant Dottie disappearing into thin air or what happened to Junie. But it didn't matter because they were both real bad things. "I won't ever let anything happen to you. You know that."

I couldn't stop thinking about how Rasmussen had touched Junie when she hadn't wanted him to. How scared she musta been. "Are you sure about that?" I asked. "About that molesting part?" I stopped rubbing her back because just then the thought of touching skin made me feel a little sick to my stomach right below my wishbone.

"Fast Susie says that the man molested Junie and then had the sex with her and when he was done he wrapped her undies around her neck and pulled on 'em until she couldn't breathe anymore."

After Troo fell asleep, I laid there in the dark and listened to Dottie's ghost crying, hoping so bad that Fast Susie was wrong. Because I knew that if somebody didn't listen to me, if somebody didn't stop Rasmussen right away, me and Junie Piaskowski would soon have a lot more in common than our love of lanyards.

CHAPTER TEN

It was hot for late June, much hotter than it shoulda been. Ethel said that it was so hot and humid that it reminded her of Mississippi, where she was born and raised. Like we did every Wednesday, Troo and me had spent the morning being charitable with Mrs. Galecki, who Ethel had been taking good care of for a long time. The reason why we did that, besides adoring Ethel, was when we got back to school in September, Sister Imelda would make all us kids read out loud our stories entitled "How I Spent My Charitable Summer." What with everything that'd been going on, I hadn't worked on my story for a while, so I promised myself that I would do that tonight even if Hall was there. It was gettin' harder and harder to figure exactly when Hall might show up. When he did come home, you *could* figure on him being what Mary Lane called "sloshed to the gills."

After we were done helping Ethel out, she gave us each a peanut butter and marshmallow sandwich, like she always did, and then Troo and me went over to the zoo to watch Sampson get fed, which was the other thing we did every Wednesday.

We'd just come out of the Honey Creek that ran behind the whole park and the air felt cool and nice on our bare legs. Troo had recently started smoking L&Ms that she'd stolen out of Hall's pocket when he was passed out on the couch. She had also found a flat little blue French cap to wear that she said was called a *beret*. Troo just went ape for hats of all kinds. "I've been thinking," she said, lighting up.

"About what?" We were up in our favorite zoo tree and I was admiring Sampson while eating my sandwich. Troo had eaten hers on the way over.

"About Sara Heinemann disappearing." Troo took a puff off the cigarette and made the smoke go up her nose the way Mother did sometimes. "It's called French inhaling." She coughed and did it again. "I think Fast Susie is right. I think Sara has gotten herself murdered and molested just like Junie."

I thought Sara had gotten herself murdered and molested, too, but I didn't want to scare Troo by agreeing with her. And I also thought—no, I *knew*—that Rasmussen had done it, just like Junie. And that he'd also pushed Wendy down the Spencers' root cellar stairs because it had been so stormy dark out that night that he probably hadn't realized it was Wendy until it was too late. He probably hadn't gone ahead and murdered Wendy because he knew a Mongoloid couldn't point him out in a lineup, which was what happened if you got arrested in the movies.

Troo spat her cigarette down to the ground and wiggled off her tree branch onto mine. She pointed over at Sampson and made a surprised face and said, "Oh, look, Sally!" When I turned, she grabbed the other half of my sandwich out of my hand and stuck it in her mouth before I could stop her.

"Troo!"

She grinned and said with her mouth full, "Remember how Junie was found over by the lagoon?"

I didn't answer because I was mad. I'd been really looking forward to the rest of that peanut butter and marshmallow sandwich.

"Maybe that same guy who took Junie took Sara," Troo said, fingering my braid, which was her way of saying sorry. "If we could find Sara's body, we'd probably get a reward and our pictures in the newspaper like Mary Lane did when she called in that fire she set."

"It's Rasmussen, Troo. Rasmussen is that guy." I brushed her hand away, worn out with her not believing me.

A couple of other people had come for Sampson's two o'clock feeding. Two ladies with little kids I didn't know. And also Artie Latour, who was one of Wendy's brothers. Artie was two years older than me and was a really goofy tall guy with an Adam's apple that was so big all you could do was stare at his skinny neck when he talked to you, getting hypnotized by this thing moving up and down like the grain elevator out at the farm. Artie also had a harelip from when he was born. Not too much else to keep in mind about him except he walked with his toes pointed in.

Troo hopped down from the tree after me and started over to where Artie was standing in front of Sampson's cage, which wasn't really a cage at all. In the winter Sampson stayed in his cage in the monkey house. (Heartbreaking.) But in the summer, he liked to be outside where there were big orange boulders and a little pool of water and some shade off to the side where he could get out of the heat and eat his lunch in peace.

"Artie," Troo called over to him.

Probably he didn't answer because one of his older brothers, Reese, was the biggest bully in the whole world. Reese was always picking on Artie and had given him a good whack on the side of the head at the playground last year after he lost to Artie in Battleship. His ear swelled up to the size of a peach and now Artie didn't hear so hot sometimes.

"Artiiieee," Troo screamed.

He jumped away from the black iron railing. When he saw who it was, his face turned the same color as an orangutan's butt. Artie had what Fast Susie called "the hots" for Troo.

"Wendy okay?" I asked, coming up next to him.

Artie shrugged. "She got some stitches." He was such a good brother to Wendy, not like Reese, who always called her the idiot. Reese Latour would go to hell eventually, on this I would bet a million dollars.

Sampson was eating a banana, not singing while he ate, showing a lot better manners than those Latour boys. Troo had snuck us in for supper a couple of nights ago with the help of Mimi Latour, who was in the same grade as Troo. The Latours were having something called slumgoodie, which was in this big glass bowl and couldn't hold a candle to Mother's tuna noodle casserole. There was also a big stack of Wonder Bread and oleo and powdered milk to drink that tasted so much like I imagined melted chalk would. Reese Latour stared at Troo the entire supper, smiling at her like she was a piece of cherry cobbler.

Artie asked, like he didn't care at all, "What're you doing for the Fourth of July, Troo?"

The man who was feeding Sampson was Mary Lane's father. I thought he should take some of that food home and feed it to Mary Lane so she wouldn't be the skinniest darn kid in the world anymore.

Troo said, "The Fourth? Why, Sally and me wouldn't miss the bicycle parade for all the tea in China." She winked at him and Artie's Adam's apple gave his gum a little ride down his throat, he got so flusterated. He'd come in second last year to Troo in the bike-decorating contest and had won a subscription to a magazine called *Boys' Life*. Troo had won a new set of streamers for her bike and a five-dollar certificate to the Five and Dime since the bike-decorating contest was sponsored by Kenfield's Five and Dime . . . We Have What You Need!

Artie pulled on his bad ear, which he did all the time because he was sorta high-strung, like a racehorse. "Did you hear about Sara Heinemann bein' missing?"

Troo was resting her arms on the iron railing, watching Mr. Lane toss Sampson's lunch to him. "Yeah."

"The cops came by this morning and said to make sure we lock our doors." Artie bent down and began rolling up his pants legs. He was probably gonna go do a little cooling off over in the Honey Creek just like we had. "You and Sally should be careful. My ma says she's not gonna let my sisters go out alone anymore after the streetlights come on. She says it's not safe. That there's a nut runnin' around with a couple of loose screws."

I was staring at Sampson and thinking about how he could keep anybody safe. How just to see his big hands and black hairy arms you'd know he'd never let anything bad happen to you. And then, like he knew what I was thinking, he looked at me and waved. And I waved back.

"Quit it," Troo said, and knocked my hand down and

looked around to see if anybody was watching. Her little blue French cap fell over her eye and she shoved it back. "He's not saying hello to you. He's just a gorilla batting at a fly, for Chrissakes."

"No, Troo," I said, reaching as far as I could over the railing toward him, wanting so much to stroke his smooth hair. "He's much, much more than just a gorilla." I waved one more time, and in answer Sampson ran to the edge of the pit and looked me straight in the eye and beat his chest over and over. "He is magnificent."

CHAPTER ELEVEN

"How I Spent My Charitable Summer"
by Sally Elizabeth O'Malley

Almost every Wednesday this summer, me and Troo, which is short for Trooper and not for Trudy, which everybody thinks, go to Mrs. Galecki's. Troo's real name is Margaret. Our daddy, before he died, gave her that name, Real Trooper, because she didn't cry when she stepped on that rusty nail in the Ambersons' backyard and had to have that shot. Then the whole family started calling her Trooper and when that took too much time to say, Troo. I also call her Troo genius, because she is really, really smart and knew all the state capitols by the time she was seven years old. So Troo and me almost every Wednesday go to Mrs. Galecki's to help Ethel take care of her. I read books to her once Ethel gets her into her wheelchair out on her back screened-in porch where Mrs. Galecki likes to stare at that crab-apple tree. Her head is wobbly but her mind is still smart and not like the other grandmother of ours, who had hardening in her arteries and for a while

made us call her Gramma Marie Antoinette. That
was my daddy's mother. She's dead now. Both our
grampas are dead. Our mother is dying. Troo and
me go visit our other granny up on Fifty-ninth Street,
who is not dead yet but is getting closer by the minute. She is eighty-four years old and can't bend down
anymore or go to the grocery store, and she has arthritis and palpitations so we have to pick things up
off the floor for her and wring out her underwear
and Uncle Paulie's socks. Uncle Paulie is not exactly
right in the head because of his brain being damaged, so he has to live with Granny where she can
keep an eye on him. Here is another charitable thing
I did. I wrote a letter to my mother. They don't let
kids in the hospital unless someone is pounding
down heaven's door so I have to send it in the mail
and I don't have any money for a stamp, but as soon
as I can find one I am going to send it.

DEAR MOTHER,
    HOW ARE YOU FEELING? A LOT OF THINGS HAVE BEEN
GOING ON AROUND HERE. DADDY TOLD ME TO TELL YOU HE
FORGIVES YOU. I MISS YOU. PLEASE COME HOME.
    YOURS IN CHRIST,
    YOUR DAUGHTER,
    SALLY O'MALLEY

That's what I wrote that night before Troo came back
from the bathroom and Nell came in smelling like the brew-
ery over near County Stadium, where before the baseball
games Daddy and I used to sing the "Star-Spangled Banner"

that ended with: The laaand of the free and the home . . . of
the . . . *Braves.*

Nell was leaning on the door to our bedroom. "Where
you two been all day? I just ran into Hall comin' up the
block and he's mad as a hornet and drunk as a skunk." Nell
talked in the croaky voice she must've inherited from her
father.

Troo pulled the sheet over her head and yelled, "Aw,
shut up, Nell. Can't you see we're trying to get our beauty
sleep here?"

Nell tripped on her way over to the bed, then kicked at
it and tried to grab for Troo, whose side was closest to the
wall. "Damn your smart mouth, Troo O'Malley."

"Fuck you," Troo said from under the sheet. "Just fuck,
fuck, fuck, fuck you." Fast Susie had recently taught her that
word and she absolutely adored it because Troo had always
been in love with *all* words that started with the letter *f.*

Nell kept hitting at the sheet and Troo kept laughing
harder and louder, and then Nell just gave up and smacked
me because I was closer. "That's a little present for your sister. Give it to her for me, won't you, Sally dear? And by the
way, you numbskull"—she stuck her pointy red nails into
my shoulder—"it's not Earl Flynn, it's *Errol* Flynn." And
then Nell stumbled out and slammed the door to her bedroom hard enough to make the crucifix above our bed rattle
like a train.

"What a pill," Troo said, still laughing under the sheet.

I put my hand over where I thought her mouth was and
said, "Shhh."

Hall was coming up the front steps. He was singing.
And falling down. And getting back up. I got under the

sheet with Troo. For a minute it was all quiet and I thought that maybe he'd passed out so I took my hand off Troo's mouth, but then he crashed through the front door at the top of the landing and smashed into the piano and hollered, "Fer Chrissakes!" when he slammed his hands down onto the deep end of the keys and a horrible ear-aching sound echoed down the hall.

He was coming through the living room. The floor creaked in the dining room. I could hear muttering and singing and things skittering across the wood floor. And then it all stopped. He was just there. Leaning in our bedroom doorway the way Nell had. I could smell the beer. Troo grabbed my hand and squeezed it with everything she had.

"Where the hell you two been?" he yelled. I put my fingers back up to her lips, letting Troo know not to answer.

And then he started singing again. "Ninety-nine bottles of beer on the wall . . . ninety-nine bottles of beer. If one of those bottles should happen to fall . . . well, well, well. Who do we have here?" Hall ripped the sheet off us. All we had on was our underpants.

He was breathing in the dark like somebody had been chasing him and we didn't dare move or open our eyes, but then Troo finally said, "We're sleeping, Hall. Get out and leave us be."

Hall reached over me and pulled Troo out of bed with one hand.

He threw his beer bottle down and it spun round and round on the bare floor. He had Troo up against the bedroom wall, holding her there like he was trying to hang her like a picture. "What did you just say?" he snarled.

Troo stuck her tongue out and Hall yelled, "Don't you

dare . . . ," and then he lifted her off the wall and smacked her against it again.

I knew if I didn't stop him, he would hurt her bad. I'd seen Hall in this mood before when he was drunk and gave Mr. Hopkins, who used to live next door, a fat lip and kicked him when he was down.

"Hall?" I said softly, swinging my feet out of bed.

He didn't say anything. His breathing was comin' faster and faster, and Troo's arms were turning redder and redder.

"Ninety-nine bottles of beer on the wall . . . ," I sang.

Hall went way in close to Troo's face and yelled, "Your mother ain't here to protect you now. You ever talk to me like that again, I'll beat you so bad you won't walk for a week, you little—"

"Let go of me, you fu—"

"Ninety-nine bottles of beer on the wall," I screamed out so Hall wouldn't hear what Troo was about to say. "Ninety-nine bottles of beer. If one of those bottles should happen to fall, there'd be how many bottles of beer on the wall?" Keeping my eye on him, I grabbed for a nightie that was balled up next to the bed. "Hall?"

He let Troo slide down the wall like he'd forgotten all about her and sang out, "Ninety-eight bottles of beer on the wall."

I took his hand and led him into the living room. We sang together until we got down to eighty-eight bottles and he passed out on our red-and-brown couch.

When I finally looked up, Troo was sitting on the piano bench, one of Mother's long knives in her hand.

CHAPTER TWELVE

Kenfield's Five and Dime had to be the best store in the whole wide world. It even smelled good because it had this case with a glass window full of tons of candy, like little wax bottles full of red liquid and pastel buttons on white paper and B-B-Bats and off to the side a little machine that made fresh popcorn all day long.

The wood floors were a wavy dark yellow color and the aisles were skinny but full of things that Mrs. Kenfield musta collected over the years and then sold to people. She was the nicest one of the Kenfield family. And, of course, Dottie was nice when she was still around and hadn't disappeared into thin air. Mr. Kenfield was a sour man. Mother said he was that way because he never got over what happened to Dottie. When I asked her, "By the way, whatever *did* happen to Dottie?" Mother gave me one of her do-you-smell-dog-poop looks and said mind your own beeswax.

Kenfield's even had a pet aisle where Troo and me had bought a turtle once that we called Elmer, and there were garden seeds and pencils and bars of Ivory soap. All the ladies in the neighborhood would come to shop at the Five and Dime with brush curlers in their hair so they would look good for their husbands when they came home from the factory, so sometimes the store also reminded me of a beauty parlor.

We walked down aisle three and found the boxes of Kleenex stacked on top of one another. Troo was keeping her eyes peeled for when Mrs. Kenfield got busy with Mrs. Plautch, trying to help her select some new hot pads for her kitchen. Troo had a way with Kleenex flowers. This summer, she was going to snitch the bobby pins she'd need to make the flowers out of Nell's Future Hairdresser Kit, which Hall had paid for and said would be a good trade for Nell since everybody had hair, like everybody had feet. Hall had taken her up to Yvonne's School of Beauty and enrolled her last week. Nell came home with a pink hatbox full of scissors and pins and combs and, of course, her favorite, permanent rods and papers and the solution that smelled like death warmed over. Worse, even, than Dr. Sullivan's breath. That was smart of Nell, to ask Hall to enroll her when he was shnockered.

I watched Troo sneak a box of Kleenex under her shirt, and then we left by the back door that slammed hard enough for Mrs. Kenfield to take notice and call out, "Hope your mother is feeling better, girls."

Taking that Kleenex made my conscience feel bothered, so when we got out in the alley I said, "We gotta take that back. It's not right to steal."

"Aw, quit being such a goody-goody. The Kleenex is a consolation prize because our mother might be dying. A consolation prize like they give those women on those game shows that Helen used to watch when she ironed. Remember that?" It made me so sad to think of Mother that I wasn't able to say anything else about the Kleenex.

On the way back home, like Troo promised, we stopped

at the park lagoon. I'd brought my fishing pole. I never caught anything, but I liked to fish once a week next to the willow tree in the shade. I have this picture of my daddy and me fishing when I was about three years old out at this lake near the farm. His hair is blown by the breeze into these two little horns. Mother said he looks devil-may-care in this picture, which I thought was a pretty funny thing to say.

"Hall must think Mother's gonna die," I said, scrounging around in the lagoon mud for a worm and finally finding one.

Troo had found an old Kroger bag in the trash can and stuck her Kleenex in it and now she was sitting on the bank dangling her feet in the water. That girl just loved to go barefoot and never worried about stepping on a rusty nail again, which I really admired. "Hall who?" she said.

Troo hated to talk about any kind of dying and always changed the subject like that. I changed the subject back because I needed to know what she thought.

"Hall must think Mother's gonna die or he wouldn't be gettin' some from Rosie up at Jerbak's and getting so darn drunk." I took a bobber out of my pocket and slipped it on my line. "Since he and Nell are the only ones that get to see her, maybe he's right." I dropped the line into the lagoon right into the center of some willow leaves. I could see myself in the water. My face was swimming about a foot away from my body.

Troo splashed with her feet and made me disappear. "Well, you know what Doris Day says, *Que sera, sera*. That's French, you know."

Troo was just doing some of that whistling in the dark. I bet deep down in her heart she missed Helen as much as

I did and I'd been missing her so bad. All of her. Even her yelling and her warbly singing but especially the way she looked on Sunday morning in church when she was all dolled up and the best-looking woman in the Communion line. Her white dress pressed with sharp creases and her matching white high-heel shoes. Her great hair caught at the back of her neck in a gold barrette. I even missed that sad look she gave me when she thought I wasn't looking. And the smell of her breath and the feel of her cool freckled hand on my forehead.

I felt a little tug on my line but brought it up too fast and discovered the worm was gone. "Darn," I said, and turned to Troo, who was bending over the water and making faces at herself. That's when I saw him. Rasmussen. He was parked across the street, staring at us from the window of his squad car. When he knew I'd seen him, he drove off suddenly.

"Did you see him?" I jumped up and pointed down Lisbon Street. "That was Rasmussen. He was watchin' us."

Troo looked but you couldn't barely even see the car anymore. "That wasn't Rasmussen. And even if it was, why would he be watchin' us anyway?" She slipped her tennis shoes back on and then crawled into the deepness of that weeping willow tree. It was one of Troo's favorite summer places. She loved the way she could sit in there and nobody could see her but she could see them, and how when the sun landed just right on those leaves they reminded her of those beaded curtains they had over at the Peking Palace, where we got chicken chop suey once last winter after Hall sold a lot of shoes in one day. Troo had lit up an L&M. The smoke was wiggling out through the willow branches.

I sat down on the bank and threw my line back in even

though I didn't have a worm. I started thinking about the
fish down there and what my red bobber must look like to
them, floating above them, watching them like Rasmussen
had been watching us.

"Oh God. Oh sweet Jesus, Mary and Joseph," Troo yelled,
crawling out from under the tree. She had a tennis shoe in the
palm of her hand.

"Holy cow," I whispered. Troo set the shoe on the
ground and poked at it with a stick until it flipped over and
you could see somebody had stitched a little pink butterfly
near the heel. "It must be Sara's. Look at that blood. We
should tell somebody."

It occurred to me that maybe Rasmussen hadn't been
watching us. Maybe he'd been waiting for us to leave, because right before he fell asleep last night he remembered
this shoe with the little butterfly on the heel that he had left
behind when he'd murdered and molested Sara. He'd come
back for it. The laces were still tied. And the blood spots
made a kind of connect-the-dots pattern.

"It's definitely Sara's," I said, inspecting it.

"How do you know that?" Troo asked.

"Whose else could it be?"

"Aw, c'mon. It could be anybody's. Like . . ." She couldn't
think of anybody's name so instead she just stood up and
flicked the willow leaves off her shorts. "It's probably just
mud anyways."

I was sure we needed to call the police. But that would
mean Rasmussen would show up, and wouldn't that be just
hunky-dory for him? Here I was, the girl who he was trying
to murder and molest, poking at the bloody shoe he'd been
looking for. It would be a two-fer for him.

Then I had an idea. Me, not Troo, who usually had the ideas since she was so outgoing and a genius. I put the shoe down next to the lagoon bank, setting it upright so it looked real sharp, like the ones up in Shuster's window. Then I walked to the firebox and said, "I'm gonna pull this thing."

The wind changed direction and the sweet smell of chocolate chip cookies came floating in on the breeze, which was making little swirls on top of the lagoon. Troo closed her eyes and breathed in the smell and said, "You better not. Remember how mad they got the last time?"

I'd pulled this exact same fire handle last summer right around this time. And boy, were those firemen steamed when they found out there was no fire. I'd done it cuz Mary Lane said she'd give me a dime if I would and, after all, she *was* our best friend.

"I'm gonna pull it so somebody finds this shoe," I said. "It's a clue. Like in *Cinderella*. Ready?"

I yanked the little black handle down and Troo grabbed her Kroger bag and we took off across the street and hid behind a garage. About three minutes later the sirens were wailing down Lisbon. We watched as the firemen jumped off the truck and looked around for the smoke. Then one of the guys took his fireman's hat off and threw it on the ground and said loud enough for us to hear, "Those goddamn kids. That's the third time this month." But just like I planned, he saw the shoe next to the lagoon and then called over another short fireman, who picked it up, and they got back into the truck and drove off. For a second there, I thought the fatter one saw us and I picked up Troo's hand to hightail it out of there.

Now somebody had that shoe who might think it could

be Sara's, and thank goodness that somebody was not Sally O'Malley. That was a big relief because I had enough other things to worry about. Like staying two steps ahead of Rasmussen.

We took the shortcut home through the Von Knappens' backyard, and when we turned the corner to head down Vliet Street I saw something that I wished I hadn't. Right then I knew I had a lot more to worry about than I'd originally thought. In fact, I knew right then that Troo and me were, like Hall said all the time now, "Up the Shit Creek without a paddle."

CHAPTER THIRTEEN

A squad car was parked right in front of our house. Rasmussen was sitting on the steps closest to the street. His stork legs were stretched out, his elbows on the step above him. Behind him, Mrs. Goldman, the landlady who lived downstairs from us, was peeking out her lace curtains, probably checking to see what all the commotion was about.

The cop had two soda bottles in his hands. "Hello, girls," he said politely.

I didn't say anything but Troo said, "Hi, Officer Rasmussen," as she eyed those Cokes. The hair around her forehead had gotten curlier than usual and she smelled from the walk home the way she did when she got real sweaty, which was sort of like your hand did if you held a nickel in it too long.

Rasmussen patted the step next to him. After Troo sat down, he handed her the soda and she guzzled the entire bottle down. Rasmussen smiled at me and said, "Well, what have the two of you been up to today?" He waggled the other Coke in front of me. I shook my head no, so he gave it to Troo, who burped real loud for an almost ten-year-old and then drank that one down, too.

"Cat got your tongue, Sally?" Rasmussen was dressed all in his heavy blue cop uniform. I watched as a bead of sweat crawled from beneath his hat and skimmed over that vein in his temple.

Troo said, "We been over to the zoo."

If I'd had something other than a piece of Dubble Bubble in my stomach, I would have thrown up. How could my own sister speak to him?

"The zoo, huh?" Rasmussen said. "Well, if my memory doesn't fail me, the zoo is close to the lagoon, isn't it?"

I dared not take my eyes off of this Frankenstein monster with very big dimples sitting on our front steps.

"Sally? That's right, isn't it?" he asked. "The lagoon is just across from the zoo?"

What a faker. He knew we'd been over there. He'd been watching us.

"And how was Sampson today?" Rasmussen asked.

Troo said, "We didn't go see Sampson."

"Don't get around much anymore," I said before I could stop myself.

Rasmussen stopped smiling. "What was that?"

"Don't pay too much attention to her, Officer. Sally imagines things. Like don't get around much anymore." Troo giggled. "She thinks that's what Sampson is singing to himself all the time."

Rasmussen laughed loudly and it was such a good one, a little like the way a bowling ball sounds when it goes down an alley.

"Oh, so you have an imagination then, Sally?" he said. "That's a good thing. My sister Carol has an imagination and she ended up writing books."

Mother thought my imagination was a bad thing and that always made me feel real hopeless because if I coulda changed it for her, I woulda.

Mrs. Goldman was still in her window, watching. Thank God Almighty. If I had to grab for his gun and shoot Rasmussen, Mrs. Goldman would hide me in her attic just like the Anne Frank girl in that book she gave me last summer for helping her and Mr. Goldman out with their garden.

Rasmussen turned to see what I was looking at and then tipped his hat at Mrs. Goldman, who let the curtain slide back. When we were working together earlier that morning pulling weeds, I'd almost told our landlady that Rasmussen was after me since she didn't seem to like cops all that much and sometimes she called them the Gestapo. Now, I wished I'd told her.

Rasmussen pointed to the step below him. "Why not take a load off, Sally?"

I took a step back.

He looked at me kinda funny and said, "Somebody pulled the fire alarm over near the lagoon a little while ago. Fire Chief Bailey told me he thought he saw two girls hiding behind the Wahlstroms' garage."

He'd murdered Junie Piaskowski at the end of last summer. He'd probably murdered Sara. And I knew how he'd gotten away with it. Because Troo was right, Rasmussen acted nice. He even volunteered up at the school's paper drive that we had every year to raise money for the missionaries. He was strong, too. I remembered how he picked up the load of papers I'd brought up to school in my Radio Flyer and swung them up onto the scale like it was nothing to him. And how he'd said, "Congratulations, Sally. You're the big winner for the day." Then he handed me a quarter and a free pass to the fish fry that we had every Friday night in the school cafeteria even though I didn't have half as much paper as Willie O'Hara, who was so good at collecting things.

"Sally?"

I looked over at Troo.

"Are you having a little flight of imagination?" She was getting herself worked up like she'd gotten drunk on that Coke. She was also giving me that smile where just one corner of her mouth went up. It was a bad smile. A teaser's smile. "Officer Rasmussen wants to know if you pulled the fire alarm."

"You already know you could get into serious trouble for making a false alarm. You were warned about that last year, right?" Rasmussen took off his cap again and ran his fingers through his hair. "I'm glad to hear it wasn't you, Sally. Always felt you were a girl of excellent character."

He was trying to butter me up. Trick me into confessing. I looked down at his shoes. They were brown and scuffed with run-down heels. Not like the black ones he had on the other night when he chased me down the alley. And he had on white socks with blue dots on them. Not the pink-and-green argyle ones. But he could not fool me.

"Well, I'm going to ask around the neighborhood about that alarm. Maybe it was a couple of the Latour girls. You two remember what I told you last year about talking to strangers, right?" He stood. Goodness, he was a tall, tall man.

"Why haven't you found Sara yet?" I blurted out.

"I'm sure she'll turn up soon and there is nothing in the world to be worried about." Rasmussen sounded heartbroken when he said that, which only made me feel more disgusted with him. He walked down the last two steps and brushed against my arm, which made me shiver. Then he pointed at the Kroger bag and said very seriously, "You gotta pay back Mrs. Kenfield for those Kleenex, Troo. Remember the Fourth Commandment."

Troo's eyes got real big, almost as big as Granny's thyroid eyes. "Yeah, I was goin' to do that," she said, trying to put the bag behind her back like out of sight, out of mind.

"See that you do," Rasmussen said. "And I'm sorry that your mother is sick. Maybe one of these days, you can come over to my house. Got a new puppy who likes little girls a lot."

"Thank you, Officer Rasmussen," Troo said. "The next time we go to see Ethel and Mrs. Galecki, Sally and me will stop by." She was being what Hall called a little brownnose, like that new guy named Jim who was working up at Shuster's.

After Rasmussen started up the block toward the Latours', Troo laughed and said, "Well, that was a close one." She rolled over onto the grass and when she did her tummy made this erupting noise. "I'm famished."

I was still watching Rasmussen. He was talking to Willie O'Hara, who was pointing to his bike tire. Rasmussen knelt down to look at it and said something to Willie, who was nodding. Then Rasmussen stood up and cuffed him on his head. Willie smiled up at him like he was the bee's knees. Like Daddy always said, the devil can take any form he wishes.

"How 'bout we head over to Granny's?" I said, feeling safe since I knew Rasmussen would be grilling the Latours for the next half hour. I was hungry, too, and Granny would at least give us a cuppa. That's what she called cups of tea. And if Uncle Paulie was there, he'd probably just ignore us and work on one of those Popsicle stick houses he was always building. Granny had about a ton of those Popsicle stick houses all over her little house. Everywhere you looked, there was another one. Troo liked Granny, but Uncle Paulie gave her the creeps. Especially when he wanted to play peek-a-boo, which was his very favorite game. Troo said it was just cooties, but I thought I finally understood why she didn't like him. O'Malley sister mental telepathy. Uncle Paulie reminded Troo of the crash.

Troo said, "I don't have time to visit with Granny. I gotta start up on my Kleenex flowers."

In two more days there would be the parade of bicycles and relay races and a picnic and finally, the fireworks over at the lagoon. Fourth of July was the best holiday of the year next to Halloween and Christmas.

"Where you two been?"

Troo and me looked up. Nell was standing above us on the steps. Her hair was brown just like Troo's grocery bag and came a little lower than her neck and she was now wearing it in something called "the bubble," which was also what Nell's figure looked like. That might be a slight exaggeration. Mother said Nell was voluptuous. (This is like lush.)

"Around," Troo said, searching for a four-leaf clover, which is something she did sometimes when she got around grass.

"I've been looking for you all morning," Nell said. "You wanna go see Mother?"

"What do you mean, do we wanna go see Mother?" Troo asked like she didn't care at all.

"Eddie's aunt Margie is a nurse over at St. Joe's and she said she'd sneak you two in, if you want." Nell was dressed in clean clothes because she knew how to run the washing machine and the wringer. She looked like a grown-up in her pink pedal pushers and pink blouse. You could see her white bra peeking through the third and fourth buttons. Her bosoms were getting so big! Like all they'd needed was this hot, humid summer to grow as round and ripe as watermelons.

"Nell, your bosoms are huge," Troo said, reading my mind. "They're practically blocking out the sun. What the hell you doin' to 'em?"

Nell snorted. She knew Troo was nothing but jealous. Ever since Fast Susie had shown us her bosoms, Troo would lift up her shirt every morning at the mirror behind our bedroom door, and if she stood just right, her bosoms did look slightly bigger, but I thought that was because there was a wave in the mirror.

Nell crossed her arms across her chest. Barely. "You wanna go see Mother or not?"

Troo plucked a blade of grass from the lawn and stuck it in her mouth. She shut her eyes. She was thinking.

I jumped up and said, "I'll go." Since I couldn't find the money for a stamp for my letter, I needed to tell Mother in person what Daddy had told me before he died. That he forgave her. Because if she really was dying, she'd want to know that happy news when they saw each other in Heaven.

"You comin'?" I asked Troo.

"Naw." She picked up her bag of Kleenex and walked toward the backyard.

That got me worried. Troo, who was braver and prettier and smarter and more outgoing than me, thought it might not be a good idea to see her dying mother. That gave me second thoughts and I almost went after her.

But then Eddie Callahan pulled up in his Chevy car. It was turquoise and white and had fins so if you should accidentally drive it into the lagoon that would be okay. Nell had told me Eddie got a really good deal on this Chevy car because the old owner was in big trouble with the bookies. I was pretty sure that had something to do with the Finney Library. Maybe the old Chevy owner didn't pay his dues, which could really get Mrs. Kambowski riled up, and that was why the bookies had to sell the car to Eddie. To pay her off? I'd ask Troo later. She'd been spending a lot of time at the library lately. Probably doing some more cheatin' on the Bookworm Ladder.

"What's cookin', good-lookin'?" Eddie said to Nell's bosoms, which it seemed he was not able to take his eyes off of. I couldn't blame him. They sorta stuck out of Nell's chest like the headlights on his car.

I got into the backseat and Eddie turned up the radio real loud and we headed down Vliet Street toward the hospital listening to "Love Potion #9." When we were stopped at the corner of North and Lisbon, Eddie said, "Damn, was I speeding?" He was looking into his rearview mirror around the fuzzy dice.

I turned in my seat and looked out the back window and there was Rasmussen, his gumball flashing.

Eddie pulled over to the curb and blew his breath into his hand, which was very thoughtful since you should never have bad breath when you're talking to a cop. Suddenly Rasmussen was at Eddie's car window. He leaned his head in and looked directly at me and said, "Sally, could you get out of the car?"

Eddie, being so glad that he wasn't getting a speeding ticket, reached back and pulled me over to the front seat and shoved me out the door.

Rasmussen sat down on the curb a little ways away and called over to me, "Sit down, please." He took off his hat and I thought again what nice full hair he had, even though there was a rim around it from the hatband. The top half being darker with sweat and the bottom half more the color of sweet corn from the farm when it was ready to get picked.

"I just got done talking with Fire Chief Bailey," Rasmussen said after I sat down a few feet away from him. "Do you know the firemen found a shoe over near the lagoon and that it looks just like one that Sara Heinemann was wearing the night she disappeared?"

Glad that I'd been right, I began to pick at a scab on the cut I got from the Kenfields' prickly bushes the night I was running away from Rasmussen in the alley.

"Sally?"

Rasmussen smelled extra good. Not like Aqua Velva like Daddy, but something else that smelled like an orange does the second you take off the peel. "You won't get in trouble. Just tell me the truth. Did you find that shoe?"

I looked back at the Chevy. Nell and Eddie were not even looking my way. If he was quick, Rasmussen could grab me and stick me into the trunk of his car and when people asked later about Sally O'Malley, he would say, "Gosh, the last time I saw her she was heading down North Avenue. I think she said she had to pick up some Kleenex at the Five and Dime."

"Sally?"

I looked down into the street below the curb. There was a Popsicle stick, so I picked it up and would give it later to Uncle Paulie.

"I know what a bad time you and your family are going through," he said so kindly. "I really do."

No, he did not! Was his mother dying? Was his stepfather mean drunk all the time? Did he have a dead father he'd made promises to and a little sister to keep safe and an older sister who was being a complete moony love dope? For a second, I thought, Go ahead, just steal me, molest me, murder me. Just get it over with. And it scared me to think like that. That kind of thinking did not show the kind of stick-to-itiveness that Daddy expected from me.

"You need to tell me the truth, Sally. It's important."

"I pulled the fire alarm. Troo found the shoe underneath the big willow tree at the lagoon."

His mouth turned down on the edges. "That's all I needed to know."

He stood up and reached into his back pocket to take out his wallet. He flipped it open and got out a card. It said: David Rasmussen. Precinct 6. Badge number 343. And a phone number. "If you should think of anything else you want to tell me, give me a call here." He pointed down at the phone number. His fingernails had dirt beneath them. Probably from burying Sara. "Or if it's a real emergency, you know you can come to my house and tell me." He said kind of shyly, "I've got a garden. I hear you like to garden."

How'd he know that?

I stood up and Rasmussen handed me that card with his name and number on it. Taped to the back was a five-dollar bill. And that was pretty strange. But not half as strange as the pictures I saw in his wallet. One of them was of me in my school uniform taken last year. And in the plastic area where you can put other pictures, there was Junie Piaskowski in her First Holy Communion dress, smiling her head off. She had no idea what was coming.

CHAPTER FOURTEEN

When I got back into the car, Eddie said, "What'd he want?"

"He was just askin' me some questions."

"About what?" Nell asked, rubbing on Eddie's arm.

"Sara Heinemann."

Eddie said, "That missing kid?"

I didn't show them Rasmussen's card. And I didn't tell them about the pictures of me and Junie Piaskowski that I'd seen in his wallet. Why bother.

"I found this in the street." I gave Nell the five dollars Rasmussen had given me to buy my silence because he suspected that I knew he was the murderer and molester. Like in that movie Troo and me'd seen. I couldn't remember the name of it but it had to do with blackmail, which meant that somebody gave somebody else money to keep their big mouths shut or else. That's what that five bucks was. Blood money.

When Eddie pulled away from the curb I said, "I don't want to go to the hospital anymore."

I wanted to see Mother and let her know about Daddy forgiving her and maybe lie down with her a bit and tell her that Rasmussen had a picture of me and a dead girl in his wallet. And I hoped that she'd believe me, but she wouldn't. And that just made me feel sadder than being shipwrecked on a deserted island without my man Friday.

"Cool." Eddie snatched the five bucks out of Nell's hand as he pulled away from the curb. "Let's go to The Milky Way."

Nell seemed fine with us not visiting Mother, but she seemed fine with just about anything Eddie wanted to do. I stuck my head out the window so the air would run across my face. As we cruised down North Avenue we passed Marsha's Dance Studio and the abandoned tire building that Mary Lane had accidentally set on fire. I swear I could still smell burnt rubber.

"Sally?" Nell stuck her head out the window.

"Yeah?" I pulled my head back into the car so she did, too.

"Are you and Troo okay?"

"Yeah."

"You know about Hall, right?"

She meant about him gettin' some from Rosie Ruggins, the cocktail waitress who had a beauty mark in the corner of her lip that made her look like she'd just eaten a piece of fudge. We'd just passed Jerbak's Beer 'n Bowl. Hall's station wagon was sitting right out front. He shoulda been at work selling shoes at Shuster's.

Nell lifted her head off Eddie's shoulder. Her Brillo pad hairdo made her look like she wasn't related to me at all. One day Mother showed me a picture of her and Nell's father sitting on the fender of a car, and sure enough, Nell had her father's chin, which was sort of squarish, and that kind of nose that was popular called a ski-jump nose.

She turned around in her seat and said in a kind voice,

which really made me start to worry, "The doctor says Mother doesn't look so good. You gotta be prepared."

Eddie said, "Hey, you two, quit talkin' about this dyin' stuff. It's a drag." He'd stopped in the middle of North Avenue and turned on his blinker to turn left into The Milky Way. I had heard of it but had never been. There were boys in leather jackets and ducktails and girls with ponytails standing around and laughing and leaning on their cars and looking around to see who was looking. The rock 'n' roll music was loud and they were all trying to get the attention of girls on roller skates who were bringing food out to the cars on red trays with legs.

Eddie pulled into an empty spot and stuck something to his window that had a speaker in it and said, "Hello?"

"Welcome to the Milky Way . . . our food is outta this world," a tinny voice said, but it didn't sound like she really meant it.

"Hey, Aunt Nancy, it's me, Eddie."

The speaker buzzed.

"Whadda ya want, Eddie?"

"Gimme four cheeseburgers, no onions, four fries and four triple Mars shakes."

That's when I figured out why the place was called The Milky Way, because it had all these red and blue planets and some moons and stars hanging from these poles. And the skating girls were dressed up in silver skirts and on their heads they wore something that looked like antenna that bobbed to the left and to the right as they glided in between the cars.

"When you gonna get around to changing my oil?" Aunt Nancy said through the speaker.

"Aww . . . quit busting my hump, already. I said I'd get around to it and I will."

The speaker buzzed again and then Aunt Nancy yelled, "Four Galaxy burgers, hold the onions, four fries and four chocolate shakes. Two fifty-seven." And then she said, "Get to that oil tomorrow, Eddie, or I'll tell your ma what I saw in the trunk of your car when I was lookin' for my flashlight."

Eddie turned the same color pink as Nell's pedal pushers.

"What did she find in the trunk?" Nell asked.

"Nothin'." When Eddie lied his left eyebrow always twitched. I wondered if Nell noticed that. "Just some beer cans, but you know how my ma is about drinkin' after my da's accident."

Eddie's ma, that would be Mrs. Callahan, her husband got killed last winter over at the Feelin' Good Cookie Factory. They had an open casket at the funeral so you could see dead Mr. Callahan, who hadn't looked that great in life and looked even worse in death. Especially after that cookie press got to him. But Mr. Becker from Becker Funeral Homes had done a nice job fluffing Mr. Callahan's face back out again so he ended up looking like one of those waxy mannequins that you pay a dime to see up at the Wisconsin State Fair. Usually they were of Marilyn Monroe or Clark Gable.

Eddie checked his hair in the mirror, got out of the car and went to talk to Reese Latour, who was leaning against the railing outside a door marked DOLLS. Reese was rolling dice with some other boys. He was such bad news, always beatin' somebody up or pushin' them around or callin' them a name. But it looked to me that Eddie and Reese were friends because they were talking and then looking back at the car and laughing. That worried me for Nell. Like Granny said, you lie down with dogs, you get fleas.

Nell was staring at Eddie like he was hotsy totsy even though he was scrawny and his skin had some problems and me, I didn't think he was such a looker. But he did have nice dark brown hair that he wore in a pompadour, and Nell liking hair so much, maybe that was what they had in common. That's why people fell in love, Mother said, because they had things in common.

"Do you love him?" I asked.

Nell was looking in the mirror, smoothing on hot pink lipstick. "You writin' a book?"

And then this girl roller-skated up and Nell smiled real fast and said, "Hi, Melinda."

Melinda attached the tray full of bags of food to the window on Nell's side of the car. "Hi, Nell." Her little antenna was bobbing on her head. I wasn't sure what Melinda was supposed to be, but then I remembered the drive-in had to do with outer-space stuff, like in *Flash Gordon*, so maybe Melinda was supposed to be a space ant or something.

Nell reached over and beeped the *ah oooga* car horn to get Eddie's attention, to let him know the food had come. He laughed at something Reese Latour said and then walked slowly back to the car.

Eddie smiled real nice at Melinda as she whizzed past him, but when he got back in the car he said meanly to Nell, "I'll get back into the car when I'm damn good and ready." He looked out the windshield. Reese Latour was looking straight at him. "You don't ever do nuthin' like that to me again. Beep at me like that, unnerstand?" Then Eddie pulled Nell's hair hard enough to make her neck bend back.

"Sorry," she whimpered.

Eddie pulled just a little harder and said, "You better be, sister," and then he let go and pushed her head away.

On the ride back home, nobody talked. Just the radio DJ, who said it might rain on the Fourth of July. The bag of food made my lap warm, but as hungry as I was, I couldn't eat, thinking about what Eddie had done to Nell. Made her give in like that.

When we pulled up to our house, Nell got out of the car. Mother's yellow scarf that Nell had started wearing around her neck fluttered in the breeze. I had barely slammed the door shut when Eddie laid rubber. Nell and me just stood there together and watched him speed down Vliet Street, Dion singing about teenager love floating back to us.

CHAPTER FIFTEEN

knew Troo would be sitting on the backyard bench folding those tissues back and forth and back and forth into one chubby line and then she'd slip a bobby pin over it in the middle and slowly separate the layers of Kleenex until they looked exactly like a carnation, which was an excellent funeral flower my mother always said.

When I walked past our landlords' kitchen window, I remembered what Mr. Goldman was complaining about yesterday to Mrs. Goldman when I'd been diggin' for worms. His raised voice came through the window screen, saying Hall was *betrunkenes* and he hadn't paid the rent and if he didn't soon we would be . . . *kaput*. Mrs. Goldman said quietly back to her husband, "But, Otto, what will happen to the children?"

"Trooooo . . . ," I yelled out, so when I came around the house I wouldn't scare her. If there was anything Troo hated, it was to be snuck up on. She'd gotten really jumpy about that since the crash.

"Troooo . . ."

No answer. I got scared then. Maybe Rasmussen had changed his mind about coming after me. Maybe he'd decided to go after Troo. I ran down the path next to the pink peonies that had lost their smell and had started to fall apart. I stopped at the edge of the house and peeked my head around. Troo was surrounded by at least twenty white Kleenex flowers, like a girl on a parade float. She just hadn't heard me because she could get deaf when she was working on something. The tip of her tongue stuck out of her pouty mouth.

I watched my little sister for a minute and then because our yard butted up next to the Kenfields', one story up, I looked up at Dottie's bedroom and just for a second I could swear she was standing in the window. That even made *me* worry about my imagination.

"Whatcha doin' over there?" Troo laughed. "Seein' if Dottie wants to come out and play?"

"Very funny." I waved the bag of food at my sister. "Got you something." I slipped off my shoes and walked across the grass toward her.

"Is that you, *Liebchin*?" Mrs. Goldman popped her head out the gardening lean-to next to the garage. That's what she called me. *Liebchin* meant sweetheart in the German language.

Mrs. Goldman was a largish woman and when she was working in the garden, she sometimes wore a pair of Mr. Goldman's brown shiny trousers that were the same color as her curly hair. In Germany, she had been a teacher, but now she was just a landlady. She had on a yellow ironed shirt, rolled up at the sleeves, and the first thing I noticed like always were those numbers on her arm.

I'd asked Mrs. Goldman about that tattoo the first time I helped her water the garden last summer. I asked her if she'd been a sailor like Hall. She set her hose down and asked why I thought that. When I pointed at her arm, she gave me a rusty smile, like she hadn't used it for a while, and told me that back in Germany she and Mr. Goldman had been captured by some bad people who put them in a place called a concentration camp. Then they branded them like cattle. And those bad people were called Nazis. This was something like the Frankenstein monster for Mrs. Goldman because she shivered when she said Nazis. Like these were people that you would not want to tangle with at any time who I bet had German shepherds, which everyone knew were dogs you could never trust. (Except, of course, for Rin Tin Tin, who was the exception to the rule.)

"Do you need any help, Mrs. Goldman?" I asked, because I knew that Troo was thinking uncharitable thoughts and maybe by me being charitable it would somehow cancel them out. Troo didn't like our landlords because our lease said we couldn't have pets so her dog, Butchy, had had to stay out in the country with peeing Jerry Amberson. Troo held that against the Goldmans.

"Come to the garden. I want to show you," Mrs. Goldman said, stepping all the way out of the shed.

Troo crossed her eyes at me and went back to her Kleenex flowers when I walked past her.

"See?" Mrs. Goldman pointed, kneeling down in the dirt. "It is the fruit of our labor. The first of the tomatoes."

I said what I always said when something sprouted up like that. "That is such a miracle."

To plant those little tan seeds and then after a while something good to eat or smell would grow. It amazed me, every time. And it made me remember how out on the farm Daddy would plant in the muddy spring and by summer there would be tall corn waving around in the field that at night

I could hear rustling through our bedroom window, saying *shush . . . shush . . . shush.*

"Yes, you are right," Mrs. Goldman said, kneeling down and gently rolling the little green balls between her fingers like they were emeralds. "It is a kind of miracle."

"Marta, come here," Mr. Goldman called to her out the back door and then went right back in. Mr. Goldman wasn't much for talking. His English was not so good.

I helped her up and my fingers wrapped around her tattooed arm and I hoped that didn't hurt. She said, "A garden is also a way to be prepared. You never know what can happen. But no matter what, it is nice to know you will have the fresh vegetables." Mrs. Goldman and Daddy, they woulda gotten along just great. She brushed the dirt off her pants and then took my chin in her hand and said in her school-teacher voice, "You must be careful, *Liebchin*. Life, it is not simple like a garden, where flowers are always flowers and weeds are always weeds." And then she walked slowly toward the house, saying to Troo as she passed her, "Beautiful."

Troo pretended she hadn't heard her.

I'd forgotten all about the burgers and fries and shakes. I walked back to the bench and dropped the glassy-looking bag down next to Troo.

"Where'd you get this?" she asked.

"Nell and Eddie took me to The Milky Way. We gotta go there sometime. It's very modern." Troo absolutely adored modern stuff. "They got a girl on roller skates up there named Melinda who is called a carhop and skates the food out to you when it's ready."

"Really?" Troo opened the bag and took out the fries. "That's what I'm gonna do when I grow up. Work in a modern drive-in like that and make money and go get Butchy from peeing Jerry Amberson." She looked back when Mrs. Goldman let the screen door slam shut and gave it a raspberry. "Whatta ya think?" She pointed at her bike.

"Looks good." She'd wound red, white and blue crepe paper through the spokes. And more around the handlebars. It was a blue Schwinn that used to be Nell's. Mother had given it to Troo after hers disappeared. I didn't have a bike and I wasn't sure why. I guess everyone figured Troo would share hers with me, but whoever figured that didn't know Troo all that well.

She dug our Galaxy burgers out of the bag and handed me mine. "Did you see Mother?"

"Uh-uh." Suddenly, I wished I had. I was feeling real bad about not telling her that Daddy forgave her, and soon it might be too late. "But I did see Rasmussen, who gave me this." I reached into my pocket and pulled out the card he had handed me and told her all about what had happened when Rasmussen had stopped us up on North Avenue.

"So he got it out of you, huh?" She gave me the do-you-smell-dog-poop look that was *exactly* like Mother's because Troo never would have told Rasmussen. You'd have to stick bamboo under her fingernails to get her to tell something like that. "You sure you told him you pulled the fire alarm?"

I picked up one of her Kleenex flowers and put it in her hair. "I had to. He ambushed me."

"What else did he say?" Troo asked, sticking a fry in her mouth.

"He said he had a garden and that he'd heard I liked to garden."

Troo opened her mouth real big and laughed and some of

the fry flew out. "How'd he know that? I bet you about shit a brick." She wiped her mouth off on her hand and then on her blouse. She smelled like the inside of a tennis shoe right when you took it off. I wondered if I did, too. Maybe we should have listened to Nell and taken a couple of baths. I didn't think either one of us had changed our clothes in about a week and you could kinda see all over Troo's shorts how we'd been spending our time. There was Coke dribble and some of the Latours' slumgoodie stuck to the front and a small piece of Dubble Bubble holding on to her pocket. "Just shit a brick."

"Shut up, Troo, or I'll make you shut up."

"You and what army?" Troo crunched up the bag and threw it at me. "Help me tape these flowers on, will ya?"

I didn't tell Troo about Junie's and my picture being in Rasmussen's wallet because I was getting a little sick of nobody believing me. And she'd probably just laugh at me and maybe even call me a fruitcake.

We spent the next half hour not talking much, just taping the carnation flowers to streamers that we stuck all over her bike.

"Do you think if Mother dies we'll have to look at her in her coffin like they made us do to Mr. Callahan?" I asked. Troo was standing back, admiring her Schwinn.

"Probably. Maybe we'd even have to kiss her." She made this mushy noise with her lips. "They made Eddie kiss his dad right on the lips. Remember that?"

My daddy had a closed casket because Mother said she thought open casket funerals were gruesome. But if I'd had the chance to give Daddy one more Eskimo kiss, I would have. Gladly.

There was the smack of a ball against a bat and fun yelling. Those sounds comin' off the playground always reminded me of that story about temptation that Sister Imelda told us about in catechism class. Those Sirens luring sailors to their island.

"I'm gonna go over, you comin'?" Troo asked, tipping her head.

"Can't. I told Wendy I'd come by." I really hadn't told Wendy that, but I wanted to go down in the basement of our house where it was cool and maybe write another letter to Mother or get my charitable works story out from under the bed and work on it some more. The basement was where I went when I wanted to be alone.

Troo looked at me funny. Usually if Troo wanted to do something, I went along with it. But I was a little sick and tired of Troo that day. (Sorry, Daddy.)

She glanced over at her bike, smiled one more time and took off at a dead run, her ponytail swishing back and forth.

I followed after her to make sure she went all the way over because sometimes Troo could be tricky like that. Sneakin' back up on me. I waited until she got in a talk with Bobby the counselor, who was watching the tetherball game, and then I walked toward the back door.

"Hi, hi, hi, Thally O'Malley."

I jumped and looked around but didn't see her.

"Thally O'Malley."

Maybe I was starting to hear voices like Virginia Cunningham. But then I turned around and there she was, Wendy Latour, sitting in the swing over on the Kenfields' front porch like she had heard me fib to Troo and showed up so I wouldn't have a lying sin this week.

"Come, Thally O'Malley," she sang louder. Wendy mostly sang everything she said, which was proof once again that when God took something away, he gave you something else, because Wendy was almost always *real* happy.

I was gonna just ignore her and get down to the basement to my hiding place, but then I remembered to be charitable to people who are not as lucky as me, even though lately I'd been feeling not quite as lucky as an Irish girl should.

I climbed the Kenfields' front steps. Wendy was swinging hard so I knew something was bothering her. Whenever she got worked up, swinging calmed her down.

"Thally O'Malley, my ath hurts," she yelled, although I was only about a foot away from her.

I looked back over at Troo on the playground, where she was beating the ever-lovin' tetherball snot out of Bobby. Barb, the other counselor, and Willie and Artie were watching and laughing real hard.

"Wendy," I said, "stop doing that swinging or you're gonna fall out and then your ass really will hurt." She stopped almost instantly. Troo always teased me about how Wendy liked me. I think she might've been a little jealous because mostly everybody liked Troo better than me because of her outgoingness. Troo said Wendy only liked me better because my name rhymed.

I sat down on the wooden swing next to her. Wendy was always pretty clean because Mrs. Latour paid some extra attention to her. And she had the shiniest shoe-polish black hair. "Wendy, where are your shoes and socks?"

"Nith to meet you." She reached over and gave me one of those bear hugs.

"Okay, Wendy, that's good now," I said after I'd counted to ten. She hugged me tighter. "I can't breathe."

She let go and set her head down on my shoulder. I could smell her Prell hair. "My ath hurts."

"That's okay. My ass hurts too." I'd figured out a long time ago that if I repeated back to Wendy what she just said to me, she would sometimes stop saying whatever she was saying over and over.

She lifted her head. "Right?"

"Right."

"Troo? Mad?" She pointed across the street at her.

"She sure is."

My sister was yelling something at Bobby, the playground counselor. I couldn't hear what it was, but she was stomping her foot like she did when something didn't go her way. Bobby was teasing her, waving the tetherball above her head so she couldn't reach it. She was getting madder and madder by the second, almost ready to blow. I felt sort of bad because it was making me feel gladder and gladder by the second to see Troo not get her way, which was not a charitable way to feel at all.

"Wendy, you need to put your thinking cap on. I gotta ask you some questions." I needed to know what'd happened over at the Spencers' root cellar when she fell down. What Rasmussen had done to her. Even though she was a Mongoloid, she was a pretty smart one. Mother said Wendy was just a little Mongoloidish, not as bad as some of them. "You ready for the first question?"

She bobbed her head up and down.

"How'd you get that?" I pointed at the Band-Aid above her eyebrow.

She started rocking the swing slowly at first and then quicker and quicker. I stomped my feet down so it'd stop. "Wendy?"

"My ath—"

"I know." It always took a couple of tries to get Wendy to listen to you. "How'd you get that boo-boo?" She looked at me with her head to the side like the way that RCA dog did. I pointed to her bandage again. "Did a man do that to you?"

"Fell."

"Fell?" I yelled because I just wanted her to say Rasmussen hurt her so bad and then there would be two of us and maybe somebody would believe us. "You better not be lyin' to me."

Wendy started to cry because she cried real easy, especially if you raised your voice to her. "My ath—"

"I'm sorry, I'm sorry . . . oh, don't cry." I picked up her stubby hand. Someone had painted her fingernails watermelon pink and there was that plastic Cracker Jack ring that she always wore on her wedding finger.

"Was it Officer Rasmussen, Wendy? Did he push you and that's why you fell?"

"Weeeeennnndy."

Wendy perked up. It was her ma calling her. If you had to call thirteen kids for supper every day, that would give anybody the lungs of an opera singer, Mother said, and you could tell that even though Mrs. Latour and Mother were in choir together up at church, Mother thought that anybody who had thirteen kids, even if they were Catholic, was dumb as a curb.

"Weeeeeendy."

She got up and started toward the Kenfields' steps. "Going to Ma, Thally O'Malley."

"Okay," I said, giving up, but then I thought I better try one more time. "Was Rasmussen down in the cellar with you?"

She nodded her head yes and then she shook her head no so I didn't know which she meant, but it was too late to ask her again cuz she'd already hopped down the steps.

She stopped at the bottom and said, "Rathmuthen," and then cut across the Kenfields' grass toward home.

"There's a bad man out there. Keep your eyes open, Wendy," I called after her.

She turned and opened her eyes really big and then took off again in that crazy-legged way of running she had. I sat there for a while and rocked and felt pretty good because now at least I had Wendy Latour on my side, even if she was a Mongoloid. After all, she'd pretty much just told me that Rasmussen had tried to murder and molest her.

CHAPTER SIXTEEN

The first time I came down to the basement by myself was the night after Mrs. Callahan's birthday party, when Mother and Hall were screaming so bad. Mother wanted Hall to stop drinking so much and Hall wanted Mother to shut the hell up about his drinking. Troo was sleeping over at Fast Susie's and Nell was at a school dance. I was alone in my room reading *My Friend Flicka* when they started in on each other and then Dottie's ghost began crying and I just couldn't listen to all that. So I snuck out of bed and went on the tips of my toes through the kitchen, making sure I didn't step on that piece of linoleum right in front of the stove that always made a sound like it had a stomachache, and down the steps past the Goldmans' back door and down one more flight. I had my flashlight so it wasn't as bad as it sounds.

When I got there, I sat on this hard brown suitcase that belonged to Hall when he was a sailor and had stickers all over it from faraway countries. I was gonna stay in the basement and read until the shouting coming down through the radiators stopped. I propped the flashlight up against this old lamp and made finger shadows on the wall for a while. I could do a bird and another kind of bird. When one bird was flying across the basement wall, it came across a picture of a lady in a hat sitting on a bench. Since I'd just been down there that afternoon helping Mother put shirts through the wringer, which I just loved to do because sometimes she made jokes about how she wished Hall was still inside one of those shirts, I couldn't believe I hadn't noticed this picture. I got closer. When I touched it, it slid down the wall and behind where it used to be hanging was a hidey-hole. I could see the tip of something that looked like a shoe box. Then something squeaked like a mouse, which didn't scare me, but then I thought it might be a bat and those did scare me because of this movie me and Troo saw called *Horror of Dracula* and it really was pretty horrible. So I waited until I didn't hear the sound anymore and then stuck my hand inside that hidey-hole and lifted out the box and wondered whose it was. Mrs. Goldman's? I checked the side and it said "Shuster's Shoes, size 7," so it had to be Mother's because Mrs. Goldman had to wear special sturdy shoes, size 10, because her feet had gotten so bad in the concentration camp. And Nell wore a size 5. I lifted off the top. Two pictures and a little ring made out of a crinkly cookie wrapper like they put those chocolate chip cookies in up at the Feelin' Good Cookie Factory were laying on the bottom. One picture had kids in gowns and those flat hats with the tassels on them, the kind that Nell wore when she graduated. Only it wasn't Nell's picture. It was more old-fashioned and the kids had funnier hair than Nell's, which I had no idea was possible. "Washington High School . . . Class of 1940 . . . Jim Madigan Photography Studio" was written in swirly letters across the bottom.

So that afternoon, after talking to Wendy, I got to the

bottom of the basement steps and took the shoe box out of the hidey-hole and sat down on the old brown suitcase. I slipped the cookie wrapper ring on my finger, but it fell off right away like it always did, so I stuck it back in the shoe box under the other picture. My favorite. The one of Mother with her wavy hair and freckles sitting in a rowboat down at the lagoon. She was about Nell's age in this picture and she had on shorts that showed her pretty legs and trim ankles and she looked so very, very happy, a kind of happy that I couldn't ever hardly remember seeing in her since Daddy died. Seeing her smile like that made me want to cry in that damp basement that smelled of coal clinkers. Cry and not have anybody to tell me to shut up with that crying. For goodness sake, why did God give you tear ducts if you weren't supposed to cry?

The other picture, the graduation one, didn't make me sad. It made me feel good because I knew a lot of the people in it. There was Mrs. Callahan and Mrs. Latour and Mr. Kenfield and Mr. Fitzpatrick from the drugstore. And then I noticed two other people. A homely-looking boy whose ears kinda stuck out, but I couldn't really tell who it was cuz he had turned his face away from the camera. Who was that? I knew I'd seen him before, but it wasn't exactly him. And then way up on the top of this graduation picture, I noticed somebody who was tall. And had light hair. It was Rasmussen! I was shocked that I hadn't paid attention to that detail before. He hadn't changed very much. I would take this picture over to Granny's the next time I visited and ask if she could've told right off that Rasmussen was gonna be a murderer and molester. Some of the boys on Vliet Street I knew would grow up to go to jail. Like Greasy Al

Molinari, whose brother Coochie got taken away not too long ago for stealing the Cadillac car that old man Holzhauer kept in his garage but didn't drive anymore. Reese Latour would go to jail, too. You could just tell by how mean they were that nothing good would ever happen to these boys. It shouldn't anyway.

When I heard footsteps coming down the back stairs, I quickly stuffed everything back into the box.

"Who is down here?"

"It's just me, Mrs. Goldman."

"What are you doing in that dark basement, *Liebchin*?"

"Nothing."

She was quiet. Then she said, "I understand."

She went back up the steps, stopping on the landing. "When you are done with your nothing, please to come to the back door. I have made you a little something."

Her doin' that . . . I don't know what the heck came over me. I just really used those tear ducts of mine. When I was all cried out, I wiped my face off on a dirty white blouse that was laying on top of the washer and stuck the shoe box back into the hidey-hole. And then I walked up the back steps and found a green glass plate outside Mrs. Goldman's door. Six brown sugar cookies and a glass of cold, fresh milk in a jelly glass, just like Mother used to do for me, were on the floor outside Mrs. Goldman's back door.

I took the cookies and milk out to the backyard bench and looked over at Troo's Fourth of July bike and thought about Mother's happy, smiling picture down in the hidey-hole and how nice Mrs. Goldman was even though she didn't have to be, especially since those Nazis had been so *un*nice to her when they took away her little daughter for a shower and never brought her back. And even though things really hadn't been going so hot for me lately, that fancy bike and that old picture and my sweet landlady made me feel so grateful that I brought my hands together and bowed my head and did what Daddy had always said to do when I was feeling this way. I thanked the Lord God Almighty for his blessings, especially for those luscious, luscious brown sugar cookies that I stuffed into my mouth faster than you can say Jackie Robinson. I didn't save even a crumb for Troo.

CHAPTER SEVENTEEN

Troo liked Willie O'Hara even though he collected stamps and was always asking everybody to bring him used-up envelopes. I thought that was sort of a dumb hobby, but it wasn't his fault. His mother was an artist and that's what made Willie weird. Mrs. O'Hara made things out of clay. Busts, Willie called them. I was sure that was a lie because *busts* was another word for bosoms. Willie probably just made that up to make Troo laugh, and I couldn't blame him. My sister, she had a laugh that sounded kinda like that "Chopsticks" song she played on the piano. It made you feel great just to hear it.

Willie was blubbery, but he called it big-boned, and had a funny way of talking. It was called a Brooklyn accent, Troo told me. He'd moved from New York onto the block last summer because his father had run away with his hubba-hubba secretary and his mother had relatives around here who were helping Mrs. O'Hara out until she could get on her feet again. Which it looked like she had, because she was going out to supper clubs with Officer Riordan, and Fast Susie said they might get hitched.

The streetlights had gone on so we were all sitting out on the O'Haras' front steps, getting ready to start playing red light, green light, hope to see the ghost tonight. I didn't know then that it was the last time we'd play for a while.

Willie announced, "They found Sara Heinemann's body at the red rowboats today and my ma is so glad that I'm not a little girl because she doesn't think she could stand to live without me."

We were all quiet until Troo licked her lips and asked, "Was she murdered and molested like Junie?"

"Yeah." Willie bent over and tied his shoes with two knots. Willie was not very coordinated, and last week he had tripped and fallen down these very steps and gotten a nasty cut on his arm that he kept showing to everybody every five minutes. "That's what Officer Riordan told Ma anyway."

Artie Latour was sitting next to me and Wendy next to him. Fast Susie had stopped playing red light, green light, because she was getting too old she said. She was across the street at the playground, sitting on one of the green benches, bouncing one of the red rubber balls while she talked to Bobby and Barb.

"Sara was going to make her First Holy Communion this year," Artie said. "I bet they'll bury her in her white dress. That's what they did with Junie."

That was so sad that none of us could even look at each other.

"My ma says not to worry," Willie said. "That they'll catch the guy soon because we have excellent policemen in Officer Rasmussen and Officer Riordan."

Oh, poor Willie. I guessed mothers who were artists were not all that smart because I thought if everybody would just take a breather and think about it for a minute, they would see clear as day that Rasmussen was not what he pretended to be. Everyone was judging that book by its cover, was what Granny would say.

I looked over at Wendy and she threw me a kiss with a big smacking sound like Dinah Shore on her "See the USA in Your Chevrolet" show.

"How's your ma doin'?" Mary Lane asked, from the step above me. I knew she was talking to me and Troo because somebody asked us that at least once a day.

Troo said, "She's a lot better," even though she had no idea how Mother was doing, because Nell had stopped talking to us for a couple of days because she and Eddie were having a bad fight. I'd heard her yelling at him. Heck, the whole neighborhood heard Nell yelling at Eddie last night since she was chasing him down Vliet Street waving a bra and screaming at the top of her lungs, "Melinda? Melinda? You went to second base with that outer-space skank Melinda?"

It wasn't beer at all that Aunt Nancy had seen in the trunk of Eddie's car. (Told you his eye twitched when he lied.) Nell had taken Eddie's car keys out of his jeans pocket when he was taking a nap after they had done their daily exercises in her room. She was planning to empty out those beer cans for him as a charitable thing to do so Eddie wouldn't get in trouble with his ma. Nell found the bra under the spare tire. She'd been in her room crying since Tuesday, so she hadn't gone up to St. Joe's to check on Mother. And I knew that Hall hadn't because he was too busy gettin' some from Rosie up at Jerbak's, and everybody knew about that now because there were no secrets in this neighborhood. Everyone had started to look at me and Troo with even bigger pity eyes and stopped talking when we came up to them.

Troo and me didn't care about Hall gettin' some with

Rosie since it would be fine with us if we never saw him again. We agreed that we absolutely did not want Rosie Ruggins to be our new mother because she had these twin boys that were the worst. Rickey and Ronney not only picked their noses but did practical jokes like putting whoopee cushions on your desk seat or pulling out the chair just when you were going to sit down. What freams.

"Looks like it's gonna storm again," Artie said. The smell of it was coming through. I looked over at Troo, who was rubbing her arm. Across the street Fast Susie began helping Bobby and Barb pick up the balls and bats and bases that hadda go into the shed because the playground closed when it rained so nobody would get hit by lightning.

We all agreed to try and get in one game before it started to rain so we did rock paper scissors to see who would be the first ghost. It was Artie.

He took off across the O'Haras' front lawn while the rest of us counted loudly together. "One Mississippi . . . two Mississippi . . . three Mississippi."

I really loved this time of night, when the parents were on their porches listening to the radio and maybe having beer in tall glasses and talking, like Mother and Daddy used to, catching up on what each of them had done that day.

"Ten Mississippi . . . eleven Mississippi . . ."

If someone led me to each of these houses, even if I was blindfolded, I would be able to tell you whose house it was by how it smelled after suppertime. The Fazios and their garlic and the Goldmans and their sauerkraut and the Latours and their slumgoodie and the O'Haras and their corned beef and cabbage.

"Fifteen Mississippi . . . sixteen Mississippi . . ."

I peeked down to where Mr. Kenfield was sitting on his front porch swing just sort of staring out at the street in front of him like he did every night, probably thinking about how Dottie had disappeared into thin air.

"Twenty-two Mississippi . . . twenty-three Mississippi."

I wondered what Mother was doing. I wished I could brush her hair a hundred times with her gold hairbrush like she let me do sometimes.

"Twenty-five Mississippi . . . ready or not . . . here we come!"

Wendy got caught right off like she always did. Artie had hidden in these bushes beneath his bedroom window, and when Wendy walked by singing, "Red light, green light, hope to thee the ghoth . . . ," he jumped out at her and yelled, "Boo!" But for some reason instead of laughing like she always did, Wendy started to cry, so we had to wait while Artie went into the basement of their house and got a Popsicle out of their deep freezer, which was this enormous thing that had venison and a lot of other food just in case we got attacked by the Russians. Mr. Latour had also built a bomb shelter in their backyard, so Troo and me stayed friendly with them just in case. When we lived on the farm, Troo and me wanted to have a bomb shelter, but Mother said we didn't need one because that bomb business was a lot of silly nonsense and we had a lot of other things to worry about besides the Reds. Daddy laughed at that and said, "And we don't have to worry much about them either. Not with the way Lawrence has been pitching."

The second time around, we skipped the counting and just looked away from Willie and Wendy when they ran off and hid. The playground was lit up like County Stadium.

A light drizzle started to fall. Eddie and Nell were snuggled in the corner of the school where they thought nobody could see them. I guessed they weren't mad at each other anymore because I could see that Eddie was sliding into second base.

Troo yelled, "Ready or not, here we come," and then we all took off again. I was walking between the Fazios' and the Latours', saying not too loudly, I admit, "Red light, green light, hope to see the ghost tonight. Red light, green light, hope to see the ghost tonight."

I had just circled behind the Fazios' side bushes and could see and smell through their back window that Nana was at the kitchen window making those yummy cannolis. I pinched myself so I wouldn't forget to tell Troo because those were her favorite and she would wanna eat over there tomorrow just to get those for dessert. Another thunder grumble rolled over my head, but beneath that there was a shout, like somebody had been caught by the ghost, so I turned to run toward it, and when I did somebody grabbed me by my braid and swung me down to the wet grass. Real hard. I could feel something come off him. Like a feeling. Like how you feel if you are afraid. And in a flash of lightning, I saw the pillowcase he had over his head with places cut out for his eyes and his mouth and it moved ever so slightly like the sails on a ship when he stood above me, his black spongy-soled shoes on either side of me. The rain started coming down hard, but I could hear Rasmussen just fine when he bent down to my ear and said, "Sally, dear, I love you," so, so sweetly that I almost believed him.

CHAPTER EIGHTEEN

Nana Fazio screamed *Il mio Dio . . . il mio Dio* and ran toward me in her long black dress, swinging her bosoms belt over her tiny head like a lasso. Rasmussen laughed a little and said, "Until we meet again," and ran off toward the alley. I felt something moving around in my head like you did if you stood up too fast and I saw some shooting stars even though it'd started raining so hard. Troo told me later that I'd fainted dead away just like Scarlett O'Hara in *Gone With the Wind*.

When I woke up, we were coming down the Fazios' front steps. I thought that Rasmussen had probably dodged Nana and run behind the Spencers' garage and taken off that pillowcase, and here he was with me in his arms and nobody was doing a darn thing to stop him. Where is Troo? I wanted to scream but nothing came out. I tried to push off him, but he acted like he couldn't even feel that. Like I was a bug and he didn't even notice. Then I relaxed a little because I figured out that he'd never murder and molest me in front of the whole neighborhood. Oh no, not tricky Rasmussen.

Held close to his chest, my face pressed against his badge number 343 as the rain came down, I sniffed his uniform, which smelled like my socks did after sledding, and that made me think of Mother and hot cocoa. And maybe it was be-cause I was so tuckered out, or maybe I wanted to imagine for a little while that I was wrong and Rasmussen really was the good egg everybody said he was. So I'm sorry to have to say this, but I gave up, and didn't struggle. I just snuggled up to him, felt his breath going in and out of his chest, and tried to figure out what tune he was humming.

Right in front of the Kenfields' house Rasmussen looked down at me and asked, "Did he say anything to you, Sally? Did you recognize him?"

Ha! Like he didn't know what he said and he didn't know what he looked like.

I bent my head down and said, "Did you know Dottie Kenfield?" I was trying to get a look at his shoes. They were those brown ones he usually wore. He musta changed out of the spongy black ones he had on when he bushwhacked me.

Rasmussen looked over at Mr. Kenfield's cigarette burn-ing red in the dark and said so low I almost couldn't hear him, "That is a sad, sad story that you are too young to know about." And then he said louder toward the Kenfields' porch, "Evenin', Chuck."

I never looked Rasmussen in the eyes because I was too afraid what I might see there. Daddy always said the eyes are the windows to the soul, which didn't make sense because I thought your soul was located sort of near your heart and not your eyeballs, but if Daddy said it, it was true and I didn't ever, ever want to see into Rasmussen's raggedy soul.

I didn't have to worry because his eyes were covered by his police hat where the rain had beaded up on the rim, but the streetlight was shining on his lips. They were soft-looking like baby blanket satin. He had murdered Junie. And Sara.

Like Granny said, three's the charm. The next time he would murder me, so a little "Ohhh" escaped out of me.

"You okay, Sally?" he asked like he cared.

The rain was starting and stopping like it couldn't make up its mind. I looked over at our front porch. Troo was sitting there with a jar full of fireflies. She was the most amazing firefly catcher. Fireflies flocked to Troo, probably because they began with the letter *f*. I knew she'd tried real hard to catch some quick to make me feel better because that's what she always did when I was out of sorts. The fireflies were flashing off and on in the jar that she held beneath her chin, and when she saw me she gave me a double thumbs-up. Daddy used to do that, so that made me finally cry. Because here I was in the arms of the man who wanted me dead and there wasn't one thing I could do about it. I felt like a leaf going down the Honey Creek after a storm.

Rasmussen walked me up the steps near the house and set me down next to Troo and said, "Make sure she gets a bath," and then he just walked away like he had something urgent to do. Probably to go cover up the footprints he'd left in the Fazios' yard.

Troo said, "You like 'em?"

I said with a shocked voice, "Rasmussen?"

"No, you fruitcake . . . these." She shoved the jar of fireflies into my hand. I could tell she was scared.

I looked down at the jar and said the first *f* word I could think of, "Fantastic." And that made Troo stop licking her lips.

It was only later, when I was floating in the warm bath that Nell had run for me, that I recognized what that tune was that Rasmussen had been humming on the way home from the Fazios'. It was "Catch a Falling Star" by Perry Como, which was my favorite song last year. Me and Troo would put on a little show in the living room and sing and pretend we were catching falling stars and putting them in our jama pockets, saving them for a rainy day, until Hall screamed at us to shut the crap up.

Later, between the sheets, while she rubbed my back longer than she ever had, Troo said, "I figure it was Greasy Al who grabbed at you over at the Fazios'. You know how he's always bullying."

I didn't even bother telling Troo that I was sure it was Rasmussen. What was the use?

"Don't worry," Troo said from the dark, the heat of her body mixing in with mine, the fireflies flashing on our dresser. "I got a plan to get him back. And my bike, too. Night, Sal." She slipped her fingers into her mouth, squeezed her baby doll to her chest and turned over hard and quick like she couldn't wait until tomorrow because tomorrow was the Fourth, the most exciting day of the summer next to the block party.

"Night, Troo."

When I was sure she was asleep, I got up and went into Mother's room and pulled her yellow nightie out from the bottom drawer of her dresser, and then I got Daddy's Timex from the dressing table and put it on my wrist. After I said my prayers and told Daddy I was sorry like I did every night, I laid down at the foot of Mother's bed and drifted off to the sound of rain that was strong enough to be good for the crops, and tried and tried to remember the last time I felt safe.

CHAPTER NINETEEN

"Saaally . . . Saaally." The sound of her scream chased my dream away. I tried to jump out of bed, to get to her, to help her. Was Hall after her? Rasmussen? "I'm coming," I yelled back, fighting to get untangled from Mother's yellow nightie.

Troo came running from the back stairs into Mother's room and flew up onto the bed next to me. "Wake the hell up, it's almost seven thirty and we gotta be at the park by eight sharp." She smacked me in the head with the pillow and then walked over to Mother's dressing table. She didn't ask me what I was doing sleeping in Mother's room, but from her reflection in the mirror I thought maybe she already knew and was just daring me to say something about what she was doin'. She slid some blue eye shadow over her lids and ran a bit of the cherry red lipstick across her pouty lips and tipped the Evening in Paris bottle upside down and put some on her wrists. And then she got up and hit me one more time with the pillow and said, "I'll meet you downstairs. Hurry. I got something to show you," and ran off.

Just like Hall, Nell hadn't come home last night. (Troo added that to her tattletale list with a bunch of patriotic stars.)

I pulled Mother's nightie off and kissed Daddy's watch and put them back where they belonged. When I was all dressed, I chased down the back steps, pushed on the screen door and had that radio weatherman ever been wrong. July Fourth, 1959, was beautiful. Today my Troo would win that bike-decorating prize because, boy oh boy, did her Schwinn look grand! She musta got up early and worked on it some more. I didn't think she'd be able to ride it over to the park cuz it was so covered in flowers and streamers and crepe paper.

Troo was standing in front of the bike holding on to something that looked like a giant ice cream cone made out of that old Kroger bag she'd found down at the lagoon. She also had a crown or something on her head made out of aluminum foil that came to a bunch of points that reminded me of Butchy's old dog collar.

She stood up extra straight and looked off into the distance with a serious face and when I didn't say anything, she said, "Don't you get it? I'm the Statue of Liberty."

"Ohhhh," I said, not wanting to get too close to that pointy crown, which looked like it could definitely poke your eye out.

"It's the *pièce de résistance, non?*" Troo laughed. "I looked up a picture of it over at the library and Mrs. Kambowski has been teaching me some more French words. Did you know the statue was a present from France?"

I wished I had a Brownie camera. I would've taken a picture of Troo and run it up to the hospital to Mother. Troo looked so beautiful and so . . . foreign.

"Do you like my *chapeau?*"

I searched around for whatever the heck a *chapeau* was.

She pointed at the crown.

"Ohhh," I said again. "But what's the ice cream cone got to do with it?"

Troo shook it at me and said, "It's not an ice cream cone, you nitwit. It's her torch. I found an old sheet for her dress but I took it off because I kept trippin' on it and fallin' down."

She carefully wheeled her bike through the backyard and down the front hill, me trailing behind. Looking at Troo that morning as we walked toward the park, the sun bouncing off her shiny *chapeau*, I knew what I had to do to protect her. I had to come up with some sort of a plan for my little Statue of Liberty. Why hadn't I thought of this before? Because if Rasmussen murdered and molested me, she would never be able to stand it. Nobody could whistle in the dark that loud, not even my Troo. So a scheme was what I needed. Like in one of those movies at the Uptown. Just like that Humphrey Bogart. He always had a scheme.

Yes, what I needed to do was get the goods on Rasmussen. Spy on him, catch him doing something that he shouldn't or find some evidence, and then I could reveal him to everybody for what he really was. But maybe I wouldn't start that until I had a chance to talk to Mary Lane, because she was the best spy in the neighborhood. Mary Lane was a regular Mata Hari. Or maybe I'd wait until after Sara Heinemann's funeral, which was going to be tomorrow. Would Rasmussen go to the funeral? Sometimes in movies after somebody murdered somebody they would go to the funeral. Mary Lane always hung around after she lit a fire. Just stood there and watched it burn until there was nothing left but the smell and the smile on her face.

What a show!

Hundreds of kids and bikes and dogs with bows around their necks and even some baby buggies covered the big grassy area that ran along the banks of the Honey Creek. There were balloons hanging from the trees and picnic benches scattered around with paper tablecloths the same color as the flags on little sticks that everybody was waving around. The day was the hottest yet this summer and everybody was saying thank God for the shade. The Fourth was always hot around here, you could count on that. But this was even hotter than what you could count on.

The Everly Brothers were blaring out of loudspeakers, trying to wake up Little Susie, until someone came on and said, "All children under twelve should meet under the oak tree with the red ribbon around it." Troo jumped up off the grass and said, "One for the money, two for the show, three to get ready, now go, cat, go."

I trailed behind her as we shoved through a crowd of older kids, one of them being Greasy Al Molinari, who was probably just there to steal some kid's bike when they went to the bathroom.

Greasy Al pointed at Troo's crown and torch and said, "What ya s'posed to be, O'Malley? A TV-antenna-eatin' ice cream cone?" His beady greasy eyes stared out from beneath his clumpy black eyebrows. His mouth hung half open like it always did. "I been lookin' for you."

"Oh, yeah?" Troo smiled and said, "What would a spaghetti for brains like you want with me?"

The big muscles in Greasy Al's arms twitched. He and his brothers liked to lift weights in their garage on this bench they had sitting below this picture of Ava Gardner in a leopard-skin bathing suit. "What did you just call me, you little mick?"

Troo smiled her even better smile, the one where she shows every single one of her teeth. "You heard me. Or are your ears as gimpy as your polio leg?"

Greasy Al pushed off the tree and walked up to us. "Nice bike."

"Don't even think about stealing this bike," Troo snarled. "And if you ever come after my sister again, I'll—"

The voice crackled over the loudspeaker. "Last call for the under-twelves bicycle-decorating contest. At the oak tree with the red ribbon."

"Let me by, you dago," Troo said, trying to push past him. Greasy Al had her front bike wheel in between his legs.

And then real fast, Greasy Al took out his switchblade knife from his back pocket and cut all the white Kleenex flowers off Troo's handlebars with one hand and with the other ripped off her crown. He hunch-limped away laughing, smashing the shiny aluminum foil between his fingers.

"Last call for the under-twelves," the voice said again.

If this had happened to anybody else but Troo, like me for instance, I'd be bawling my head off. But not my Real Trooper. She stared after Greasy Al, and if looks really could kill, Greasy Al woulda been deader than a doorknob.

Then out of nowhere Rasmussen showed up with a ribbon on his T-shirt that said JUDGE. No matter where we went or what we did, it seemed like Rasmussen was just around the corner.

"Morning, girls," he said. He looked different out of his policeman's uniform. More like some of the other men from the neighborhood. "You better get over there, Troo, the judging is about to begin." He took out some Scotch tape from his pocket and then quickly picked up the white flowers off the ground and taped them all back on to Troo's handlebars.

Troo pushed her bike past him and made her way over to the oak tree. She forgot to thank Rasmussen because I knew she was busy thinking about how she would find Greasy Al later and do something really hideous to him. My sister had her cruisin' for a bruisin' wild look on her face.

Rasmussen smiled down at me and said, "You feeling okay? Recovered from last night?" I didn't look up, but I nodded. "Glad to hear it," he said, and him and his clipboard moved over to a group of mothers with decorated baby buggies. Too bad Rasmussen liked to murder and molest girls because if he didn't he probably would've been considered a good egg. That's why Junie and Sara went off with him, because I also learned from those movies that when a crime was committed it was always somebody that nobody suspected. Like Jeeves, the good egg butler.

The smell of hot dogs and hamburgers and Italian sausage and bratwurst on the grills hung in the air even though it was early in the morning. After the sack races, Troo and me planned to eat so much food they'd have to take us home in a coaster wagon. Like camels, we'd be able to go a few more days without eating, and then on Thursday night Willie had invited us to have supper with him and his ma and Officer Riordan, who I thought I would tell about Rasmussen after all. If the timing was right.

Over thirty kids had entered but everybody there could tell right off that this was a two-horse race, just like it'd been last year. Troo was smiling at one of the judges, who was Mary Lane's father. I guessed since the zoo was right next door, maybe since he wasn't feeding Sampson, they made him come over and judge the bike-decorating contest.

Mr. Lane was looking over Artie Latour's bike. Holy Magillacuddy! Artie had really gone all out. Way out! He had streamers trailing off his handlebars and baseball cards in the spokes and sitting in his basket was a giant cardboard picture of Abraham Lincoln, who looked—I'd never noticed this before—quite a lot like Nana Fazio, but much, much taller.

Mr. Lane came up to us and said, "How's your mother feeling?" He bent down to look at the flowers that Rasmussen had taped back on Troo's handlebars.

Putting on her absolutely best manners and her dolly voice, Troo said, "She's doing fine, Mr. Lane. Thank you so much for asking."

"Top-notch decorating, Troo. Top-notch." Mr. Lane wrote something on his clipboard and moved down the line.

The loudspeaker crackled again and the man said, "Five minutes, judges. Five minutes left."

Greasy Al Molinari was sitting on a picnic table using his switchblade to carve something into the brown wood. Troo couldn't take her eyes off of him even after Rasmussen went over and started talking to him. I watched as Greasy Al slapped his switchblade knife into Rasmussen's hand and limped off toward the Honey Creek, kicking Troo's crushed-up crown along the ground.

"Before the sack race, let's go down to the creek and cool off, okay?" Troo said, wiping the sweat off her forehead with her arm.

"Yeah, the creek sounds real good." I knew she might lose this year because Artie's bike was a lollapalooza and I would've done anything to make her feel better, even go down to the creek with her and throw stones at Greasy Al.

The loudspeaker buzzed back on. "All right, everybody, all the judging is final. If you hear your name, please go over to the judges' table next to the picnic area to pick up your prize."

Wendy Latour won the prize for the best-decorated wagon. When she saw me she sang, "Thally O'Malley. Hi . . . hi . . . hi," and then threw me some of her Dinah Shore USA kisses.

Mr. Mahlberg, who was doing the announcing, told everyone that some kid I didn't know named Billy Quigley won for best tricycle. And then he said, "The twelve and unders were tough this year. Real tough." *Oh no. Oh no. Poor Troo.* "Will Artie Latour and Troo O'Malley please come to the judges' table?"

Of course I went with, and when we got there, Mr. Lane smiled and said, "Congratulations, Troo. You and Artie tied." I thought the judges made it into a tie like that because our mother was dying, because Artie really deserved that first place. But a tie was good. That way nobody was going to spend the rest of the day shooting daggers out of their eyes at one another. But Troo wasn't any too happy with that tie. I could tell by her too-wide, fake smile. "Go claim your prize," Mr. Lane said, pointing behind us.

A big Kenfield's Five and Dime banner hung behind the prize table. Mrs. Callahan was congratulating the winners.

"Hello, girls," she said when we came up. "Congratulations, Troo."

Betty Callahan got up from the folding chair and put her arms around us. She had on a sleeveless white blouse, navy Bermuda shorts and gold earrings. She also had a lot of oomph in her hair that she had recently changed. "You two doin' all right?" she asked.

Mrs. Callahan smelled so good that I almost started crying, but then I looked over at Troo and she shot me a don't-you-dare look. She must've also smelled that Evening in Paris.

"I visited your mother yesterday," Mrs. Callahan said.

Troo was getting antsy, looking over at the prize table and not even listening. I knew what she had her eye on. It was a genuine Davy Crockett coonskin cap. Being the lover of hats that she was, she'd been admiring them up at the Five and Dime for the last week and now Artie Latour was running his hand through the fur.

"My sister, Margie, who's a nurse up at St. Joe's, told me that Helen is holding her own," Mrs. Callahan said.

Troo wandered toward the prize table and got up right behind Artie and whispered something in his ear. Probably threatening to drown him in the Honey Creek if he didn't let her have that coonskin cap.

"You sure everything is okay at your house, Sal?"

"Everything is fine, Mrs. Callahan." Now Artie had that coonskin in his hand and Troo was grabbing the coonskin tail and if I didn't do something, this would turn into the kind of roll-around-on-the-ground fight that Troo had a bad reputation for.

I started to hurry toward them, but then I stopped and turned my head back to Mrs. Callahan. "Is that true what you just said about Mother? That she's holding her own?"

I wasn't sure what that meant but it sounded pretty good and I wished she really was holding her own. Mrs. Callahan looked me directly in the eye and couldn't say another word, so I pretty much knew she was just saying that to make me feel better.

"Fight!"

I turned and there were Artie and Troo wrestling and rolling in the dirt. She had the coonskin cap tucked under her arm and wouldn't give it up, and then she kicked Artie a good one in the leg right before Mr. Lane came by to pull her off. Mr. Lane picked up the coonskin and set it on Troo's head. I looked back at Artie Latour doubled over on the ground holding his leg. His shirt had got ripped and dirt caked his sweaty arms, and I thought in some special way our mother dying was working out okay for us because we were gettin' cut all sorts of slack.

Troo was thinking the exact same thing. Because she got up off the ground, flipped the coonskin tail at Artie and took off laughing, waving her ice cream torch back and forth and yelling, "Give me your tired, your poor. Your huddled messes."

CHAPTER TWENTY

For fifteen minutes or so I lost Troo in all the red, white and blue, so I had a nice visit with Ethel, who had the day off from taking care of Mrs. Galecki. Ethel'd come with her gentleman friend named Mr. Raymond Buckland Johnson, who said we could call him Ray Buck for short. He was from the South just like Ethel. Georgia, I think he said. Ray Buck was a city bus driver and his skin was as black as a bad luck cat. Much blacker than Ethel, who was the color of a Hershey bar. Ray Buck was also tall, thin and a little hunched over in the shoulders, so when he turned sideways he looked like a question mark. Troo and me, we just adored Ethel and were getting to know Ray Buck a little bit better and were beginning to adore him as well.

Some people around here didn't like the Negroes. Like Hall. And Reese Latour, who called me and Troo nigger lovers every chance he got. Troo and me had asked Ethel about why that was. She'd told us she didn't know why for certain, but that it was true that some white folks didn't care too much for coloreds. Down in the South there was even this club called the KKK that was really mean to Negroes. They dressed up in sheets and burned crosses on the Negroes' front lawns to hurt their feelings, which made me wonder for a second if Rasmussen belonged to the KKK because of that pillowcase he had on his head when he'd tried to grab me at the Fazios'.

"So, Miss Sally, how's your mama doin'?" Ethel asked, after she suggested that Ray Buck go off to the refreshment stand to get her a cool drink. Ethel always called us Miss Troo or Miss Sally because she had the best manners and liked manners in others. I just loved to listen to her talk. She was another one with an accent, but not like Willie's Brooklyn one or the Goldmans' German one, which were hard sounding, like they were just about to get in a fight with you. Ethel's accent flowed like the Honey Creek water, and one time when I was helping her hull strawberries for shortcake I fell dead asleep on the kitchen chair because come to think of it, that's what her voice really sounded like. A lullaby.

"Mrs. Callahan just told me that Mother is holding her own, Ethel, thank you for asking," I said.

I pulled myself up onto the first limb of the tree that Ethel was sitting under, so I could get a better lookout for Troo.

"That so? Your mama's holdin' her own? Well, Lordy, that is good news to these tired ears." Ethel was below me in a plastic chair, barefoot and fanning herself with a newspaper, which she said she liked to read because it was important to be educated to the goings-on. She turned to gaze up at me. "How come you and Miss Troo ain't been by lately?"

"We been busy." I wanted to tell Ethel how Rasmussen was trying to murder and molest me and I hadn't felt much like coming by since she lived right next door to him. But as Mother always said, there was a time and place for everything. "How is Mrs. Galecki feeling?"

"She's been askin' for you. And so has Mr. Gary."

"Mr. Gary's here?" I asked, excited.

Mrs. Galecki's son, Mr. Gary Galecki, lived in California and would come and see his mother every summer. The last time he was here he played old maid with me and Troo for over two hours out on the screened-in porch and that made Troo say that she thought Mr. Gary especially must like kids because damn, you couldn't hardly get a grown-up to do anything with you at all. Mr. Gary Galecki was another good egg.

"Mr. Gary's feelin's are real hurt that you and Miss Troo ain't stopped by to say hey." Ethel looked scrumptious today. She had on a little straw hat with creamy pansy flowers and her dress was lemon colored and made her chocolate skin really stand out quite nicely. That's why Ray Buck was looking at Ethel the way he was when he brought her back a cup of iced tea. She really did look good enough to eat. Ray Buck could see we were visiting so after he gave Ethel her drink and a wink, he moved over to the side with his smooth walk and lit up a cigarette with a snap of his lighter.

"We'll come by real soon, I promise. Troo was just tellin' me today how much she was looking forward to seeing Mr. Gary."

"All right then, I'll tell him he can be expectin' you." Ethel took a long drink out of her cup and then moved around in her chair a little to get comfortable because she believed in being as comfortable as possible at all times. Life had enough uncomfortable in it, she always said.

"Are you little gals bein' careful? I been readin' in the newspaper that there's a crazy man out there and I heard tell that somebody grabbed at you over at the Fazios' yard the

other night. You best pay attention when you're out and about."
Ethel sounded like she knew what it meant to be grabbed at.
"Alls I gotta say is thank the Lord that Mr. Rasmussen lives
next door to me. Gives me a feelin' of such safety."

Should I tell her? Shouldn't I tell Ethel, my dear Negro
friend, how very smart she was about certain things like
how to take care of sick people and how to make the best
blond brownies and how she had the singing voice of all the
cherubs in heaven, but that she was wrong, dead wrong,
about Rasmussen?

I looked out over the crowd while I was deciding about
that and spotted Troo's Statue of Liberty torch. She was
talking to Uncle Paulie, who probably wasn't working today
at Jerbak's Beer 'n Bowl setting up pins for one dollar and ten
cents an hour because the lanes were closed for the Fourth
like everything else was. The other thing Uncle Paulie did to
make money for himself and Granny was collect soda bottles
out of people's garbage cans and take them to Delancey's
Corner Store. Mrs. Delancey gave him two pennies for the
bottles and Uncle Paulie always counted them real carefully,
like maybe Mrs. Delancey was trying to gyp him.

Uncle Paulie was looking at the ground and pointing at
something. Troo bent down and handed it to him, and then
he ran around her and put his hands over her eyes. I could
see his mouth moving. I knew he was saying "Peek-a-boo."
Troo pushed his fingers off her face and ran.

"Did you hear what I said, Miss Sally?"

"Pardon me?" I had to use manners around Ethel or she
would get after me.

Ethel sighed, and when she did her bosoms went up and
down just like Artie Latour's Adam's apple. "I said you and

Miss Troo should come over to see the puppy that Officer Rasmussen got. I know how Troo is still missin' that Butchy dog of hers." She had probably told him about how we had to leave Butchy out on the farm. Rasmussen probably bought that puppy to trick me into trusting him. It was common knowledge that me and Troo had a fondness for animals of all kinds.

"What happened to Officer Rasmussen's wife?" I asked before I had even figured out I was gonna do that.

Ethel turned quickly back toward me. "Dave Rasmussen don't have a wife. He's a bachelor man."

"Why do you think he doesn't have a wife?" I was swing-ing my feet back and forth up in that tree. I was getting ner-vous now, talking about Rasmussen, because I already knew why he didn't have a wife. Rasmussen didn't like wives. Ras-mussen liked little girls. From up in the tree crook, I could see what everybody was doin'. Troo had found Willie. They were holding hands, walking toward the gully that led down to the Honey Creek.

Ethel said, "Come down here, Miss Sally. This twistin' and turnin' is givin' me a pain in my neck and Lord knows, I don't need another one of them."

I always did what Ethel told me to do so I hopped out of the tree and landed on the grass next to her. She ran her hand down my hair and told me it reminded her of a bag of just picked cotton.

"You know, my mama, she died young," Ethel said qui-etly. "It's a sad thing when a woman gets sick and dies 'fore she's done doin' her mothering. It just ain't right and not in the order of things. So you say a lot of prayers that your mama gets better, okay?"

I nodded and then Ray Buck came over and said, "Time to take a stroll over," and pointed toward the zoo. They were going over to see Sampson because that was what everybody liked to do over there. Admire the King of the Jungle.

"I'll see ya later, Miss Sally. Maybe at them fireworks." Ethel stood, pulled her lemon dress down and smiled at Ray Buck when he offered her his arm. "You give my best to Miss Troo and tell her that Mr. Gary brought along his old maid cards and he's a-rarin' to go."

"You say hello to Mr. Gary for us and you can count on us this week to help you with Mrs. Galecki. I have a new book from the library with some beautiful pictures I think she'll like. It's called *Black Beauty*."

Ethel grinned and said, "Why didn't nobody tell me that somebody done wrote a book about me?"

Ray Buck started laughing so hard he had to clear his throat and spit.

I didn't get the joke until the two of them were walking on the path over toward Sampson, and then thought I better get down to the creek and get Troo because they just announced that the sack races would begin in five minutes. I'd tell Ethel later that was a good one.

Mary Lane, who I think musta been on her third or fourth Eskimo Pie, because she had four of those sticks lined up in front of her, called me over and said, "Take these and give 'em to your uncle Paulie so I can put that in my charitable works story."

Everybody in the neighborhood knew about Uncle Paulie and his Popsicle sticks. Just like everybody knew that Mrs. Goldman wouldn't ever wear the color gray and Ethel wouldn't drink Coca-Cola unless she could drop peanuts in it and that Mrs. Latour was not going to have any more kids because she'd gone into the hospital and had an operation where they took all her insides out and threw them away.

"Yeah . . . okay," I said, picking up the sticks. Mary Lane didn't want to give the sticks to him herself because Uncle Paulie was so odd. The way he always walked with his head down like he was searching for something. And the way he talked, which was real slow and sometimes didn't make sense. And he also smiled too much, particularly at stuff nobody else smiled at. Like at that dead bird I found in Granny's backyard. Before he had the accident and got his brain damaged, he hardly ever smiled. Granny used to warn me to steer clear of him, to not get on Uncle Paulie's bad side because "That boy can get his Irish up." The way she said it, I could tell she was afraid of her own son.

I stuck Mary Lane's sticks in my pocket and felt like a bad Catholic for sometimes not liking my own uncle, so I made up my mind to go look for him. But first I wanted to cool down with Troo and make sure she wasn't throwing anything at Greasy Al.

"Three minutes . . . three minutes, everybody, until the sack races . . . find a partner," came over the loudspeaker.

Everybody was laughing and eating and sweating and the sun felt so scorchy, like if we stayed out in it long enough we'd all melt like ice cream and there'd be nothin' left of us to see but people puddles.

I ran into Nell on my way to the creek. She seemed a little drunk because she was acting way more nice than Nell usually acted in the morning, or anytime really. She even hugged me, which was not something Nell generally did. But then she cried a little. When Eddie brought her over a cup of root beer, she started laughing again real quick. Clearly, Nell was going crazy. (Well, she certainly had the hair for it.)

I stood on top of the hill and looked down at the creek. Kids were hopping across the rocks and sometimes falling in and laughing and then getting right back up, and then I saw Troo. She and Willie were sitting next to the little waterfall and even though it was so hot she had on her prize-winning coonskin cap. I yelled to her, "The sack races are getting ready to start."

She yelled back up, "Hold your horses."

When I turned to walk back to the race area, I ran smack dab into Reese Latour and his flat-as-a-frying-pan face. He was staring down at Troo, grinning and rubbing the front of his pants. Reese was always doing that. Fast Susie Fazio said that Reese'd told her he had a magic genie in there and he was making a wish.

"What were you talkin' to those two niggers about?" he slobbered out. Reese'd been drinking something that I thought might set my hair on fire, that's how strong he smelled.

Before I had a chance to tell him to mind his own beeswax, Artie came running up next to me and said, "Hi, Sally."

Without a word, Reese reached behind me and shoved his brother down on the ground. The bike-decorating prize Artie'd picked out, a silver bike bell, flew through the air and landed at my feet, making a noise like the ones at the beginning of a boxing match. "Can't you see that her and me are talkin'?" Reese groused. "Aren't you supposed to be watchin' the idiot?"

Reese was Nell's age, almost grown up, and shouldn't be shoving around someone younger than himself. I helped

Artie up and handed him back his bell after Reese started singing, "Harelip, harelip, harelip," loud enough for people to start looking at us. Then he took another swallow out of whatever was in that brown paper bag and got up close to me and said, "Why don't you just marry a nigger if you love 'em so much," and walked off.

"Two minutes . . . two minutes, everyone. Get your partners and pick your sack."

"You wanna be my partner, Sally?" Artie acted like Reese pushin' him down was no big deal because it happened every day, and then I realized it probably did and felt so sorry for him.

I looked back at where Troo should've been coming up the gully. Well, the heck with her. Let Willy watch over her for a bit. "Yeah, that'd be fine, Artie."

Artie and I went over to the pile of sacks and found one that looked strong and didn't stink too bad. (Each year at the Fourth of July sack race, Mr. Lane said they used the same sacks they used since the American Revolution.) We slipped our legs in and Mrs. Callahan tied us together with a rope and we hopped over to the starting line. It was funny to feel Artie's sweaty, hairy leg against mine. Troo was gonna be so mad if I did the race with him and not her. I wanted to say to Artie I changed my mind, but then I thought he'd think I didn't want to partner with him because he was a harelip.

I looked for Troo again and started to get worried. She loved the sack race and had been looking forward to it all year long since we had won it last year. Mr. Lane said, "On your mark . . ." Too late now to go lookin' for her. "Get set . . ." I looked down the line at our opponents. Way on the very end was Troo. With Willie. She waved to me and gave me her teaser smile. And then more than anything I wanted to win that sack race.

"Go!"

Much to my surprise, to make up for that harelip, God had made Artie Latour a fast hopper. Real fast. Before I knew it, I was on the ground at the finish line and Mrs. Callahan was smiling and putting blue ribbons over our necks. Everybody was yelling congratulations. 'Cept for Troo.

"A new record in the sack race, folks!" Mr. Lane yelled. "That's Sally O'Malley and Artie Latour. Let's give them a round of applause." Everybody clapped and then Mr. Larsen, who owned the Tick Tock Coffee Shop over on Burleigh Street and seemed to be in charge of the cookout, hollered out, "Come and get it!" and waved a flag toward the picnic area, where you could eat for free and have watermelon and ice cream Dixie cups for dessert.

Artie headed over there with me like we were still in the sack tied together. Troo was sitting on the edge of a picnic table a ways away, giving me the evil eyeball, so I thought I better go talk to her.

I said, "I'll see you later, Artie."

He adjusted the ribbon around his neck and said, "You're a nice girl, Sally." Then he got in the hamburger line. And now maybe Artie Latour had the hots for me.

Her arms crossed over her chest, her toe tapping, Troo looked very fired up. I knew what she wanted me to say and do. She wanted me to apologize for winning the sack race and give her the blue ribbon.

I sat down next to her on the picnic table and tried to

put my arm around her, but she shrugged it off. "You coulda waited for me, you know," she said with flaring nostrils.

"I called for you. Twice. You didn't come and I was feelin' bad for Artie since Reese pushed him down and called him a harelip."

"Suit yourself," she said, and walked away. Troo gave up so fast and didn't start a real fight because we both knew later that night, I would give her that blue ribbon that said CHAMPION on it in gold letters. That was the way it was with her and me. Just the way Daddy woulda wanted it.

After the egg race and two hamburgers and a hot dog and a little dunk in the creek, we laid down in the grass under a big maple tree and I sniffed my sunburned skin, which I had always found to be a nice smell. We played crazy eights with Mary Lane and Mimi Latour until it started to get dark, and then Nell and Eddie came and found Troo and me and we went over to the lagoon to sit on a soft blanket next to the water and watch the fireworks.

As I watched those red, white and blue stars burst up in the sky, I wondered about two things. The first was, how bad did it hurt when you got murdered and molested because we were sitting not far from the willow tree where Troo'd found Sara Heinemann's shoe. And the second thing I wondered as I sat there, Troo's head in my lap, a warm lagoon breeze running across my cheeks when all the fireworks went off at the same time and everybody's faces were lit up and tilted toward the sky, I wondered could Mother see these fireworks from her hospital window and if she could, was she missing me the same way I was missing her?

CHAPTER TWENTY-ONE

When all that was left of the fireworks was the smoke, Nell gathered up the blanket and said for me and Troo to walk home with the Latours because she and Eddie were going down to Lake Michigan to watch the submarine races. That was fine with me. It was a warm night and I liked to walk and look into people's houses through their picture windows when their lights were on and there was a mother and the father and some kids and sometimes they looked just like a painting. I wasn't a peeper like Mary Lane. I didn't like to look *that* close. I just liked that feeling . . . that feeling of everything being the way it was supposed to be.

Up the block the rest of the neighborhood was making their way home and I could hear Mrs. Latour yelling at one of her kids to shut up and quit their whining. Troo said, "I let Willie give me a smooch down by the creek." I thought smooching with a boy was more disgusting than when Wendy Latour ate that dusty wiener she found underneath the picnic table today so I changed the subject.

"Did you see Ethel and Ray Buck?" I asked. We were walking past the Fitzpatricks', who lived a block down from their drugstore. Nobody home.

"Yeah. Ethel says that Ray Buck is a fantastic bus driver. He has routes all over the city and has to remember them all by heart." Troo kicked a rock. "And she told me that Mr. Gary is in town and asking about us, which is kinda nice because Mr. Gary is flush, Sally. We could ask him to borrow us some money after Mother dies and Hall gets into some trouble, because you know he's going to, and then we can move to France."

And that's why she was called a Troo genius because, you see, I never woulda thought of that. It was better than a good plan. Troo was especially right about Hall. I'd heard him talking to himself two nights ago in the bathroom when I was laying in bed, my sheets smelling like this bird's nest I found once in the backyard. "That manager," Hall said and then stopped to puke. "That big Shuster's manager from Cincinnati, he's got nooo idea who he's dealin' with. They'll regret this when the best shoe seller west of the Mississippi is gone." In the morning I found him asleep in the bathtub. Hall was very bad at directions.

"Mr. Gary has very dreamy eyes," Troo said in her sleepy voice, the one she got when she listened to Bobby Darin on the blue Motorola transistor radio that Mr. Gary brought us last year all the way from California for no reason at all. I thought that maybe Troo had a crush on Mr. Gary even if his ears stuck out and . . . Eureka! That's who the other boy was in Mother's graduation picture. It was Mr. Gary! I had no idea that he knew Mother. He'd never said anything. I should've paid attention to details because all you had to do was look at those ears that stuck out of his head like rowboat oars. I became extra excited to see him because I'd ask him questions about Mother and probably, because I had to know, the guy who was standing in the top row. Rasmussen.

When we walked by Fitzpatrick's Drugstore, we waved through the window at Henry Fitzpatrick, a boy in my class. The drugstore had a soda fountain and Henry was sometimes the soda jerk, which was not a very nice thing to be called. I felt bad because Henry also had some disease called homofeelya and he had to be careful not to fall down on the playground because with this homofeelya you could start to bleed until all your blood was gone. So Henry was kind of pale and knobby and was especially careful when he opened a can of any kind.

But Henry liked to read just like me, so sometimes we sat on the front step of the drugstore and talked about books. A lot of the other kids called him Homo Henry, I think because of his bleeding disease, so he didn't have a lot of friends. He wanted to be a pilot when he grew up so he read a lot about airplanes, which reminded me of my Sky King. But Henry had to know that no homofeelyas would get to be a pilot because what if he crashed or something and started bleeding all over the place and left a trail into the woods so the Russians could find him and then torture him to tell government secrets. I figured that Henry would grow up to be a pharmacist like his father and I bet he knew that too, and that's why he looked kind of sad most of the time.

Henry stuck his head out the drugstore door and said, "Come on in."

I waited while Troo propped her bike up on the side of the building and then I pulled open the drugstore door and it was so cool inside, just like the "Icy Cold Refrigeration" sticker on the door promised. Henry was sitting at the countertop and sipping on a chocolate phosphate.

"You want one?" Henry asked, pointing down at his glass.

"That'd be swell," I said.

"How were the fireworks?" Henry got up off his stool and went behind the countertop. He took two glasses from a stack, wiped 'em off with a towel and set them on the counter.

"Better than last year," Troo said. I think she must've known that Henry hadn't gone and was too afraid it might have something to do with his bleeding disease, so she didn't ask why because Troo wasn't all that good with sick people. Except for Mrs. Galecki, who was stiff with oldness and got me and Troo mixed up sometimes, but did not look sick.

Henry squirted some chocolate into the tall glasses. I could see his face in the big mirror above the stack. Henry was darn good-looking. A little ghosty, but darn good-looking. If Troo and Willie were going to be girlfriend and boyfriend, then maybe Henry and I could do the same. No smooching allowed, though.

Henry used a long, skinny spoon to stir up the bubble water and chocolate. "Are you going to Sara's funeral tomorrow?"

It felt funny to be sitting in Fitzpatrick's Drugstore like this at night, the lights down so low and that witch hazel smell and the air conditioning making my arms bumpy in a good way. I wished I could've slept right there on that freezing cold counter instead of going home.

I took a sip of my phosphate and was impressed with what a good job Henry had done and was pleased that he had handed mine to me before he handed Troo hers. "Are you?"

"Yeah. I have to," he barely said. "Sara Marie was my cousin."

"Oh," I said. "We're definitely going to the funeral then, right, Troo?" Not paying attention to me, she'd slipped her hand into the Dubble Bubble bowl next to the soda fountain and was helping herself.

"The funeral is at nine o'clock," Henry said. I looked over to where Mr. Fitzpatrick usually sat handing people their medicine. I thought I saw him just for a second, or maybe that was just a shadow from the big glowing red Coke clock that hung on the wall.

And then all of a sudden Henry's thin homofeelya shoulders started bouncing up and down like one of my fishing bobbers. I got up off my stool and walked around the end of the counter and got up next to him. I just stood there for a minute trying to think of something to say. "Don't cry, Henry. Just remember what Sister Imelda always tells us in catechism class. How when people die it's okay because they go back home with God. That's probably how Sara feels right this minute, like she just got home after a hard day. Her and God are probably just laying around on clouds watching *I Love Lucy*."

That only made him cry harder. Might be that Henry Fitzpatrick was sensitive just like me.

In the mirror above the soda fountain, I could see Troo stuffing her pockets with things she was taking off the shelves.

"We gotta get goin'. So we'll see ya tomorrow morning, okay?" I patted Henry on the back and went back to my stool because it'd felt so awful to be behind the counter. Like when you do or say something you're not supposed to and you get that dumb feeling in your stomach. I had that dumb feeling about what I'd said to Daddy the day of the crash.

"Yeah, see ya tomorrow, Henry," Troo called, waiting at the door for me, her pockets bulging with stolen goods. I bet Troo never got that dumb feeling in her stomach.

We left him there like that, his head still on the counter. He didn't really say good-bye, because he was probably thinking of his cousin in her small coffin, the same kind Junie Piaskowski had. That worried me at her funeral because I'd thought coffins only came in one size, grown-up. But somebody knew that kids died all the time and that was their job, to make little coffins for dead kids that were lined inside with pink and had a pillow of stiff lace.

I looked back at Henry through the drugstore window. He hadn't moved his head off the counter. It must feel great on his hot eyes. I bet by now he probably felt real bad about crying like a girl because everyone knew that if boys cried it meant they could be what Willie O'Hara called "light in their loafers," which was another way to say homo, and maybe that's why the other kids called him Homo Henry after all, which would certainly put the kibosh on us being boyfriend and girlfriend. Willie said he'd seen light-in-their-loafers men in New York City. He'd even taken a taxicab ride once with one of them who was dressed up like a woman and called him kitten! I knew that being a homo meant you loved other homos. But why would a man do that? Get all dressed up like that? Willie had to be wrong.

The man in the taxi had probably gotten all dressed up like that for a play. Like with Father Jim. One night Mary Lane went up to church to pray for her mother to make fried chicken, and when she was done she decided to do a little peeping. So she creeped over to the rectory and peeked in the window and there was Father Jim dressed up in a fluffy white dress with petticoats and high heels, dancing around the living room to "Some Enchanted Evening."

When Father Jim saw Mary Lane, he invited her in and made her a big ham and cheddar cheese sandwich on rye bread, even though it was Friday. He told her that the church's Men's Club was putting on a play and made her promise not to tell anybody that she had seen him dressed up like that because the play was a surprise and she would wreck it if she told. Mary Lane promised by crossing her heart and hoping to die, but the next day she came over to our house and told me and Troo the whole story. And she's still alive. So that whole "Some Enchanted Evening" story was probably just another one of Mary Lane's big fat lies.

"So," said Troo, balancing her bike against her leg and lighting up an L&M from a new pack she had taken from behind Fitzpatrick's cash register, "Henry and Sally sitting in a tree, k-i-s-s-i-n-g." Her face grew bright in the match flame. I knew she'd bring up Henry giving me my phosphate first. Troo was famous for never lettin' go of something. "First comes love, then comes marriage . . ." I stopped walking and lifted my CHAMPION ribbon over my head and slipped it over Troo's because it was more important to her than to me and I also knew she'd stop singing that stupid song if I did. But most of all I did it because Daddy was right this minute looking down from Heaven and giving me a double thumbs-up.

Troo ran her finger down the ribbon and had another puff of her cigarette and said, "You know what, Sal? You are the best big sister in the whole world and don't you forget. . . ." And then something jumped out of the bushes and Troo was knocked flat onto the sidewalk and a big black shape stinking of pepperoni was all over her, grunting and pinching at her, the muscles in his arms tight like a tug-of-war rope.

Greasy Al was sitting on top of Troo and holding her hands to the sidewalk. I jumped on his back and he flipped me off like a bucking bronco. I landed face-first in the bushes that he'd been hiding in next to the drugstore. Troo tossed and turned and yelled, her legs marching up and down. "You fucking dago, let me go."

"You want me to let you go, you little mick? Your wish is my command." Greasy Al let go of Troo's hands and hauled off and socked her. And then he got up off her. Troo had dropped her bike on the ground and he was limping his way toward it, but then like he wanted to beat on Troo some more, he limped back. He was laughing his greasy laugh. I ran at him, and then Troo, who had gone quiet, moaned, so I stopped, not sure who to go to. Then a voice in the darkness said real softly, "Leave her alone."

At first I thought I hadn't heard right and that I'd made it up because I was always imagining getting saved. But then he stepped underneath the streetlight and I saw his white skinny legs and my eyes traveled up his body to his chest that was barely wider than a cigar box. He was holding a gun in his two pale hands. Henry Fitzpatrick said louder, "Leave her alone, Greasy Al." And then the whole world stopped and all you could hear was us breathing hard and all you could smell was Troo's cigarette burning in the grass and that's when Mr. Fitzpatrick came out of the drugstore and ran over to see what was happening.

He took the gun out of Henry's hand and said, "It's okay now, son. I can take it from here," and he moved Henry behind him.

Greasy Al got up and hunch-limped off into the dark.

Mr. Fitzpatrick looked after him to make sure he wasn't coming back and then said, "I'll call Dave Rasmussen as soon as we clean Troo up here." He picked her up in his arms and Henry ran ahead of him to hold open the door. I looked down and there were my and Troo's handprints that we had done last summer when Mr. Fitzpatrick had the sidewalk patched because it had a big hole in it and he said he didn't want anybody to twist an ankle. Our hands looked so small next to Troo's coonskin cap laying there like it was dead.

Henry stuck his head out the drugstore door and said, "You better get in here. Pop says we might have to take Troo to the hospital. She could have a broken nose." Then he went back inside.

I was holding on to Troo's beautiful Schwinn for dear life. I didn't want to go back in there. I just wanted to run home and go down into the basement and crawl into that hidey-hole because I had let something bad happen to my little sister.

Henry came out of the drugstore and walked over to me. "It's okay. She's going to be okay. Pop says now that maybe it's just a bad lump. He's gonna go get the car and take the two of you home and you won't ever have to worry about Greasy Al again."

That wasn't true. Because last year Greasy Al stuck Teddy Mahlberg in the leg with his switchblade and nobody did a darn thing about it. I was there at the playground when it happened. Saw the whole thing. Greasy Al got mad because Teddy beat him in the Mumbly Peg knife game they played sometimes on the grass next to the steps. Bobby called the fuzz, but nothing happened to Greasy Al because Mr. Molinari of Molinari's Ristorante Italiano was friends with police sergeant D'Amico and they laughed and said boys will be boys and slapped each other on the back right in front of me.

I let Henry lead me back into the drugstore. Mr. Fitzpatrick had laid Troo out right on the soda fountain counter. How nice of him not to mention all the stuff falling out of her pockets. Band-Aids and Dubble Bubble and that pack of red-and-white L&Ms like somehow she knew she might need them later. She turned her head toward mine when I sat down on the red counter stool. "Stop crying," she said, all persnickety. Henry went over to one of the shelves and picked up a box of Kleenex and brought it back to me. Mr. Fitzpatrick put some ice he got from behind the soda fountain on Troo's nose and then said he had to go make a phone call. "Did he get the bike?" Troo whispered. "Did he?"

I shook my head.

Troo smiled, and if she coulda she woulda laughed out loud, because that's the way Troo was. She didn't ever seem to feel pain all that much. But it would have driven her Virginia Cunningham insane if Greasy Al had limped off with that bike.

With the drugstore lights real soft, I thought how much Henry looked like Earl Flynn, who was Earl Flynn no matter what Nell said. No, not actually looked like him. But Henry had that kind of bravery. So right at that moment I knew I would marry Henry Fitzpatrick even if he was a homo because nobody could ever impress me the way he had when he stood up to Greasy Al Molinari. I picked up his hand and held it hard until what little blood it had went somewhere else in his body, hopefully to his heart.

And then the lights from Mr. Fitzpatrick's Rambler shined into the store and Henry and me helped Troo off the counter.

When we got outside, Rasmussen was there waiting for us. He had Troo's coonskin cap in his hand, his foot up on the bumper of his squad car.

"Girls," Mr. Fitzpatrick said, getting out of his car, "you know Officer Rasmussen, right?"

"Yes, we know Officer Rasmussen, don't we, Sally?" Troo musta been feeling better because she said that in her teasing voice. She snatched the coonskin cap outta Rasmussen's hand and put it back on her head.

Rasmussen was staring at me. No matter who else was around, it always seemed he only had eyes for me. Couldn't everybody see that? "Was it the Molinari boy, Sally?"

I nodded but refused to look at him.

"I'll go look for him," Rasmussen said. And then he pulled Mr. Fitzpatrick off to the side of his Rambler and said something to him. Mr. Fitzpatrick shook his head after a few minutes, then looked back at Troo and me and said, "God Almighty. Those poor kids."

I hadn't heard all of what Rasmussen had told Mr. Fitzpatrick but I did hear him say, in a soft voice, "I'm so sorry about Sara. I know how you're feeling. How's Alice holding up?"

"Alice is okay, trying to be strong for her sister," Mr. Fitzpatrick said back.

Rasmussen looked over and said, "Sally, Mr. Fitzpatrick

is going to give you a ride to your granny's. She'll know what to do about Troo's nose."

They said a few more things in low man voices and ended it off with Rasmussen saying, "I'll see you tomorrow morning, Lou."

Mr. Fitzpatrick shook Rasmussen's hand with both of his and said, "Thanks for everything, Dave. Really appreciate it."

Rasmussen gave me one more look and drove off.

While I watched the taillights of the squad car scurrying through the night like an Edward G. Robinson dirty rat, I promised myself that when I was able to prove how Rasmussen had first murdered Junie Piaskowski and then Sara Heinemann, I would make Rasmussen get down on his knees and apologize to Mr. Fitzpatrick right before they strapped him into the electric chair and baked him blacker than Nell's tuna noodle casserole.

CHAPTER TWENTY-TWO

On the ride over to Granny's, Henry and I sat in the backseat of his Rambler that still had that certain smell of newness about it. I had not let go of Henry's hand and it was beginning to sweat but I didn't mind that at all. That was how I knew I was in love with him, because I didn't even like to hold Troo's hand when it got that clammy. Troo was feeling better. Her nose was just a lot bigger. She was sitting in front with Mr. Fitzpatrick, her head resting against the back of the seat. The breeze coming through the car window was drying off the sweat that had popped up on her forehead below her coonskin. She looked like she was almost asleep.

"Sally?" Mr. Fitzpatrick said quietly. He was looking at me in the rearview mirror. Henry's dad was a white-looking man so it made me wonder if Henry got the homofeelya from him. Mr. Fitzpatrick wore thick black glasses and was almost bald so he had the forehead of a baby but a chin made of stone. I wanted to say to Troo, "Fitzpatrick?" And I hoped she'd say, "Irish."

"Yes, Mr. Fitzpatrick?" I said.

"Officer Rasmussen just told me that there's been a little problem with Hall. You need to stay at your granny's tonight and then tomorrow Nell and Eddie will come and get you."

I knew this was going to happen. Hall was dead, I bet.

Henry squeezed my hand a little tighter when I rolled down my window to get some of that nice thick summer night air. When I was ready, I asked, "What happened to Hall?"

I looked at the back of Mr. Fitzpatrick's neck. He must've just had a haircut because there was a red rash running along the edge of his white pharmacy jacket. Mother used to tell Daddy that Vaseline was good for that.

Mr. Fitzpatrick put his eyes back on the road. "Hall got himself into a little bit of trouble and he's down at the jail right now."

Troo, who it turned out was not sleeping at all, said, "Did he get in a fight?"

Mr. Fitzpatrick said, "Hall hit Mr. Jerbak over the head with a beer bottle and now Mr. Jerbak is in the hospital."

"And he's in jail for that?" Troo asked, surprise in her voice. Kids were always getting hit and nobody had to go to jail.

"Charges are being pressed against Hall," Mr. Fitzpatrick said. He turned on his blinker, which made that soft *tick tick tick* noise. We turned down Fifty-ninth Street and went past Delancey's Corner Store, which made me think of poor Sara Heinemann going to get her mother some milk and maybe have a glass of Ovaltine before she got tucked into bed and instead she ended up dead. A couple people in shorts and T-shirts were still sitting out on their front steps, drinking out of beer bottles and listening to the radio that was playing some boogie-woogie. One of them waved to Mr. Fitzpatrick and he waved back.

"Can I press some of those charges against Greasy Al?" Troo asked.

Mr. Fitzpatrick shook his head and frowned. "Don't you worry, the Molinari boy won't be bothering you again, Troo. Officer Rasmussen will see to that."

I could tell from the way he had talked to him at the drugstore that Mr. Fitzpatrick admired Rasmussen. I so wanted to tell him how it was Rasmussen who had murdered and molested his niece Sara. Because of that rash on his neck and because his boy had homofeelya, it made me think he'd understand about some things. "Officer Rasmussen . . . ," I started to say.

Mr. Fitzpatrick's eyes moved back to the rearview mirror. "What about Officer Rasmussen?"

"He's . . . he's . . ."

"Yeah . . . he's a great guy, isn't he?" Mr. Fitzpatrick said. "Dave's been a real help to the family during this hard time."

I squeezed Henry's hand so hard that he yelped out.

"I want to go home," I said the second he parked in front of Granny's.

Mr. Fitzpatrick put his arm along the top of his seat and turned toward me and Henry. He had a nice gold watch and his arm was hairy on his white skin. I had to keep myself from laying my face on that arm because it looked so much like Daddy's. "I'm sorry, Sally. Officer Rasmussen doesn't think it's a good idea for you to go home right now."

I bet he didn't. Rasmussen just wanted to know where I was so later, when it got good and dark, he could tell Granny he'd come to take me home, and because she was so old she'd just hand me over to him like a day-old newspaper.

Mr. Fitzpatrick looked at his watch. "I've got to go pick up my wife now, girls. You'll be fine here for tonight."

Troo, who must've gotten punched a lot harder than I thought because she was being way too quiet, said, "Okay." Mr. Fitzpatrick got out of the car and opened Troo's door for her and gave her nose a quick look-see and said, "Keep ice on that tonight. It should feel better tomorrow."

I turned to Henry and gave him my best smile, the one where my dimples got so big you could hide a piece of Dubble Bubble in 'em. Henry said, "See you at the funeral tomorrow, Sally." And out the window he called, "Don't worry about your bike, Troo. Pop put it in the store to keep it safe. And your ice cream cone, too."

Troo said, "It's not an ice . . . aw, forget it," and turned toward Granny's.

I felt astounded, because suddenly I knew why Troo wanted to do that smooching with Willie. More than anything I wanted to feel my lips against Henry Fitzpatrick's fuzzy pale cheek and whisper thank you for rescuing us from Greasy Al. But Mr. Fitzpatrick was right there and I wasn't sure how he'd take that.

After the car pulled away from the curb, Troo said, "You like him?"

"Yes," I said. We watched the Rambler go down the street. Henry's white hand was flapping good-bye out the back window.

"Does it hurt?" I asked, looking at her nose.

"I've had worse."

She was thinking about the car crash because she always got this look on her face that was different from all her other looks. A sort of Statue of Liberty look.

"Do you miss him?" I asked.

She knew I meant Daddy but she pretended she didn't. She threw the ice down on the grass and reached into her pocket for an L&M. She lit it and then took a deep puff, blowing it into a ring that floated over my head. She grinned at my amazement. "Fast Susie showed me how to do that. It's called a French smoke ring." The smoke floated above her head like a halo. "Let's go see Ethel. I wouldn't mind playin' some cards with her and Mr. Gary. In fact, that would be a fantastic thing to do right now, go play some old maid. And maybe we could get Ethel to give us some of those blond brownies. I'm famished."

I was so relieved. Troo was feeling lots better because she had just said four *f* words. I was also relieved that I would not have to sit in that old chair of Granny's by the window and watch Uncle Paulie gluing Popsicle sticks together while he whistled old-timey songs, knowing that Rasmussen knew where I was sleeping. So I said the one thing my sister never got sick of hearing. "Troo genius."

CHAPTER TWENTY-THREE

We were standing on Mrs. Galecki's front porch. After we rang the doorbell, nobody answered and I got worried that they might all be asleep. From where I stood I could see the top of our house and the Kenfields' and I knew there would be some Dottie ghost-crying going on in her bedroom. And, of course, I could see Rasmussen's house because I was standing ten feet away from it. His house was bigger than Mrs. Galecki's. Not a duplex, but a house where only one family lived, like our old one out in the country. I so missed that house. Even peeing Jerry Amberson. Things seemed a lot safer out there, if you didn't count the farmers that were always getting an arm or leg whacked off by an International Harvester like what happened to Mr. Jerry Amberson, who had a hand that was hard and hollow and the fingernails were painted a fancy lady pink. But at least out in the country there wasn't a murderer or a molester. Who was a cop. Whose house I could touch right this minute.

"You know, it's gonna be the block party soon," I said to Troo, who looked awfully tired from our seven-block walk over from Granny's. I always mentioned the block party when I wanted to cheer her up because it was her favorite thing about summer. That's when she'd been crowned Queen of the Playground, her favorite part being that rhinestone crown I had told her more than once did not look good with her snowsuit.

Troo didn't answer.

"And the state fair." I added on her third favorite thing about summer.

Troo was sniffing the air. The wind was blowing those chocolate chip cookie smells our way. Those ovens baked day and night, night and day up at the Feelin' Good Cookie Factory. Mother always said the smell of those cookies gave her a stomachache. Maybe that smell was what had made her gallbladder so bad.

"Troo?"

"Shhh . . . I think I hear something." She stepped back down off the porch and looked back up at the house. Then I heard something, too. I followed her around the side of Mrs. Galecki's that was so close to Rasmussen's. Laughter got louder with each step.

Sitting in the screened porch that Mr. Gary Galecki had built for his mother right after the Fourth last summer, so she could enjoy the rest of the summer nights without getting bitten up by the skeeters, were Ethel and Ray Buck Johnson and Mr. Gary. Me and Troo had watched while Mr. Gary built that porch for his ma. The wood smelled so good when he cut it on that buzzing saw. We would get him drinks of water when he asked us to and he told us stories about California and how he had oranges that grew on trees right in his backyard and that he had the loveliest rosebushes, over twenty of them. Mr. Gary said that maybe someday Troo and me could come out there to visit him and he would take us to Disneyland.

"Well, who do we have here?" Ethel said when we came around the corner, even though she darn well knew who we were.

Mr. Gary got up and opened the screen door to let us in. He was on the tallish side and a lot stronger than he looked. And he had the most beautiful hands you've ever seen. Narrow, with strong clean fingernails. Of course, he had those ears that were a lot like Dumbo's, so God had to give him those hands to make up for those ears. Ray Buck was sitting on a little straw couch and smoking a cigar. Ethel was waving a punk back and forth to keep the skeeters away just in case one got in there because Ethel absolutely despised skeeters and called them God's worst idea. They had the record player on in the house and Nat King Cole was singing "Mona Lisa" through the kitchen screen door onto the porch.

Mr. Gary gave us both a really good hug. "It's about time you showed up. Thought maybe you didn't like old Mr. Gary anymore." He wasn't old, he was just making a joke. He was the same age as everybody in the graduating picture in my hidey-hole. The same age as Mother. Thirty-eight years old. "My, how you two have grown," he said like he was surprised and maybe a little disappointed.

We hadn't seen Mr. Gary for a whole year. The last time he was here was last summer, right around when Junie Piaskowski turned up dead, that's all anybody could talk or think about so we hadn't really gotten to spend much time with him. Mr. Gary only came to visit during the summer because the winter cold made his teeth ache, which was why he'd moved to California in the first place.

"How old are you two now?" Mr. Gary placed his hand on Troo's shoulder. He had no way of knowing that she didn't like to be touched unless you were part of her family or one of her very, very best friends. But Ethel knew that so she jumped right up off the chair cushion and said, "My Lord, Troo, what happened to your nose?" She pulled Troo over to the light that was coming out of the kitchen. Troo tipped her head up toward Ethel. "Oh my goodness. Who did that to you, darlin'?"

Since Troo was looking too pooped to participate, I told them the story about what had happened with Greasy Al and how Hall was in jail and we weren't sure where Nell was and how Mr. Fitzpatrick drove us to Granny's but (I lied here, so I'm sorry about that, God and Daddy) Granny didn't answer her door so we came over here.

"Well, of course you did," Ethel said, and gave a worried look to Ray Buck and Mr. Gary. "I'm sure it'd be fine if you slept right out here on the porch tonight."

Mr. Gary said, "Absolutely. We wouldn't want you wandering the streets with all that's been happening around here."

Ray Buck got up and gave Troo his seat on the straw couch when Ethel went back into the house, probably to check on Mrs. Galecki. The fireflies had come out. Ethel told me once that fireflies had followed her up from Mississippi. And it was true, wasn't it? How special people more than others attracted special things like fireflies and crickets and shooting stars and four-leaf clovers.

Ethel came back out with a plate. Ray Buck took a

brownie but Mr. Gary said no thanks. Me and Troo had two each of those best blond Mississippi brownies.

When he was done chewing, Ray Buck kissed Ethel on the cheek and said, "Must be goin'. Early bird catches the worm." We all said good night to him and then Ethel walked him to the front of the house, where he'd catch the bus that stopped on the corner. It would take him home to the Core, where all the other Negroes lived. Ray Buck got to ride the bus for free because he was a bus driver, so that was good for him.

Mr. Gary stood and stretched his arms up and when he did his shirt rode up and I could see his stomach, which was as flat as an ironing board and sunny California brown with black curls around his belly button that went down in a line to the top of his pants. He said, "It's getting late. Gotta hit the sheets. How about some old maid tomorrow, girls?"

"Sounds good, Mr. Gary," I said, already planning to ask him if he knew my mother and if they were friends in high school. Maybe I'd even ask him a few questions about Rasmussen. "Night."

"Don't let the bedbugs bite," he said and walked toward the porch door, but then he turned and smiled kinda sadly at us. Mr. Gary looked like he had something on his mind, but he didn't say nothing. He just rubbed his hands on his pants and went in, passing Ethel when he did.

In her arms, Ethel had pillows with pillowcases that were ironed and smelled of Tide laundry soap, and even though it was warm out she covered our bare legs with a clean white sheet. Troo asked if she could please have a glass of milk and Ethel went and got that for her. Then Ethel lowered herself down in the chair and all the lights were out except for the fireflies and all the noise was low except for the crickets that got loud on those hot summer nights and the Moriaritys' barking dog, and then she said, "Little gals, you're havin' a hard row to hoe right now. Let's pray some together."

Ethel was not a Catholic. She was a Baptist. So every Sunday afternoon she went down to church in the Negro neighborhood while Rasmussen kept an eye on Mrs. Galecki, and wasn't that ever so nice of him to do? Bah.

When I grew up, that was what I was going to be—a Baptist. Ethel let me go with her every so often during the summer. It was the most fun I ever had at church. Reverend Joe preached with such pep. Even peppier than Barb the playground counselor, who was a pretty darn peppy paper shaker. After the service there was always a get-together in the backyard of the church, which really wasn't a church but an old appliance store that still had the sign hanging out front that said in worn away letters: JOE KOOL'S SMALL AND LARGE APPLIANCES FOR THE DISCRIMINATING. They had a ton of fried chicken set out on top of red-checkered tablecloths next to some colored greens, which were like spinach but better. On the number 63 bus on the way back home I once asked, "Ethel? When we come down here again, could we please bring Mary Lane along because fried chicken is her absolute favorite?" Between laughs, Ethel said, "That's a real thoughtful idea. Miss Mary Lane could use a little fattenin' up. That girl is skinnier than a poor relation."

Now, I closed my eyes and so did Troo as Ethel said in her praying voice, "Dear God, these little gals sure could use some help." Ethel went on to tell Him that we were good girls and that our mother was sick and maybe could

He please spare her for a little while longer so she could come back and take care of us. I got so sad in my chest then. A deep sadness, more like a wanting so badly of something. A starving sadness. I must've started crying because Troo kicked me.

Ethel got up with an *aaahhhmen* and kissed both of us on our foreheads and went back into the house with a slam of that screen door, her sweet lilies of the valley perfume staying behind to sit with us a while longer.

My head was on one end of the straw couch and Troo's on the other and her bare feet were next to my tummy, so I rubbed them a little for her until she fell asleep, which was almost right away. Then I got up as quiet as it is when you can't sleep at night. I stared down at Troo's red waves streaming out of her coonskin cap. It was a full moon night and some of its glow was falling across her face and made her look like a saint. I pulled the sheet right up to her chin and then walked over to the edge of the screen porch so I could get a good look at Rasmussen's house. It was all dark except for a light on in what I thought might be the kitchen. Maybe Rasmussen was out looking for Greasy Al Molinari like he told Mr. Fitzpatrick he would. Or maybe he was hiding right around the corner, waiting and watching for me like he had that first night when he chased me down the alley. After Rasmussen did away with me, Troo would be all alone. Even though she acted so tough sometimes, I remembered what she was like after Daddy died. She couldn't take something like that again. She'd turn into a nutcase and have to go out to the county looney bin and live there with Mrs. Foosman from over on Hi Mount Street, who had tried to drown her two kids in the bathtub because God had told her they were little devils. I couldn't let that happen. I could never let Daddy down like that. I'd rather be dead, that's how much I loved my Trooper.

To keep her safe, I needed to make my scheme come true. I was going over to Rasmussen's house and look around a little to see if I could find Sara's other tennis shoe or Junie's St. Christopher medal she got for her First Holy Communion, which Fast Susie Fazio said had never been found. And then I would come right back to the house and wake up Mr. Gary and he would take the shoe and the medal and drive them over to the police station and then the cops would come to get Rasmussen and electrocute him ASAP.

I wanted to ask Ethel for help, but I didn't. Because I knew she *really* liked Rasmussen. She even did charitable things for him. Like watering his garden if it had been a hot day and he couldn't come home from the police station. Or if he had to leave very early, Ethel would bring his milk and butter in from the chute and put it in his refrigerator.

One night, I asked Ethel while we were playing go fish why she liked Rasmussen so much. She leaned forward, quickly plucked three cards out of her hand and placed them facedown in front of me. The first card she flipped over was the jack of hearts. "See that?" she said. "Let's say that's Dave Rasmussen." Then she flipped over the middle card. "And then let's say"—she tapped the queen of hearts—"let's say that's . . ." She almost said a name, but caught herself. I slit my eyes at her. Ethel had her no-how-no-way look on her face, so I knew there was no use asking who had just been sitting on the tip of her tongue.

"You know why that jack of hearts has such a sad-lookin' face?" Ethel asked.

I studied the card. "Because he has to wear those dumb-lookin' clothes?"

Ethel snorted. " 'Sides that."

I am usually very good at guessing games because of my imagination, but for the life of me I couldn't come up with anything. "I don't know, Ethel. Why's he look so sad?" He really did look awful.

"Well, it's all because of this here queen." Ethel picked the card up and waved it at me. "She was deep in love and wanted to marry this jack." She put the cards together like a couple walking down an aisle. "But this jack"—she put it right up to my face—"even though he was deep in love, too, he told the queen he couldn't marry her." She *tsked . . . tsked . . . tsked*. "So the queen done went off and married someone else." She turned over the last card. It was the king of diamonds. "So now the poor ole jack has got a permanent fracture of the heart."

Sometimes I had to pay very close attention to Ethel and her stories. They could be as confusing as one of those soap opera stories she listened to on her kitchen radio while she was ironing.

"Ethel, are you tellin' me that Rasmussen loved a woman with all his heart and soul and all the stars in the sky and starfish in the sea and she married somebody else?"

"That's 'xactly what I'm tellin' you, Miss Sally," she said. "Truth be told"—she leaned in so close I could see the hairs in her nose—"that queen got married to somebody 'sides that jack more'n once." And I could tell by the wrinkle that came between her eyebrows that the whole story had made Ethel, who was a real romantic woman, feel just terrible for Rasmussen.

Oh, poor Miss Ethel Jenkins from Calhoun County, Mississippi. Rasmussen had even fooled the smartest woman I knew. But he couldn't fool me. I pulled carefully on the creaky screen door that led out of the porch so it didn't wake Troo. Then I walked out of Mrs. Galecki's yard into the alley because a white picket fence full of sleeping yellow roses separated the two yards and I didn't want to come back later all scratched up. That would make Ethel suspicious in the morning. I held my breath and looked around. Nothin' seemed like it shouldn't, so I walked around Rasmussen's garage and tried to peek in. I bet when he stole girls he brought them here to molest them. Because those girls were both taken right off the sidewalk. Sara had been on her way to get that milk for her mother and Junie, I heard, had been on the way to her dance class at Marsha's Dance Studio, where they had children's tap and ballet lessons. And they weren't found right away after they disappeared. So Rasmussen had to have brought them somewhere after he grabbed them. He probably had a car like Mr. Gary. Hardly anybody had one around here. Most people took the bus or walked to where they had to go every morning, like to the Feelin' Good Cookie Factory or to church or to the Kroger.

I snuck into Rasmussen's backyard, slowly, slowly closing the gate but leaving it unlatched in case I had to make a fast getaway. I couldn't believe my eyes! There was the garden Rasmussen had told me about. Oh, it was a sight. There was a birdbath with water and a little birdhouse on a stick. And carrots and tomatoes and radishes in rows. And small green beans growing on large poles that looked like a tepee. And so many different kinds of flowers, some I'd never seen before. It was truly a Garden of Eden. Mrs. Goldman would just go crazy for this garden. So would Daddy.

I walked on the grass real quietly up to the house. I leaned against his back door waiting for my heart to stop fluttering like a kite on a windy day. Then I crossed myself and slowly pulled the handle down. And it was then that the whole backyard lit up like daytime. A car was pulling into Rasmussen's garage. I dropped down and belly-crawled as fast as I could toward the garden because that was about the only place to hide. It seemed like forever until Rasmussen pulled that garage door down with a *clickety clickety clickety*. I could hear his footsteps, but I couldn't see him. I'd gotten inside the green bean tepee to wait for him to go into his house, to hear the slam of the door, but nothing happened. After a few minutes or so, I peeked. I shouldn't have. They always tell you not to do that when you're hiding from someone, but I had to know where Rasmussen was because he was tall enough to look over his fence and there would be Troo sleeping in the screen porch. Easy pickin's, as Ethel would say. I held my breath and looked through the green bean leaves. And in the light of the moon, right next to the yellow roses, Rasmussen was sitting in his glider, rockin' slowly back and forth. Crying his eyes out.

CHAPTER TWENTY-FOUR

When that puppy of his began barking from inside the house, Rasmussen blew his nose into a handkerchief and said, "Okay, okay, hold your horses, Lizzie, I'm comin'."

After I heard the door clank shut, I sat in that green bean tepee counting up to sixty Mississippi until I thought it was safe to come out. A smart thing to do would've been to go back to Mrs. Galecki's and get back under that sheet with Troo, but I guess I really wasn't that smart like Nell always said because I didn't do that. I had a scheme and I was sticking to it.

I looked around the yard for something to stand on so I could peep in on him. Next to the back door was an orangish flowerpot like the one on the front porch that was full of red geraniums, which I had noticed because they were Mother's favorite flower. But this pot was empty so I kinda dragged it over to the side of his house, right below a window. I crouched up on it and straightened a little at a time. I could see right into Rasmussen's house! There he was opening a can of something that must've been dog food because that puppy was jumping all over his leg like Butchy used to do when I'd feed him. All I could see was the kitchen. I needed to see more of what Rasmussen was doing, how a murderer and molester got ready for bed. Maybe he would take Sara's shoe or Junie's St. Christopher medal out of their hiding place.

I tiptoed down the path and then set the pot down outside another window that looked into the dining room, which seemed a lot like ours but didn't have Pabst Blue Ribbon beer bottles all over the shiny wooden table. But it did have something else. Something so astounding that I wasn't sure if I was imagining it. There, on the dining room wall, surrounded by a golden frame—and I could see this so clearly because there was a little light above it like a lamp—there was a picture of Junie Piaskowski in her First Holy Communion dress. It was the same picture of her that Rasmussen had in his wallet, only a lot bigger. I ducked down when he walked through the dining room. He didn't even stop to look at the picture. Just went past it like it was no big deal.

I closed my eyes and thought maybe I had lost every one of my marbles. But when I opened them, there she still was—Junie. Then Rasmussen walked by again, now in his underwear, which were the boxer kind, and a bare naked chest. He turned off all the lights except for the one above Junie's First Holy Communion picture and disappeared again with that little dog. I looked back at Junie again. She was smiling on an island of white light in the dark, her hands folded on her lap like she was praying the rosary she had wound around her fingers.

Rasmussen was the worst kind of creature there could ever be! Not only had he murdered and molested Junie, he had her picture hanging in his dining room like he was bragging. Like Mr. Jerbak did about those deer heads hangin' on the wall up at the Beer 'n Bowl.

I had to go wake up Ethel and tell her immediately. Here was the proof! Maybe now she wouldn't think Rasmussen was such a good ole boy. I didn't even put the flowerpot back. I just ran right through the garden, back into the alley and through the screen door, past Troo and into Mrs. Galecki's house. Ethel's bedroom was off the kitchen like Nell's was in our house and I didn't even think of knocking, that's how scared I was. I jumped right onto her bed and began shaking her by the hip. "Ethel . . . Ethel Jenkins . . . wake up." Which I hated to do, because I knew that she was not good at this sort of in-the-middle-of-the-night scariness because that KKK club had given her some very bad memories. That's when Ethel said the KKK liked to come. In the black velvet cloak of the night.

Ethel sat right up real fast. She had something over her hair like a hat or something. And she had on a white frilly nightie. "What's wrong!?"

"Oh Ethel, you have to come see. You have to come see." I pulled on her hand and she tossed back the sheet. She slid her feet into the slippers that she called mules and then let me pull her along out on the screen porch.

Ethel whispered, "Is it Miss Troo? Is she feelin' poorly?" She looked over at Troo, who hadn't moved one iota on the little straw couch.

"Troo's fine," I whispered back. "It's Junie Piaskowski."

Ethel looked at me when I said that and then put her hand on my forehead to check if I had a temperature. "You know, you're beginning to worry Ethel."

"Just come with me real quick, Ethel. Real quick. I have something to show you that you are not going to believe!" She looked at me again and then back at Troo but followed me back to Rasmussen's, her mules slapping. Ethel stopped for a second after we went through the gate into his garden and did a whistle and said, "That man has a green thumb like I never seen." She picked off a small tomato and popped it into her mouth, and then because she was getting more awake now and wondering what the heck I was doing, she said, "Miss Sally, I believe you are havin' some kind of nightmare or walkin' in your sleep. Let's go back to bed."

In my most serious voice, one I didn't even know I had until right then, I said, "Ethel, *no!*"

Ethel frowned down at me because I was not using my manners, but she came along to the side of the house anyway. I stood back up on the flowerpot, but she didn't need to do that because she was taller than a lot of men. I pointed at Junie's picture and figured I didn't need to say anything else. That picture, like Granny said, was worth a thousand words. When Ethel saw Junie in her little white Communion dress and veil, a mixed-up look came over her face. She looked down at me and said, "What is wrong with you, child?" acting like it was la de da normal that Rasmussen had a picture of dead Junie Piaskowski hanging on his dining room wall.

I got so mad and sad all at the same time that I burst right into tears.

Ethel said, "It's okay. It's all right." She ran her hand carefully down my back, like I was one of Mrs. Galecki's china dolls. "Miss Junie's with Jesus in Heaven."

"Ethel, d-d-don't you understand?" I pointed at Junie's picture again. "I saw them together last summer at the Policemen's Picnic and they were flying a kite and Rasmussen was lookin' at Junie in a certain kind of way . . . like he loved her or something . . . and he even had his hand on her shoulder and he was touching her and then she turned up dead. He's the murderer and molester. There's the p-p-proof."

Ethel's mouth dropped almost down to the sidewalk. And then she said in her lowest voice, the one that sounded like a box fan on a hot day, "Oh my, my, my, my, my."

What was wrong with Ethel? Why wasn't she running to wake up Mr. Gary, who would call the police on Rasmussen?

Ethel lifted me up off the flowerpot and set me gently down on the ground. "We need to have a talk, Miss Sally."

I jerked my hand out of hers and whisper-yelled, "Ethel!"

"Come here to me." She pulled me into her bosoms and swatted me a little one on my butt. "Now just settle down so I can tell you what's goin' on here. It ain't what you think."

I let her lead me around the corner of the house and over to Rasmussen's green glider that still had a slight smell of that orange aftershave he wore. We sat down and she rocked us a few times and then said, "You have gone and done some jumpin' to conclusions, which is a bad business to be in."

"But, Ethel . . ."

"Just hush up for one minute." I was so jumpy mad that I tried to get up off the swing, but Ethel grabbed me by the arm and reeled me back down. "The reason Mr. Rasmussen was lookin' at Miss Junie like he loved her was cuz he did. He was Miss Junie's uncle. I thought you knew that."

"Excuse me?" I asked, because I was sure I'd heard her wrong.

Ethel said slowly, pronouncing each word very carefully, "Junie was Mr. Rasmussen's little niece. His sister Betsy's girl."

I just couldn't believe it. This man was the evilest thing walking around on two feet.

Rasmussen had murdered and molested his own niece!

I couldn't talk for a minute because suddenly I didn't trust Ethel, which made me feel really deep down slimy. "Poor Dave. Little Miss Junie was the apple of his eye." She stopped rocking us and said, "For land's sake, why'd you go and think he'd murdered her? Why, Mr. Rasmussen, he can't even murder one of God's worst ideas, that's what a good man he is."

"I'm sorry to have to say this, but you are so wrong, Ethel. Rasmussen did murder Junie and he murdered Sara Marie, too." My mind felt like the inside of a beehive. "And he's got a picture of me in his wallet so that means he's coming after me next."

Ethel let out a little surprised whoop. "Oh, wait 'til I tell Ray Buck." And then she really broke out laughing hard, maybe because she was tired or maybe to make me feel better because she knew how much I loved to hear that laugh that sounded like a million bucks, deeply rich and no end to it. "I always tol' you that imagination of yours was goin' to get you into trouble someday and today is that day, Sally."

Even though she was laughing I could tell she was a little upset with me because she had forgotten to call me *Miss* Sally. I leaned into her when she put her warm arm around me and said, "I promise you this. Mr. Rasmussen, he's the best man around here. A true gentleman. He wouldn't never hurt nobody and somehow you just gotta make yourself stop thinkin' like that."

The smell of Rasmussen's roses was getting mixed in with

that smell of chocolate chip cookies and they made a wave of sweetness that I wanted to do a swan dive into. It woulda been so nice to believe Ethel. To think that somehow I had gotten the idea about Rasmussen being a murderer and molester into my head the same way I'd thought Mr. Kenfield was a spy and that Butchy was the devil in a dog disguise. Seeing Rasmussen look at Junie over at the park when they were flying that kite and thinkin' he was up to something, and how he was always so nice but looked sad sometimes when you'd walk past his house, and how he never got married and all those other things I'd been thinking . . . it was all my imagination?

"Maybe it's because your mother is sick. The worry of that can make a body's brain think somethin' that might not be right," Ethel said. "And your daddy dyin' not that long ago. I seen this happen before. Folks can go off their head for a bit because they's so upset 'bout somethin'."

Rocking with her in the moonlight that made everything seem like it was really just a dream, with edges wispy and soft, I couldn't tell where things started and where they ended. Maybe I had gone off of my head just like she said. But then I realized that if Ethel was right and Rasmussen wasn't trying to murder and molest me . . . somebody else was. Somebody had chased me down that alley. Somebody had pushed me down in the Fazios' backyard during red light, green light. You could even ask Nana Fazio.

"You feelin' an ant's worth better, Miss Sally?" Ethel said from far away.

I wanted to say, "Yes, Ethel, I feel fine. Everything's going to be okay. I see now that what you said about Rasmussen is the honest to God's truth. That he's not the murderer and molester." But I just couldn't do that. I loved Ethel to bits and I never lied to her.

"You just go ahead and sleep, sugar. Best thing for you. Ethel's gonna go ahead and say 'nother little prayer for you." Soft and clear in her sweet voice that hung over that garden of goodness, she said, "Now I lay me down to sleep, I pray the Lord my soul to keep. And if I die before I wake, I pray the Lord my soul to take."

Last thing I thought before I drifted off was that I'd need to have a little chat with Ethel tomorrow about her prayer selection.

CHAPTER TWENTY-FIVE

I woke up in Ethel's bed the next morning, thinking about last night and what she'd told me about Rasmussen and how he was a good man, a true gentleman. A nice loving uncle to Junie. Definitely not a murderer and molester. That was so hard for me to believe. Impossible, really. I would have to have a case of amnesia to believe something like that.

Ethel peeked her head through the bedroom door and said, "Time to get your tail a-shakin'." She had some toast on a see-through plate and a cup of milk with Ovaltine in it that she'd bought just for our Wednesday visits because we just adored Ovaltine. Ethel had grown to just adore it, too. Who wouldn't? She set my breakfast down on the small bedside table right next to her Bible and a Sears and Roebuck catalog that had some folded-over pages.

Ethel went over to the bedroom window and pulled up the yellowed shade that looked right into Rasmussen's garden. I already knew he was out there and that Troo was with him because I heard their voices coming through the screen window. I saw that Troo had on a big starched shirt that was probably Mr. Gary's because it looked like a dress on her. I could tell she'd had a bath from the way her hair looked all fresh with the gold jumping around in it like Mother's.

"How you feelin' this morning?" Ethel sat down on the edge of the bed and I rolled her way.

"I'm feelin' fine this morning, Ethel. Thank you for asking. Did you tell him?" I nodded toward the window.

"No, I most certainly did not. I 'spect that might hurt Mr. Rasmussen's feelings, tellin' him you think he's a murderer and molester, don't you?" She was out of her nightie and into her Sunday clothes even though it was Tuesday. "I happen to know that Mr. Rasmussen thinks very highly of you, Miss Sally, so you gotta train your mind, get it to stop thinkin' the way it's been thinkin' about him."

I would have to work very, very hard to train my mind not to think the way it'd been thinking about him. But if Ethel was right, that's what I had to do. Because if it wasn't Rasmussen, I hadda start keepin' an eye out for whoever else it was that was trying to do away with me.

"What time is it?" I asked her. I took a bite out of the toast and it was so good with those strawberry preserves spread on top of it. "Troo and I have that funeral to go to today. I promised Henry Fitzpatrick."

"It's just after seven." Ethel got up off the bed. "I already gave Troo a bath and you're next. I'm gonna go run the water. You finish up your toast, includin' the crusts."

I rolled onto my other side and watched Troo throw the ball for the little collie dog, who looked like it was having so much fun running around Troo's legs with its tongue hangin' out. Rasmussen was bent over at his waist, laughing at the two of them.

I could hear Ethel start up the bathwater on the other side of the wall. Before Mother got sick, I didn't care much for baths and would complain the whole time, but now the idea of getting clean in that tub sounded just heavenly to me. Ethel would put bubble bath in it because that was what she always did for Mrs. Galecki. Bubble bath that came in a little yellow Avon bottle and made the whole house smell like vanilla ice cream. So I stuck the rest of the toast in my mouth, includin' crusts, and got up to see if Mrs. Galecki was around. I thought I could read her a quick story or something for lettin' me and Troo stay overnight at her house.

"Well, good morning, Sleeping Beauty." Mr. Gary was sitting at the kitchen table with his mother. He was dressed in a nice white shirt and shorts. Mr. Gary almost always wore white clothes. He took such pride in his appearance.

Mrs. Galecki said, "Good morning, Sally."

"Morning," I said to her smiling face. She absolutely adored her son and talked about him all the time when he wasn't here, told me little stories about him. Like how Mr. Gary was something called a late bloomer. And how he used to get picked on at school by bad boys who called him a ninety-eight-pound weakling. But how her Gary was doing so well after such a rocky start and she was so proud of him. So, of course, Mrs. Galecki musta been just Christmas-morning excited that Mr. Gary was sitting next to her at the round wooden breakfast table with cups of tea and toast and even some grapes.

"Come join us," Mrs. Galecki said, and waved at me with her little gnarled-up hand.

"Just for a minute would be okay cuz I really gotta take a bath." I could barely stand to be around myself, that's how bad I had begun to smell, and sitting in Rasmussen's green bean tepee in the dirt last night had not helped one bit.

I sat down next to Mrs. Galecki, who had a lot of lines

on her face, especially around her mouth. But she had pretty eyes of a brown color that I had never seen before. Like the water down at the lagoon. Light muddy colored.

Mr. Gary was reading the newspaper to his mother. His ears didn't look quite as bad as they had in that high school graduation picture in the hidey-hole. They still stuck out but his face had grown wider. "Today is the funeral of that little girl they found in the park. Did you know her, Sally?"

"Not really," I said, popping a grape in my mouth. "Sara was younger than me and Troo. A third-grader."

Mrs. Galecki shook her wobbly head back and forth and said, "How sad for her mother. You remember Cathy Miller, don't you, Gary? She married Frankie Heinemann. Sara was Cathy and Frankie's little girl."

Mr. Gary shook his paper and said, "Of course, I remember Cathy Miller. Prettiest girl in school. Lovely, lovely girl."

"I think the whole world is heading to you know where in a handbasket, don't you?" Mrs. Galecki said. "What kind of monster would hurt poor defenseless children?"

Yesterday I woulda thought right away that Rasmussen would, but I was trying not to think like that anymore. Just as a favor for Ethel. But I was pretty sure this mind training would take some time. Like learning a new card trick.

I was getting ready to ask Mr. Gary about Mother and what kind of girl she was in high school and were her and him friends when Ethel called, "Miss Sally . . . bath is ready!"

"Thank you for lettin' Troo and me stay over." I pushed my chair back and said, "We appreciate it so much."

Mr. Gary set his paper down on the table and said in

that soft, light voice of his, "What nice manners you have, Sally."

I must have blushed because he added, "And such wonderful coloring. You know what that means?"

I shook my head.

"You have green eyes and blond hair and skin with the nicest bit of peach tone," Mr. Gary said. "That's called your coloring." He picked up his paper and said from behind it, "You're a beautiful girl."

"Miss Saaallly, get your behind in here 'fore this water gets cooled down," Ethel called.

Then Mr. Gary said something behind his hand to Mrs. Galecki. I caught the words "Troo" and "coloring," and they had a little laugh about that.

I went to the bathroom door and there was Ethel sitting on the edge of the tub waiting for me. "Just take off them clothes. I'll wash 'em for you."

"But what'll I put on then?" I handed her my shirt and shorts and undies. Granny woulda said those clothes looked like something the cat dragged in.

"I called Nell. She'll be here in a shake of a lamb's tail with some clean clothes for you and Troo. She'll be takin' you to the funeral in Eddie's car and givin' me a ride, too." So that's why Ethel was in her Sunday clothes. She was going with us to the funeral, which shouldn'ta surprised me because Ethel never missed a funeral. She said it was important for the dead person's family to know how many people were gonna miss 'em.

I slipped my leg into the tub and it felt so good, that warm water and those bubbles. Ethel put a brand-new cake of Ivory soap on the side of the tub and I stretched out and floated a bit. "Behind the ears, too," she said. "And wash your hair." After Ethel closed the door, I thought about Nell and her bubblehead. Even though Nell was doing such a bad job taking care of Troo and me, before Mother got sick Nell really was only about the third worst sister in the world. I would keep that to myself, though, because I knew Troo thought Nell was the number-one worst sister. Even when she was a baby, Troo didn't like Nell one bit. Except as somebody she liked to bite when she got her teeth. And there was no reason for it. It was just Troo being ornery. And maybe just a little green-eyed jealous of Nell.

There was a shave-and-a-haircut-two-bits knock. "Sorry to bother you," Mr. Gary said through the bathroom door. "I need to get an aspirin out of the medicine cabinet for Mother. May I come in?"

I sunk down deep into the bubbles and said, "Sure," even though I didn't want him to. It was his house, after all, and woulda been poor manners to say no.

Mr. Gary came in and got the pill bottle and then snapped the medicine cabinet shut and looked at me through the mirror. "Bet that feels good, huh, Sally? I just love the water. Back home in California I live at the beach and every morning I go for a swim." He came to sit on the side of the tub down on the end where my feet were. I checked again to make sure all of me was under the bubbles. "It's a wonderful way to start the day. Always makes me feel good and clean and just born again." He gave me a little splash.

I thought about that and said, "Yeah. You're right, Mr. Gary," but I wished he'd leave or at least stop smiling because he had this one eye that crossed over a little and made him look a little off. His "coloring" was sort of like mine. Tan skin with blond hair, but instead of green eyes he had eyes the same color as his mother's, lagoon brown. And his blond hair was so blond, it looked, like Nell would say, out of a bottle. And she should know because she was in her second week now up at Yvonne's School of Beauty on North Avenue.

Ethel came back and found Mr. Gary and me talking. She gave him a little push toward the door and said to me, "Did you wash your hair?"

I slipped below the water but I could hear Ethel say something to Mr. Gary and when I came up he was gone.

Ethel knelt down next to the tub and picked up the bar of Ivory and ran it between her big brown hands until there was a lather. My head was kinda under the water and I didn't really hear her, just saw her lips moving. Ethel had wonderful lips. On the larger side. And she always wore this bright red lipstick called Fire Engine Number 5. I bet that would be what Mary Lane wore when she got older.

She pulled me up out of the water by the back of my neck and worked the lather into my hair, kneading my scalp like it was bread dough giving her a hard time. "I said what was Mr. Gary sayin' to you?"

"He said how much he loved water and how it made him feel like he was just born again."

Ethel rolled her eyes and said, out of patience, "That boy has some fanciful ideas and I don't want him gettin' your imagination all worked up again." She scraped the soap off her hands and arms and shook it into the tub. "Dunk yourself and get out."

I didn't want to get out. I wanted to stay in there and float forever and feel like Mr. Gary said, just born again, but

Ethel flapped a fluffy fresh towel at me and said, "Time's a-wastin'." I got out and let her wrap me up. "Go on into my room now and close the door behind you. Nell should be here any minute."

I crawled back underneath Ethel's covers, towel and all, and just stayed there like Ethel said, watching Troo out the window helping Rasmussen pick green beans and put them in a silver bowl. Rasmussen looked down at his watch and his lips moved. Then he looked over my way and waved. I pretended I didn't see him and rolled over onto my other side and prayed Nell would hurry up and get here, because even though it was such a warm day, seeing Troo and Rasmussen together like that, so chummy, I got the shimmy shimmy shakes.

CHAPTER TWENTY-SIX

After Troo and me got dressed in the faded navy blue church dresses and shiny shoes with cleats that Nell brought over, we went looking for Mr. Gary so we could say good-bye to him. We found him out on the front stoop, smoking a cigarette.

I said, "Mr. Gary, we gotta go to a funeral now, but we promise we'll try to come back soon and play some old maid."

Mr. Gary took a long draw and said, "You better make it sooner rather than later, Sally. I'm heading back to California in a few days."

Troo said, "The land of milk and honey."

Remembering this morning's bath, I said, "And water." A specific ocean of it.

Mr. Gary stood up and took a step back so he could get a good look at the two of us. "How pretty and fresh you girls look in your dress-up clothes," he said in his light-as-a-butterfly voice. He flicked his cigarette into the grass, gave us each a peck on the cheek and hopped down the stairs with a cheery, "I told Mother I'd cut some flowers for her. Hope to see ya later, alligators." Even after he took the turn into the backyard, I could still smell his baby powder.

Ethel and Nell were already sitting in Eddie's car, waiting

for us. I told Troo to go ahead, and then I yelled, "Just a minute," and went back into the house to thank Mrs. Galecki one
more time for letting us stay with her. She was asleep in her
kitchen chair, so I just wrote down a little note on a napkin
that said, "Thanks a million!" I signed it, "The O'Malley Sisters!" and propped it up on her glass of prune juice.

When I tiptoed out the front door and turned around,
there he was waiting for me on the porch steps.

"Morning, Sally."

I jumped halfway out of my skin. This man was very
good at creeping up on people. Rasmussen was all dressed up
in a fancy black suit, looking very sharp. He also had on shiny
black shoes. Not the spongy kind. "Can I give you a ride over
to the funeral?"

"No, that's okay." I moved down Mrs. Galecki's front
walk, far enough away from him so he couldn't grab me. "I
got a ride."

Because no matter what Ethel said about him, I was still
mostly suspicious of Rasmussen. And then I don't know
what came over me. I felt real bold with the sun shining and
the little dog Lizzie barking at a squirrel that she'd chased
up the big oak tree, so I squinted at him and said, "Why do
you have a picture of me in your wallet?"

That rattled his cage.

He yelled down to Nell and Eddie to wait a minute and
then knelt down next to me. "There's a lot of things going on
right now that you won't understand for a while. But I promise you, everything is going to be okay. You need to trust me
a little. Can you do that?" He tried to put his hands on my
shoulders, but I yanked back so hard that he lost his balance
and fell forward onto his hands and knees. He got up and

brushed his pants off and said strongly, "I think you need to ride over to church with me this morning. We need to talk." He waved good-bye to Nell and Eddie and off they went with Ethel and Troo, who was smiling at me out the back window of the '57 Chevy because she thought that was funny, me being left behind with Rasmussen.

"Let me put Lizzie in the house," Rasmussen said. "And then we've got to hurry over to church. I'm one of the pall-bearers."

He had such a nice house. Picturesque, I'd call it. It was red brick and had some ivy growing up the side of it and white shutters on the windows with red and white geraniums coming out of the window boxes.

After he got the puppy squared away he called to me from the porch, "I'm going to go get the car. Wait for me at the curb."

I was between the devil and the deep blue sea. Since I was gonna get married to Henry Fitzpatrick I had to get to that funeral even though it would be that devil Rasmussen taking me. So I walked down his steps and tried not to think about Junie's picture hanging in his dining room, telling myself over and over again that I was going to be okay because even Rasmussen wouldn't do something like murder and molest me on the way to a funeral. Nobody could be that bad, could they?

He pulled up and got out of his dark brown Ford and ran around the back fender, coming right for me. I managed to get back up on the sidewalk, and was halfway up Mrs. Galecki's steps before he caught me by the arm. I screamed and screamed so loud that Mr. Gary came running out from the backyard with a bouquet of pink flowers in his hand. He yelled, "Everything okay, Dave?"

Rasmussen just nodded at him.

"Sally Elizabeth O'Malley, what is wrong with you? I was just coming over to open your car door." Rasmussen let go of my arm and walked back over to his side of the car.

I remembered then how Daddy used to do that for Mother. Opened her car door and bent at the waist and said, "Your chariot awaits you, madam." I hadn't seen anybody do something that mannerly in a long time except for Mr. Cary Grant in the movies. So maybe just like Ethel said, Rasmussen was a true gentleman. Or maybe he was just a very, very good actor.

We drove for two blocks without talking and the silence was real loud until Rasmussen said, "You know that your mother and I are friends, right?"

I stared out the car window and let the breeze of the chocolate chip cookies ruffle my bangs.

"I went to see Helen yesterday." Rasmussen put on his blinker to turn onto Lisbon Avenue.

"Is she okay?"

Rasmussen didn't take his eyes off the road. "Yes, she is."

I wanted to ask him so many questions about Mother, just beg him to tell me every little detail—like if she'd asked about me and when she might come home and did she need anything like her gold hairbrush. But I wasn't a hundred percent sure he was telling the truth, and even if he was, I just couldn't bring myself to let him know that I wanted something from him.

"Your mother is out of the woods, but . . ." Rasmussen

turned onto Fifty-sixth Street. "There's been some trouble with Hall and I know this might upset you, Sally, but Hall is . . . Hall is . . . ah . . ."

"A goddamn dickhead?"

Rasmussen laughed but then he stopped real quick and tried to look very serious. "Although I don't approve of your language, young lady, I think that just about covers it."

I always looked at his chin when he talked. It had a little scar shaped like a comma at the bottom of it. I would never look into his eyes, no matter what Ethel said. If I looked in his eyes, my soul might jump right out my window and fly into his. Or maybe he would hypnotize me like that doctor did in that movie called *The Three Faces of Eve*, where that woman had too many people living inside her so the doctor hypnotized Eve and asked for a couple of them to move out. *Look into my eyes. Loook into my eyes.* No, thank you very much.

"You know that your mother and I have been friends since high school, correct?" he repeated.

I didn't want to admit it, but I sort of suspected that Mother and Rasmussen were friends because in that hidey-hole graduation picture they were standing next to each other and Rasmussen was smiling at Mother when he was supposed to be smiling into the camera of Jim Madigan from Jim Madigan Photography Studios.

"So, like I was saying, Hall is in a heap of trouble," Rasmussen said.

"I know about that already." I started twirling my hair around my finger, which I had started doing recently because it seemed to calm my imagination down. "Mr. Fitzpatrick told us that Hall hit Mr. Jerbak with a beer bottle and he's in jail and charges are gonna get pressed on him."

When we turned down Fifty-eighth Street, the Pias-kowskis' street, Rasmussen pulled up in front of their house and looked out the window. "Junie's been dead now for almost a year. Hard to believe." He shook himself a little like you do when you know you can't stand feeling the way you're feeling and you better snap out of it. "The house is for sale. Gotta get over here and work on that yard."

I looked out at the Piaskowskis' and noticed something I hadn't the day Troo and me had walked past on our way to church right after we found out about Mother's staph infection. There was a funny little blue birdhouse half hanging off the rain gutter and it had a kid's writing on the side that I couldn't read. It was twisting in the breeze.

Rasmussen was looking at it too because in a shaky voice he said, "Junie and I made that little birdhouse together. Blue was her favorite color. She loved birds. Especially blue-birds. She called them happiness with wings."

I didn't say anything but I was thinking that Rasmussen's big, strong outside didn't quite match up to his gooey inside, and it was a shock to me that he reminded me of a chocolate-covered cherry. Ethel was right. My thinking wasn't straight, but straight enough to know he was telling the truth about blue being Junie's favorite color, because I remembered how she just loved her blue Lik-m-aid so much that her lips always looked the same color as a cornflower.

"You know Junie was my niece, right? My sister Betsy's daughter?"

"Ethel told me that," I said quickly.

"Betsy had to move away because it was just too sad for her and her husband to live here after Junie . . ." He stepped on the gas and pulled away.

A half block later, Rasmussen turned into what was really the playground of the school but was also used as a parking lot when there was a funeral or a wedding or any other big occasion. I couldn't wait to get out of that car. Rasmussen was making me feel sad for him, the last way on Earth I expected to feel, and it was making me so nervous that I started sweating buckets. When he put the gearshift into P, I pulled down on the door handle.

"Wait just a minute, Sally. I've got something else important to tell you."

His hands were knotted up around the steering wheel and he looked as antsy as I felt. Maybe because we were so close to church he'd started feeling real guilty and was about to confess to the murders. That's just how he was acting. Like after the cops gave somebody the third degree in a movie and then the guy gets all twitchy and just puts his head down on the table and starts yelling, "Okay, I did it. I did it!"

Rasmussen said, "Mr. Jerbak died."

"What?"

"Mr. Jerbak died."

I wanted to say I never did like Mr. Jerbak anyway. He was always beating on his boy Fritz, who would come to school with black eyes that he said he'd gotten when he tripped over the dog but everybody knew Fritz Jerbak didn't have a dog.

"Do you know what that means?" Rasmussen asked.

I spotted Troo standing at the corner of the church next to the statue of St. Francis is a sissy. Which in St. Francis's case meant he was light in his sandals. Willie O'Hara came up with that one.

"It means there's gonna be another funeral?" I said.

"That's right, but that's not what I meant. Mr. Jerbak's death means that Hall won't be around anymore. He's going to jail for more than a few days."

I was bowled over like a strike. "Hall is going to jail forever, you mean?" If Hall didn't pay the rent from the money he made sellin' shoes up at Shuster's, we'd have no place to live. We were *kaput*. Oh sweet Jesus, Mary and Joseph. I grinded my teeth together and got prepared for Rasmussen to tell me that Troo and me were going to go live in the orphanage up on Lisbon Avenue.

"Maybe not forever, but Hall is going away for a really, really long time." Rasmussen swiped some sweat on his forehead with a folded white handkerchief he'd taken out of his front suit pocket. "Do you know what *that* means?"

I thought I did.

"It means that you and Nell and Troo will have to move out of your house. The Goldmans will let you stay another week, but then . . . well, they have to rent it out to people who can pay. Do you understand?" He had put his arm over the back of the front seat and was leaning toward me so close that I could smell orange slices.

I was looking out the window at Troo and trying not to think of the lonely faces up at St. Jude's. Me and Troo were about to become two more lost causes. "So we have to go live in the orphanage?"

"Well, that's what I'm getting at here." Rasmussen's words started to gush out of him like he'd sprung a leak. "Your mother thinks it would be a good idea for you and Troo to come and live with me until she gets better enough to come home."

"*WHAT?*" That had to be nothing but a flight of my

imagination, what he just said, because going to live with him was the most Virginia Cunningham crazy idea I'd ever heard!

There was a knock on the half-rolled-down car window. It was Mr. Fitzpatrick, also dressed in a black suit with a white carnation on the lapel. He leaned his head down and said, "We're all set, Dave."

Rasmussen said, "Be there in a sec, Lou."

I just couldn't believe this. Mother thought it was a good idea for Troo and me to go live with Rasmussen? Mother, how could you? I would have to make sure and ask Nell about this. Yes, that's what I'd do. Rasmussen was probably making this whole thing up. Of course he was.

Rasmussen opened his car door and said, "I've got plenty of room at my house. There are four bedrooms. And Ethel could come over to help you anytime you needed something that I couldn't do for you, like fix your hair." He picked up my braid in his hand that Ethel had done that morning, and for a second I thought he was going to start crying. And even though he could still be that murderer and molester, I didn't push him away. He'd probably tell Mother if I did. Now that I knew that Rasmussen and Mother were friends, I'd have to walk on eggshell feet around him.

He swung his legs out of the car and got out, but then leaned his head back in like Mr. Fitzpatrick had and said, "Talk it over with Troo. See what the O'Malley sisters think." And then he walked off to the front of the church to join the other men who were in black suits with just shaved faces that looked sad beyond belief.

I just sat there. Couldn't even blink my eyes, that's how shocked I was, until Troo came up and stuck her head in the window.

"Did he tell you?" She was hopping from foot to foot the way she did when she got so excited she couldn't stand it, or if she had to pee. "Well, did he?"

"Did he tell me what?" I didn't want to say what he told me just in case it was something different from what somebody told her. Mostly, I didn't want her to know we were going to have to go live in the orphanage because no way on Earth was I gonna live at Rasmussen's.

Troo pulled me out of the car and we started walking toward the church doors. "Hall is going to jail for a really long time because Mr. Jerbak is dead from when Hall hit him on the head with a beer bottle. And Mother is not gonna die."

"Yeah, he told me that."

"Isn't that fantastic!" Troo yelled real loud and then remembered she was at a funeral and said quieter, "So fucking fantastic!"

Part of it was fantastic. The part about Mother getting better. And even that part about Hall because all we ever got from him were some hits on the head and some slaps with his belt, and now Mother would be free to get married to somebody else because I didn't think the Pope made you stay married to a murderer. But that part about going to live with Rasmussen? I didn't think that was so fucking fantastic.

"Yippie ai oh ki aa," Troo shouted, a yellow rose from Rasmussen's garden bouncing on her head.

We walked into the church right behind the Latours, so we had to wait a while because it takes fifteen people a long time to stop at the holy water font, especially when Wendy Latour decides to wash her face in it. I asked Troo, "Who told you all this?"

"Nell told me on the way over." Troo smiled at Artie Latour. He still had the hots for her because his little harelip twitched into a smile until Reese put his fingers around his neck and squeezed until he turned back around again. The Latours had scrapple for breakfast. I could smell it on them.

"Nell talked to Rasmussen. He's a good egg, just like I been tellin' you." Troo'd lowered her voice into a whisper because that was what you had to do in the church, which smelled of incense and had stained-glass windows that calmed me down when the sun came through and made puzzle pieces of red and yellow and green lights on the floor. While we waited in line to go down the main aisle, I looked over at the Virgin Mary statue that always smiled at you no matter what, with her petal pink lips and chipped blue eyes that followed you wherever you went. Candles flickered beneath her feet, lit by people who'd dropped a dime in the tin collection box and asked Jesus's mother to have a good talk with her son about granting their prayers.

To tell you the truth, I didn't get half of what went on up at that church. With all the Latin mumbo jumbo and the Stations of the Cross and the nuns who waltzed like ice skaters wherever they went but would smack you a good one for not singing along with a hymn. I didn't even get what my First Communion was supposed to be about, even though people made a big deal about it and I got presents and my picture taken by Jim Madigan. I know it was the first time I tasted Jesus's body, which had been stuck into a little white cookie. And if you didn't let that cookie wafer melt in your mouth and you bit into it, Jesus would come squirting out and you would be in mortal sin trouble. But I still really didn't get why we had to do that. But that Virgin Mary statue that always smiled and made you feel loved no matter what . . . I got that.

Troo and me looked down the church pews until we found Ethel, who really stood out because she was a Negro and nobody else was. She also had on a huge hat that looked like a flying saucer had landed on her head. Troo and me genuflected and then said excuse us . . . excuse us . . . as we made our way down the pew.

Once we got down next to Ethel I whispered to Troo, because I just had to know, "Did Nell tell you Rasmussen wants us to come and live with him until Mother gets out of the hospital because the Goldmans have to rent the house to somebody who can pay?"

Troo grinned and nodded. I'd been able to tell she really liked Rasmussen that morning when I was watching them in the garden, because she tilted her head to the side and smiled at him in the way she did when she really liked somebody. So I figured, if he hadn't made it all up, we would do what Troo wanted to do, go live with Rasmussen. Because my Troo was on cloud nine and I just didn't want to wreck that for her by telling her what I really thought. That moving into Rasmussen's would be like showing the witch in Hansel and Gretel how to turn on the oven.

CHAPTER TWENTY-SEVEN

Everybody from the neighborhood was there to pay their respects. The Kenfields and the Mahlbergs and the O'Haras and the Fazios and just about anybody who belonged to Mother of Good Hope. Even Bobby and Barb the counselors from the playground came, which was very thoughtful of them. Bobby smiled at me from the pew across the aisle and Barb gave me a peppy wave like she was trying to cheer me up.

After Father Jim said mass, we all stood and sang "Holy Holy Holy," which Mrs. Heinemann told the congregation was Sara's favorite hymn, and just about everybody in church started bawling right along with Mrs. Heinemann. Except for Troo. She was just staring up at the ceiling and licking her lips. I couldn't blame her. I was also feeling so worried that I got bossy with the Virgin Mary, told her she better help the cops catch the murderer and molester real soon or else the next funeral she would be watchin' over would be mine.

When the whole sad thing wrapped up, Ethel put her sopping wet handkerchief back into her snap purse and said to me, "That was a real nice send-off." I could tell she had something she wanted to say because she had her I've-got-a-secret smile on her face. Once we got outside, Ethel asked, "Did Mr. Rasmussen have a talk with you?"

"He told me all about how Hall is in a heap of trouble and how Mother is getting better and how he wants us to go live with him."

"You'll be okay now." Ethel wrapped her arms around me and squeezed. "Mr. Dave is givin' me a ride back home. Go find Nell. I think she's got somethin' else to tell you." Ethel took off down the sidewalk toward the parking lot, humming "Don't Get Around Much Anymore." Her flying saucer hat bobbed in the breeze and her hips were goin' up and down like a teeter-totter. There was just such an importance to her. Like she would never die or get sick or leave anybody ever. Ethel Jenkins was the cool side of my pillow when I had a fever.

"See ya, Ethel," I called after her. She didn't turn around, just waved, her white-as-a-marshmallow gloved hand atop her cocoa-colored arm against the blue-plate-special sky.

Troo and me were standing on top of the hill outside the church doors that looked down into the street. People were getting into long black cars. Henry Fitzpatrick looked up at me and gave a little salute like he was already a fighter pilot. I saluted him back.

And as I watched the car pull away toward the cemetery, the little white funeral flag waving good-bye, I felt blessed to be breathing, to have my heart beating. I knew this would be a day I would never forget. Just like I'd never forget Junie's funeral. Today another little girl would get buried in a small white coffin with pink carnations on top.

I turned to go look for Nell, but Reese Latour came up

behind me and Troo, and cut me off. He started singing with his scrapple breath, "Did you ever think as a hearse goes by, that you might be the next to die? They wrap you up in a big white sheet, and bury you down about six feet deep. The worms crawl in the worms crawl out . . ." When Mrs. Latour heard him, she grabbed him by the ear and pulled him away and smacked him one on his back. That miserable excuse for a kid just laughed and kept singing. Troo gave Reese this little hand signal that Fast Susie had taught her, a flicking of her fingers under her chin that meant something dirty. Troo was becoming so Italian and French. More like the salad dressing aisle up at Kroger than an Irish girl. When Mother got out of the hospital, she'd put an end to that.

I spotted Nell and Eddie on the church steps. They were just finishing up talking to some girls I didn't know. All of their hair had been sprayed into beehives with about a can of Aqua Net and did not blow around at all so I guessed they were girls from Yvonne's School of Beauty. I watched Nell's little feet, so small for a girl her size, sink into the wet grass on her way toward me. Would Nell be coming to live at Rasmussen's house, too?

"I have some more good news for the O'Malley sisters," Nell said with Eddie in tow.

"Let me guess," Troo said. "Your bosoms have stopped growing?"

Eddie bent over and laughed like a donkey. I did too, but stopped real fast because I didn't think it was right to laugh on the day a little girl would be set to sleep forever in the ground.

"You're as funny as a rubber crutch, you know that, Troo?" Nell said.

After the hearse pulled away from the curb, I thought about how Rasmussen had looked when he and Mr. Fitzpatrick and two other men I didn't know carried Sara's little coffin down the main aisle of the church. Rasmussen looked like what Granny called world-weary. And poor Mrs. Heinemann. She walked behind the casket of her only daughter with a handkerchief up to her face, making a sound that I never hope to make.

As I watched Father Jim shushing Sara's mother now, I imagined him in that fluffy white dress with the petticoats and those high heels that Mary Lane told us he was wearing on that peeping night up at the church. And I felt worried for him. Because the Men's Club didn't put on plays. I'd asked Granny and she knew because her husband Charlie, my grampa, used to be the president of the Mother of Good Hope Men's Club. Granny told me that the men sat around and smoked cigars and told jokes about traveling salesmen and drank lots and lots of Irish whisky and Italian wine and German beer, but there was never a mention of putting on plays. Father Jim had just made that up, about there being a play and how Mary Lane should keep it secret so she wouldn't wreck the surprise. I didn't tell anybody else about there not being a Men's Club play because Father Jim had once given me a holy card of St. Patrick, who was my favorite saint, and he never gave me very long penances after confession. I really didn't know why Father Jim got dressed up so pretty like that, but it made me glad that it was none of my beeswax.

The funeral crowd was just about gone when Mr. Gary drove up to the curb in front of the church and ran up the hill toward Father Jim. Mr. Gary said something to him and then Father Jim yelled and kinda cried, "No matter how you look at it, it's a mortal sin, Gary. A mortal sin."

Granny always said that funerals were hard on everybody and the word *fun* should not start them out.

Nell poked me in the ribs with her elbow and said, "Did you hear me, Sally?"

"What?" I was still looking at Mr. Gary, who had put his arm around Father Jim's shoulders and was walking him back toward the rectory. Father was a little bent over at the waist and his arms were out to the side like he was walking on a circus tightrope, like if he made one false step he would tumble down to the ground and never get up again.

Nell said, "We're gonna go see Mother."

Eddie said in a very proud voice, "Aunt Margie arranged it. She said your mother is getting better."

For a second I couldn't think of one thing to say because in my heart I had already accepted that Mother was going to die, even after Rasmussen told me she wasn't.

Troo yelled out, "Hip, hip hooray!"

"Really, Eddie?" I asked.

"Aunt Margie said your mother is gonna be okay. Not right away, but she's not gonna die."

Mother had been gone almost all of June and five days of July and now she was coming back to us. My breath was taken right out of my body. Mother was going to be okay. Just like Rasmussen said. I looked over at Troo. She was hopping like mad from foot to foot.

"Eddie is going to take us right over to St. Joe's," Nell said as we walked toward the parking lot. "I had a long visit with Mother last night and she can't wait to see the O'Malley sisters."

After we got in the Chevy and drove a few blocks I was surprised by how the world looked so much better than it did yesterday. The sidewalks seemed cleaner and the cars shinier and even Paul Anka on the radio sounded better than usual.

Nell flipped down that visor above the windshield and looked at me and Troo in the backseat after she checked her makeup. "And I got some more good news."

"So your bosoms *have* stopped growing?" Troo said again. See how funny Troo could be? Even Nell laughed.

She turned toward us and put her hands on the seat. "Eddie and I are getting married."

"Oh, sweet Jesus, Mary and Joseph!" Troo said in her absolutely amazed voice.

Eddie started laughing and Nell said, "We're engaged." She lifted her left hand up close to my face and there was a little golden Irish ring on it with hands that met in the middle. "It was Mrs. Callahan's engagement ring. She gave it to Eddie to give to me."

I felt like I'd just gotten off that Tilt-A-Whirl ride they had up at the state fair, my head spinning and everything looking cattywampus. I really didn't believe one more thing could happen this summer. But it had. Now Nell was getting married.

When we turned down Fifty-ninth Street, I said, "We should stop real quick at Granny's and tell her about Mother getting better."

Eddie said, "Okey-dokey," and turned down the block that took us to Granny's, first stopping at Delancey's Corner Store to get some Camel cigarettes for himself and Cokes all around. Nell went in with him because it seemed like she wouldn't let go of his hand anymore, which Eddie didn't seem to mind. I guessed Eddie decided that he liked Nell's bosoms better than Melinda's because he couldn't take his eyes off her "thirty-six deelightfuls," as he called them. Nell was proud of those bosoms, too. So the two of them had liking those bosoms in common. Just like me and Henry had our books and chocolate phosphates and airplanes in common. Mother shoulda never married Hall, because I couldn't see one thing they had in common.

When Nell and Eddie went in to Delancey's, Troo leaned over and said, "You just go tell Granny by yourself, okay?"

"Sure." I knew she was feeling so happy about Mother not dying and us living at Rasmussen's until she got home and Hall going to jail that she didn't want to wreck all that happiness by seeing Uncle Paulie and playing peek-a-boo with him. Or by looking at those Popsicle stick houses, which could really get anybody feeling bad since before the accident Uncle Paulie had been a carpenter.

I thought right then was as good a time as ever. Maybe the best time because I had not seen Troo this happy for so long that I sorta wanted to be a shiny bow on her happiness package. "I've been meaning to tell you something." I was getting ready to tell her what Daddy had told me. That the car crash wasn't her fault.

Troo was looking out the window at some kids playing one two three O'Larry outside Delancey's. "Just forget it," she said. "I'm not listening anymore to your imagination about Rasmussen. He's not the murderer and molester." And then Troo turned to face me and came in real close with both hands on my cheeks, and whispered, "But I think I know who is."

CHAPTER TWENTY-EIGHT

When Eddie and Nell hopped down Delancey's Corner Store steps, Troo turned a pretend key on her lips and threw it out the window. It was her way of telling me to keep my mouth locked up tight about her knowing who the murderer and molester was. A warning not to say anything to Nell or Eddie. She wanted to keep it hush-hush between the O'Malley sisters.

Eddie handed me and Troo a Coke through the car window and then the other two that were left in the carton. "Give those to Granny and Uncle Paulie." I guessed that getting married agreed with Eddie, because he was sure acting more grown-up. Almost like Mr. Anderson in *Father Knows Best*.

He drove down ten houses and parked the Chevy under the big oak tree in front of Granny's house that she called a bungalow, which is just another word for the smallest kind of place that a person could live in. Granny could've used a much larger house because she was a big woman both up and out, especially in her arms, which had a lot of flappy skin hangin' off of them. But her face hardly had any lines and her hair was thick and white like homemade bread and she kept it in a pageboy. She also had perfect teeth that she kept in a glass full of water when she wasn't using them. If you ever met her you might think to yourself that she reminded you a lot of that guy on the dollar bill.

"Don't take too long, we have to be at the hospital by eleven," Nell called after I'd gotten out of the car. "Dr. Sullivan is going to meet us there and tell us all about Mother. And don't tell Granny about Eddie and me, I want to surprise her."

Seemed like nobody wanted me to tell anybody about nothin'.

I knocked on Granny's front door that coulda used some paint and waited for Uncle Paulie to answer it, which he always did, because Granny moved so slow with her crippled knees that you could be sitting on that porch until the cows came home if you waited for her. When he pushed open the screen door, I said, "Hi, Uncle Paulie."

He had on what he always had on, tan pants and a white T-shirt that showed off his pretzel-rod arms with the most pale freckles of anybody I'd ever seen. His hair was thick red and started back on his head a bit and looked like it should belong to an entirely different person.

"Peek-a-boo, Troo."

"No, I'm Sally, remember, Uncle Paulie? Troo has red hair just like yours." I sort of pushed past him and went looking for Granny. She was in the kitchen filling up her copper teapot with water.

"Hi, Granny. Got a present for you." I pulled open her refrigerator and put the Cokes inside for later. Granny loved Coca-Cola. Drank almost a whole six-pack every day. It gave her vim and vigor, she said.

Granny's thyroid-condition eyes got bigger when she

said, "Well, hello there, Sally. What a nice surprise. Care for a cuppa?" She didn't hug me or anything. Granny didn't go in for hugs.

"No, thank you. I can't stay long. Troo and Eddie and Nell are waiting for me in the car. We're going to see—"

"Peek-a-boo, Troo! Peek-a-boo, Daddy!" Uncle Paulie came up behind and put his hands over my eyes.

I peeled off his fingers that smelled of glue and sort of laughed out of politeness, but I was thinking that Uncle Paulie was getting weirder and weirder by the minute and maybe Granny should put *him* in the orphanage up on Lisbon Avenue.

"That's enough now, son," Granny said. "You go back into your room and work on your houses."

Uncle Paulie said down to the floor, "Okay, Ma."

Granny waited until Uncle Paulie shuffled off and then said, "So, to what do I owe the pleasure of your company?"

"Mother is getting better. Nell says she is over the hump," I said, excited to tell her such good news about her sick daughter.

"You're a day late and a dollar short, Sally m'girl." Granny reached up to the cupboard and took out one of those dainty teacups she had that were from the old country. "Officer Rasmussen has stopped by almost every day that your mother has been in the hospital to tell me how she was doing."

I must've made quite the face because Granny smiled.

"Why'd he do that?" I asked.

The copper pot whistled and Granny switched the burner off. "I thought you knew that Dave Rasmussen and your mother were friends."

That was one of the main things I really loved about Granny. She knew a lot of stuff about everybody who lived in the neighborhood and she was never shy about telling you. Like the fact that Brownie McDonald got kicked out of the seminary for drinking up all the Communion wine and that Mrs. Delancey from the corner store used to be Shelly the Snake Girl in a dancing club downtown. (I think that's why Mrs. Delancey gave Granny half off on her Coca-Cola, to keep that to herself.)

"So Officer Rasmussen, he's a good egg?" I asked her.

"Always has been. Even if he is Danish." Granny didn't have much use for anybody that wasn't Irish. "And his father was a good egg, too. Ernie, his name was."

Watching her pour that water over her tea bag, I suddenly realized how much I'd been missing her. It felt so nice to sit at her little kitchen table with the uneven legs and listen to her go on and on about the people we knew. Just like the good old days. I so wished for a minute that Granny was the hugging kind.

"You know the Rasmussen family used to own the cookie factory," Granny said. "Sold it to some big company from out East in fifty-five."

I could hear Eddie beeping his *ah oooga* horn.

Granny stuck her spoon down into her sugar bear three heaping times and stirred it into her cup. "You knew that Dave and Helen were engaged a long time ago, right?"

I did not! Being friends was one thing. Rasmussen and Mother engaged? Like Nell and Eddie? Granny must have that wrong. "Engaged to be married?"

"Oh, yes. They had the wedding date all picked out. But Dave's mother, Gertie, who always thought too highly of herself, by the way, told Dave that he could do better than Helen. That Helen wasn't high-class enough for him." Granny made a *tsking* noise. "Never did like Gertie Rasmussen. Always lording her money over everybody. And very vain about her legs, which were quite nice, but not that nice."

Granny poured a little milk into the cup until it was creamy tan and then came and sat down next to me. "But then Dave broke it off because as much as he loved Helen, he didn't think it would be right to go against his mother's wishes since Gertie was sick with tuberculosis by then. So your mother married Nell's father, instead."

Once again, for the millionth time, I was so amazed by the way grown-ups knew things that kids didn't and how good they were at keeping those things on the q.t.

Uncle Paulie was whistling "Pop Goes the Weasel" in his bedroom. And Eddie honked his horn again.

"I thought after Nell's father died that Helen and Dave would get married then," Granny said, blowing on her tea. "But your mother married your daddy instead because she was still mad at Dave for not going against Gertie."

You had to watch Granny sometimes. She could give you blarney and I thought I'd caught her. "If that's all true, then why didn't Mother marry Rasmussen after Daddy died?"

"Well, like I always say, my girl Helen can be as ornery as a pack mule with a bad back. She got that from her father, by the way. Stubborn runs worse in the Riley family than a pair of cheap nylons." She took a nice full sip from her cup. "In other words, Sally, your mother was too proud. She was having a lot of money problems because your daddy didn't leave her anything but a pile of bills and you girls. Helen didn't want Dave to know how bad off she was. A slice of humble pie right about then would've solved all her problems."

Granny let loose a long Irish sigh. "Helen always was willing to cut off her nose to spite her face."

Why, for God's sake, would Mother cut off her nose?

"Then Hall showed up," Granny grumbled.

Oh boy. This was goin' to take a while. Granny couldn't stand Hall. "Think of how desperate your mother must've been to marry a shoe salesman she only knew for two months. You'd think she would've been a little marriage shy by that time, eh?" She gave me a sip of her tea. "You know what I always say about that marriage, Sal?"

Yes, I did. Over and over again. "Once bitten, twice shy?"

The car horn beeped again and you could tell by how long he held it down that Eddie was getting really sick and tired of waiting.

"Exactly." Granny heard the horn, too. "Sounds like Eddie is having a hard time keepin' his shirt on." And then under her breath, it sounded like she said, "And his pants." She held up her hands. "Before you go, just rinse out those socks in the bathroom sink. My arthritis is really acting up today." Her hands did look like claws or something so I knew she wasn't faking, which she did sometimes. When she didn't want to do something, she'd tell me she was having "palpitations," and since there was no way I could tell if she was having palpitations, I did it because I didn't want to think about what kind of trouble I'd be in if Granny got palpitated to death. "Paulie needs them socks for work tonight, so hurry it up," she said, pushing me on the back toward the little hall. Granny was so dang bossy. This was who Mother inherited it from. Troo, too. And also that do-you-smell-dog-poop look that she was givin' me.

"Okay, okay." I had that dumb feeling in my stomach about not getting over to see Granny more often and also thinking mean thoughts about Uncle Paulie's weirdness, so I walked into the bathroom and stuck my hands into the cold gray water. I took out the first black sock and wrung it and hung it on this wooden drying stick Granny had in the tub. Then I reached down into the water again and pulled out another, and when I did I happened to get a look at myself in the mirror above the sink. My nose was sunburned and my hair had gotten almost as white as Granny's. I looked a little older, I thought. Eddie beeped again, this one so long that it got into my head and that was all I could hear, so I hurried and squeezed the water out of the next sock and turned to hang it up on the . . . Oh my God. Sweet Jesus, Mary and Joseph! It was a pink-and-green argyle.

CHAPTER TWENTY-NINE

Uncle Paulie is not a murderer and a molester," Troo said, trying not to let her poofy lips move. She'd seen this ventriloquist on *The Perry Como Show* and had changed her mind about working up at The Milky Way. Now when she grew up Troo wanted to be either Edgar Bergen or Sal Mineo. Either or. But with a leaning toward Edgar Bergen since Troo said that all that drumming might give you a headache and it would be real funny to be able to throw your voice like that. You could get some people in trouble if you could do that.

We were sitting on these plastic chairs with metal legs over in the waiting area. Nell and Eddie were talking to the desk lady in the lobby of St. Joe's. Troo had her Nell tattletale list rolled up in her hand.

"Big deal if Uncle Paulie has some of those socks," Troo said. "Lots of people have pink-and-green argyles. Willie had some on last week. And Johnny Fazio had some on at supper last night. Even Bobby at the playground wears 'em."

"Yeah, but . . . ," I tried to say.

"I think the murderer is . . ." Troo swiveled her head around to make sure nobody had snuck up on her, and I didn't have the heart to tell her that even if they did, they probably wouldn't be able to understand a darn thing she was saying. I sure couldn't. "I think it's Reese Latour. It's just bubbling inside him, trying to get out. Reese is evil, Sal. Real honest to devil evil." She ran her hands down her arms, trying to warm up her goose pimples. "Did I tell you that he pulled Fast Susie's bikini top down last week when she was suntanning in the backyard?"

I shook my head.

She shivered. "Reese could murder and molest with his eyes closed."

"Yeah, well, we'll just see," I said quietly, because Nell and Eddie were coming back and I didn't want to make too big a deal out of it because now I was *pretty* sure that Rasmussen was not the guilty party and I had been *so* sure he was. So I figured if I *might* be wrong about Rasmussen, I *might* be wrong about Uncle Paulie. I didn't want to get everybody all riled up. Especially since Troo was right about Reese Latour. If you opened him up and looked inside, his heart would not be red and bursting with love. It would be rotting maggot hateful black. Reese would murder and molest in a breeze. I hoped Troo was right. Everybody would be a lot better off if Reese went to jail. Especially poor Artie, who wouldn't have to listen to Reese telling people that he was a harelip, like they couldn't see that for themselves. And even worse than that was the way Reese treated Wendy and called her the idiot and made fun of the way she talked. And that was not even taking into account the way Reese always looked at Troo, like he had the hots for her . . . it gave me the honest-to-God skin-crawling creeps.

Yeah, Reese Latour could definitely be the murderer and molester.

"Okay, we're gonna meet Dr. Sullivan upstairs," Nell called over to us from the information desk.

We got in the elevator and Nell pressed the number three button. She looked so grown-up in her A-line dress and made-up face. Eddie had gotten fancy for the funeral, too. He had on a checkered sports coat that was way too big for him and a tie with a Chevy car on it, but he didn't stink of gas like he usually did. Instead he stunk of English Leather. And then the elevator doors slid open, and for a second I was afraid to get out. This was the floor that Daddy and Troo had been on after the crash. I remembered the picture of Jesus and his bleeding heart that was hanging on the wall outside the elevator. Troo did too, because she picked up my hand and squeezed it hard.

There was the *tock tock tock* of Nell's squash heels going down the hall, and that medicine smell, and the floor so shiny, and the sound of those nurses' thick white shoes. We turned into a room called a solarium that had magazines on tables and pictures of flowers on the walls. Sitting over by the big window was Mother in a wheelchair. I knew it was Mother because of her hair, but that's the only way I would've been able to tell because she looked skinnier than Mary Lane, which I woulda thought was humanly impossible. Not tan or strong at all. And something else seemed really different about her, not just the way she looked because she'd been sick.

"O'Malley sisters," Mother said real softly. She had on a pink robe that I'd never seen before and slippers with little pink pom-poms on them and her hair was tied back with a shiny pink ribbon. Dr. Sullivan was standing next to her, like he was protecting a newborn chicken.

Troo said, "Hi, Mother," but you could tell she was fantastically nervous by how hard she was licking her lips. "Nell did not take good care of me and Sally. I got a list I wanna show you."

Mother held her arms out to us and I didn't want to go into them because she looked so bony, but then I did and so did Troo. I couldn't even talk, tell her how glad I was that she hadn't died, that was how hard I was crying. Of course, Troo didn't cry. Not one teardrop.

"Doesn't she look in the pink?" Dr. Sullivan laughed at his joke and I thought it was a pretty good one considering how Mother was decked out. "Just terrific!"

Dr. Sullivan needed new peepers because Mother definitely looked a long way off from terrific, but I was just so glad to have her back that I hugged the doctor around his fat stomach, which was a lot harder than it looked.

"Why, thank you, Sally," the doctor said. (I'm sorry to have to say this, but his breath had not improved.) "How is that imagination of yours coming along?"

"Fine, Dr. Sullivan. Just fine." I really wished he had not brought that up in front of Mother. I was sort of mad now that I'd given him that hug.

He looked down at his watch that he kept hidden in his pocket on a chain and then out the solarium windows. Clouds that looked like fists had started to roll in. "It's going to rain again," he said. "Can't remember a summer we've had so much rain." Then he clapped his hands. "Well, I think that's quite enough excitement for one day. Let's get Helen back to bed. That was a close call, a very close call, girls. When your mother comes home, you're going to have to take very good care of her. Doctor's orders." And then he disappeared out the solarium door doing that penguin walk.

Nell put her hands on the back of the wheelchair and began to push, but Mother held up her hand to stop and said in a weak voice, "Nell, take Troo downstairs. I need to talk to Sally in private for a minute."

"Okay, but not too long," Nell scolded. "You heard what the doctor said." She kissed Mother on the head and said in a cute little voice, "I'm almost a hairdresser. When you come home I can wash and set your hair for you."

"That would be nice." Mother patted at her hair because she was sorta proud about it and had to know that it looked a little ratty. "Go on now, Nell."

"But what about my list?" Troo whined.

Mother said, "Give it to me, Troo. I'll look at it later."

Troo handed her the tattle list, which was pretty ripped and dirty from all the use it was getting, then she gave me a jealousy look and shook Mother's hand good-bye, which was kinda funny.

Eddie stood up from the checkered couch that looked so much like his jacket that I forgot for a second he was even there. "Nice to see you again, Mrs. Gustafson." That was Hall's last name. Maybe Mother could change it back again to O'Malley now that Hall was going to the slammer.

"It's all right if you call me Mother." Helen put her hand on Nell's tummy. "After all, we're going to be family soon, Eddie." Nell's smile put sun back into the solarium. Eddie just shoved his hands in his pockets and looked down at the shiny floor and grinned.

"Okay, let's get this show on the road," Nell said, trying to pick up Troo's hand. Troo yanked it out, gave me one more jealousy look and then turned on her heel in a huff. Troo really couldn't stand coming in second place. A minute later Nell was yelling, "Troo O'Malley, you get your heinie back here," from down the hall, and I'd just bet Troo was givin' her the finger. Another new thing she learned from Fast Susie.

Mother and me were alone and I heard some thunder. "Sally, come closer." I had been standing a little ways away from her so I could pay attention to the details, like you do when you want to get a really good look at something. I sat down in a brown chair that had a plastic cover over it, right across from Mother.

"I have something to tell you," she said. Her eyes were sorta dashing around like the minnows in the cold lake near dead Gramma's house. That was a detail I would never miss because I had never seen Mother nervous before. It was probably because she was in the hospital, which could make anybody jittery. My own stomach felt like I had swallowed a handful of those Mexican jumping beans they just got in up at Kenfield's Five and Dime. I grabbed on to the arms of the chair and got prepared for Mother to give me a good talking-to about my imagination. Somebody musta told her that I was having a hard time with it. I was in for it now.

"I should've told you this a long time ago." Mother sighed one of those big sighs she always did. "And I'm still not sure the timing is right."

It was not like Mother to be not sure. She was always sure in a mad kind of way.

She gave me that sad-eyed look that she gave me when she thought I wasn't looking and then said, "Sometimes women get lonely when their husbands are away."

Mother looked so breakable, it made me feel protective of her like I did with Troo. I needed to make her feel stronger right away, so I announced nice and loud, "Daddy told me to tell you that he forgives you."

She turned her head my way. "What did you just say?"

"Right before Daddy died he told me to tell you that he forgives you and I'm sorry I haven't told you before this, but like you always say, timing is everything and I just couldn't find the time." I hunched up in my shoulders and sunk down farther into the brown chair, getting ready for her to yell at me. I figured out too late that was a bad idea, telling her Daddy forgave her, because she was not smiling or acting at all like this was good news. In fact, Mother did the most amazing thing. I had heard it at night, but I had never seen it. She started to cry. And it wasn't just a little sobbing . . . it was a great big gully washer. Right into her hands. The wedding ring that Hall had given her was gone, but there was a little green mark on her finger where it used to be.

I placed my hands on her knees, which felt like two tennis balls, and just said, "Shhh . . . shhh . . . shhh."

Mother cried for a long, long time, her tears sliding down all over her face. But finally, she sort of sputtered out, "Thank you for telling me. That makes all the difference in the world." I was so relieved she wasn't gonna start hollering at me that I dug around in my pocket and found one of Troo's Kleenex carnation flowers and gave it to her.

"I've got a secret, too. This might be a big shock to you, Sal. A big shock. So be prepared." The clouds had let loose and the rain was attacking the windows and dying in squiggly lines. "I'm going to tell you why Officer Rasmussen has a picture of you in his wallet."

Oh no! Now I was going to have to tell her my suspicions about Rasmussen and she had already made these plans that we would go live with him and it was going to ruin everything when I told her I still thought, not as much as before, but it was still a very good possibility, that Rasmussen, her high school friend, had turned into a murderer and a molester.

She grabbed for my hands like I was an edge of a cliff she was falling off and said, "Dave Rasmussen is your father."

I waited for her to say something else, but she was just looking at me with her blue crater eyes and white, white face. "Oh, Mother, that's silly." I laughed even though I didn't think it was a very funny joke.

She opened her eyes wider and gave me the look where her mouth goes into a straight line. Her deadly serious look.

"Mother?" I got really afraid then and slid off that plastic-covered chair.

"Sally Elizabeth . . ."

Oh my Sky King. I need you!

Mother said real fast now, her words chasing each other out of her mouth, "I'm so sorry. I should have told you a long time ago . . . but for the longest time I wasn't even sure myself. It wasn't until you got a little older and . . . started to look so much like Dave . . . you have green eyes . . . but so did your aunt Faye . . . but then your blonde hair and dimples and . . . your daddy suspected . . . he didn't know for sure but . . ." She took my hands and pulled me back down into the chair and said in a whisper like it hurt her so bad to talk, "Paulie must've told Donny on the way home from the baseball game, the day of the crash . . . he must've . . ."

I was not Daddy's gal Sal. I was Rasmussen's gal Sal.

"That doesn't change how much Daddy loved you." Mother dabbed at her eyes with Troo's carnation.

Rasmussen's gal Sal. With green eyes. Which were rare, Mother had always told me. Rasmussen had green eyes? Like mine?

"When Daddy was in the air force, Officer Rasmussen and I . . . well . . ." Mother gave me a sorry smile. "We just fell in love again. Do you know what that means?"

I stared at the window, at the rain starting and stopping and changing direction. Yes, I knew what it meant. Mother and Rasmussen sitting in a tree, k-i-s-s-i-n-g. First comes love, then comes marriage . . . then comes Sally in a baby carriage. I wanted to run down the hallway into the elevator and out of the hospital and onto the street and throw myself in front of that number 23 bus.

Sky King was not my real daddy.

"But . . . ," I tried to say. Mother had to be wrong about this. The staph infection must've gotten into her brain and hardened her arteries.

"No buts about this, Sally. That's what your daddy meant when he told you that he forgave me." She looked right into my rare green eyes. "He forgave me for falling back in love with Dave and having you."

I started to cry and Mother pulled me into her lap. I lay my head on her chest.

"I know this is hard for you and you'll need some time to think about it, Baby." She hadn't called me Baby since Daddy died and that was nice to hear, like coming home after a long day and seeing her in the kitchen leaning over a pot stirring chicken noodle soup with those extra-fat noodles and fresh carrots. "We'll talk about this some more when I get a little stronger, but I wanted you to know. It's important that you know." Her heart was beating so hard that I wanted to reach in and pet it. "And I'm glad that I didn't die or you would never have known because Dave . . . I mean, Officer Rasmussen, he would never have told you because he is a gentleman in the truest sense of that word." She said this so sweetly, with so much kindness. That was the detail that had changed. Mother was happy now. Even after almost dying, she was smiling like that picture that I had of her down in the hideyhole. "Now, I don't want you to start up with your worrying," she said. "Everything is going to be okay now." She rested her head on the top of mine. "I'm so very tired, Sal. Please take me back to my room."

I wheeled her down the hall and handed her off to the old nurse, the same one who took care of Daddy. She looked at me like she didn't remember me when she helped Mother back into bed.

I was afraid to go near Helen, so I stood in the dark corner of the room. Maybe she wasn't my real mother either. Maybe Troo wasn't my sister or even Nell.

She called over to me in a weak voice, "Come closer." She sounded so desperate, I couldn't resist. "Forgive me," she whispered and then fell right asleep.

I sat down next to her while the rain streamed down her window, the white sheets gliding up and down with her slow breathing. Now I knew what that sad look was that she'd always been giving me. Mother loved Officer Rasmussen and I was part of that love. Forgive her? Not in a million years.

But then I remembered Daddy and how I'd sat in a room just like this one after his crash. And how he sounded when he told me he forgave Mother. It was with true love in his heart. So I sat there for a while and thought about it all. And then I surprised myself, and did the most charitable thing I had ever done while I watched Mother sleeping, maybe dreaming. I decided to forgive her for gettin' some from Officer Rasmussen. Forgive her like my Sky King had. After all, I knew what it meant to be lonely for someone you loved. I'd been so lonely for Daddy and in some funny way I had always been lonely for Mother. She might not look at me anymore with those sad eyes if I just forgave her. Let bygones be bygones because everybody knew that forgiveness was divine. So I leaned down and placed my cheek on hers and breathed in her breath. And when I whispered, "I forgive you," I smelled her Evening in Paris and finally understood why Troo wanted to run away to France.

CHAPTER THIRTY

On the ride home from the hospital the windshield wipers were going back and forth and back and forth like that metronome Mother kept on top of the piano to help you keep time when you couldn't keep it yourself. When we pulled up in front of our house, Nell said, "Sally . . . we're here." She did not say, "Sally . . . we're home."

Mrs. Goldman was in her front window like she was keeping an eye out for somebody. I looked over at Troo, who was looking back at me like she had something on her mind. Whatever it was, I knew she would wait until we were alone, when it was just the O'Malley sisters, because Troo still thought Nell was a drip even if she was getting married and we got to be flower girls.

"I'm gonna head over to Kroger and get some boxes," Eddie said.

Nell yelled to us, "Run between the raindrops, O'Malley sisters," as we dashed for the porch. That was what Mother always said on days like this. Nell was becoming more like Mother by the minute. Like an ugly old caterpillar with horrible-looking hair, Nell was turning into a butterfly that could be on the Breck shampoo bottle.

When Nell took her key out to unlock the front door,

because everybody had been told to lock their doors now because of the dead girls, Mrs. Goldman said through her screen door, "*Liebchin*, may I speak to you, please?" I thought I saw sad beams coming out of her like the Baby Jesus on his holy cards. In her German accent she said, "I am so sorry, I am so sorry. We have to rent to somebody who can pay. Do you understand this?"

Nell and Troo were stomping up the steps to get their things together because neither one of them liked Mrs. Goldman as much as I did. Besides the Butchy problem, they thought our landlady was a very wet blanket because she was always telling us to be quiet. But what they didn't know was that Mrs. Goldman's ears got very sensitive in the concentration camp and any sort of loud noises would make her have a headache that wouldn't go away for days.

"Yes, I understand," I said, walking toward her. "Please don't worry. Everything's going to be okay now."

She opened the door a little and handed me a plate of those chewy brown sugar cookies and a white paper bag. "Inside is a book for you. I know how you like to do the reading."

I turned to leave but then remembered my manners. "Thank you. And if Mr. Goldman wants me to come back and help him pick caterpillars off those tomato plants, I can do that." I looked into her brown eyes that had seen so many bad things. "Do you think that Dottie Kenfield is a ghost?" Mrs. Goldman was the only person, besides Troo, who'd heard the sounds coming from Dottie's window. I had to know that before we left. If it was Dottie's ghost crying, I didn't think I could move and leave her all alone.

"*Nein*, that is no ghost. Sometimes it is better to think

about things in your imagination to get away from what is really happening, no?" I knew she was thinking of the concentration camp then because she always squinted her eyes and the lines around her mouth got as deep as a garden furrow. "Do you understand this? That sometimes real life it is too frightening for people so we leave it for a while and think about other things?"

"I think I understand." She musta had to think about a lot of other stuff when she was in that concentration camp. Like her favorite things. Chocolate ice cream and cold red apples and this meat she got from Opperman's Butcher Shop called *schnitzel*. "So who is that crying in Dottie's room if it isn't a ghost?"

Mrs. Goldman turned toward our neighbors' house. "I believe it is Audrey Kenfield that you hear crying. Dottie's mother."

Mrs. Goldman looked at me like she was deciding something and then she seemed to make up her mind and then changed it again but finally said, "Mr. Kenfield made his daughter to leave his house after she became pregnant and was not married. Dottie is forbidden to come back home and . . . that is why Dottie's mother cries. She is yearning for her lost daughter and the daughter of her lost daughter."

I looked at Mrs. Goldman's eyes real hard for a minute. And then down at those numbers on her arm. "I will come to visit you all the time. I will. I promise." I knew she was telling the truth about Dottie because Mrs. Goldman would never lie to me. Especially about something like that. Since Mrs. Goldman's daughter, Gretchen, never came back to the concentration camp after her shower, she probably knew what a mother who had lost her child would sound like.

"Marta, you are letting in of the flies," Mr. Goldman said from inside the house.

"That book . . . you . . . one of my favorites." Mrs. Goldman put hands on my shoulders and pulled me into her for a bear hug, which she had never done before even after the day I picked over twenty-five weeds out of the garden. *"Off-veedersane, Liebchin,"* she said and closed the door.

I ran up our stairs two at a time and through the door that went into the living room. Newspapers were scattered across the floor and dust bunnies bulged in the corners and Pabst Blue Ribbon beer bottles lined the windowsills full of cigarette butts. It smelled of a place that nobody cared about anymore. I thought of Mother when I looked over at the stained red-and-brown couch. And how, after she thought Troo and me had fallen asleep at night, she would sit there sometimes and stare out the window, never seeming to find what she was looking for. But now maybe she had.

I sat down on the piano bench and opened up the white paper bag that Mrs. Goldman had given me. *A Secret Garden*. That was very thoughtful of Marta Goldman. Maybe I could learn more about gardening from this book, and when I came back to help them they would be amazed by what a better gardener I had become. Rasmussen, he was a good gardener, too. So maybe if I wanted to I would learn something from him. Which I wasn't all that sure yet that I wanted to. To forgive Mother was one thing . . . but to forgive Rasmussen? That might take some doing.

When I went into our bedroom to start putting my clothes into piles, so that when Eddie came back with the boxes I would be prepared, Troo was laying on our bed, spread out like she was making a snow angel in the room made dark by the storm. I tried to turn on the little lamp on the dresser but nothing happened.

Troo said, "What did Mother tell you?"

I knew this would bug Troo so I laid down next to her and told her. About how Daddy wasn't my real daddy. How Rasmussen was. And about our green eyes. When I was done, she was so quiet. I figured she was just too sad to say words. So I quickly said, "I have a secret for you, too." I knew that would make her happier because Troo loved a good secret and was most of the time good about keeping them.

We were both looking up at that crack that ran across the ceiling like the Honey Creek. I felt around for her hand and stroked it with my thumb the way she liked me to. "Daddy, right before he died," I said quietly, "he told me to tell you that it was okay." I said it right out like that because I thought that was the best way to do it, like when you went swimming and the water was too cold it was just a Chinese torture to go in slowly. Better just to jump right in.

I took her face in my hands and looked into the windows of her soul. "Daddy wanted me to tell you that the crash wasn't your fault."

Troo pulled away and turned to the wall. She wasn't making any noise, but I could tell by her breathing. It was the first time I had seen my sister cry since forever. I gently lifted her head and set it back down on my Sky King–smelling pillow.

Nell came in and said, "What's goin' on in here?" She had a mop and other cleaning things.

I said, "Nothin'."

"What's wrong with Troo?"

"Nothin'."

"I'm gonna clean this place up and then Eddie will take you over to Officer Rasmussen's."

"Today? But I thought we were just packing today." That felt too surprising to me. Too quick. "Are you going to stay at Rasmussen's?"

I thought Nell was going to say mind your own beeswax, you little brat. "I'm going to stay with Eddie because Mrs. Callahan said that would be fine now that we are getting married." She looked over at Troo, who was still thunderstorm crying because she had saved up so many tears from since Daddy was dead and she hadn't cried like I had, which was more like spring showers sprinkled here, there and everywhere. Nell didn't say anything to Troo, but to me she said, "You know, Sally, you don't always have to play second fiddle."

Since I didn't play the second fiddle or any other musical instrument, I thought Nell might be drunk again, especially since she grinned at me before she left. Yes, I was sure of it now. Nell was drunk.

I laid back down next to Troo and rubbed her back that was going in and out so fast. Since she still hadn't said anything, I thought she might go quiet and give up on talking like she did after the crash. But as always, my sister was full of surprises. "I have a secret for you, too," she said to the wall.

I wasn't really that excited to hear another secret because I pretty much had had it with secrets that day.

"I put my hands over Daddy's eyes," Troo said. "Right over his eyes."

The rain was coming down hard outside our bedroom window, a sound I usually liked, but it was too loud and a branch rubbed against the pane like it was trying to break in.

"On the way home from the game, Daddy and Uncle Paulie were fighting," Troo whimpered. "I wanted them to stop so bad. They were yelling about you and something about your birthday and I wanted them to pay attention to me so I played peek-a-boo with Daddy in the car even though he told me to stop, and that's why he ran into the tree and that sound was so bad, the sound of the car smashing." She was holding the edge of the pillow between her teeth to keep them from chattering. "I'm . . . I'm so sorry for killing Daddy."

Poor, poor Troo. What an awful shocking secret to have to hold on to for such a long time. I stroked her back and said, "Daddy said it's not your fault and he meant it. I promise you on the O'Malley sisters' hearts of love and all that is holy on Heaven and Earth, he forgave you."

When Troo was sure I was telling the truth, she said in a baby voice, "Could I have a glass of water, please?"

On my way to the kitchen, I could hear that Troo had gone back to her crying, which was not only about her sadness but the sadness she thought she caused others she loved, the worst kind of sadness. Maybe after a while Troo would forgive herself, but I knew she'd never, ever forget hearing the sound of the car going into that elm.

Just like I'd never, ever forget the look on Daddy's face on August 2, 1959.

"I'm disappointed in you, Sal," he'd said that morning. He was angrily pulling weeds out of the little vegetable garden I had begged him to plow for me. "Instead of going to the ballpark with me today, you're gonna stay home and work on your garden. I'm takin' Troo instead."

"But, Daddy," I cried. "I've been looking forward to this

game all week." We were going to sit in the hot sun and eat salty peanuts and hot dogs with mustard and relish and sing "Take Me Out to the Ball Game" during the seventh-inning stretches. It was a double-header against the Cards.

"I guess you shoulda spent less time looking forward and more time weeding. By the time I get home, it better look like somebody tends this garden. Like somebody cares about it." He wiped his hands off on his overalls and stomped off toward the house.

I yelled at his back, "But you promised."

He stopped for a second like he'd changed his mind, but then he just kept going toward the house.

"I hate you," I yelled to his back. "I wish I had another daddy."

The screen door slammed behind him.

I had visited that secret so much since he died that sometimes I worried it had left my heart in tatters that would never get mended.

Granny kept telling me time heals all wounds. I didn't know about that.

CHAPTER THIRTY-ONE

M other always said a house was nothing but a reflection of its occupants. She was right, because Rasmussen's house also reminded me of a chocolate-covered cherry, even better on the inside than the outside. It was clean and organized like a classroom. Only it didn't smell like books or poster paint or rubber boots. It smelled like all those flowers Rasmussen had growing in his garden and like that puppy dog Lizzie.

While we carried our clothes boxes through Rasmussen's front door, Nell told us that he and Eddie would move some other stuff, like our dresser and the little lamp, later on, and for tonight we could sleep over in Mrs. Galecki's screened porch. That was something everybody knew we really loved to do, especially Troo, who liked to watch the fireflies when she fell asleep, like they were a nightlight that made her feel safe and just so. Nell said that Rasmussen told her that me and Troo could each have our own bedroom, but I told her to tell Rasmussen no thank you, because I didn't think either one of us could fall asleep if we didn't rub each other's backs. But really, I was probably just being sinfully selfish because I just couldn't wake up in the middle of the night like I did sometimes with the Creature of the

Black Lagoon chasin' me all over the place and not have Troo next to me, making that noise she made when she sucked on her fingers, her baby doll Annie looking at me with those wide-open eyes like we'd just met.

So just like that, like we had been shot through space to another planet, the next morning we were sitting at Rasmussen's very modern yellow Formica kitchen table that I knew Troo just adored even though you would have to chain her down and drip water on her forehead for six days to get her to admit it. Troo felt happy about being Daddy's only girl now. But Troo wasn't so happy about Rasmussen being my father and the boss of this house. Like she might have to be second in command around here and she wasn't going to say something nice about any of it.

For breakfast, he'd made us waffles with real maple syrup from up north that were gone in two seconds. And lots of bacon, too, done nice and crispy.

Rasmussen wasn't sitting down with us; he was drinking a cup of percolated coffee and leaning against the sink in his policeman's uniform. "So how does heading over to the state fair tomorrow night sound to the both of you?"

Mother must've told him how much Troo loved the freak show and he was trying to be nice. Troo found those freaks fascinating as all get-out. I thought they were a little on the sad side, on display like that, all boxed up, but Troo said no, they were different from everybody else and deserving of extra attention, which was unusually charitable of her.

"The fair sounds good," I answered.

"Okay then. We'll head over there tomorrow night and you two can get cotton candy and go on some rides and . . ." Rasmussen was clearing his throat about every five seconds, which was a sure way to tell if someone was jumpy. "Does that sound good to you, Troo?"

She looked up at him and I could practically see the mad lava coming out of her ears. "My name is Margaret."

Rasmussen did not miss a beat. "So how does going to the fair sound to you, Margaret?"

Before Troo could go spouting off, I said quickly, "Goin' to the fair sounds good to her, Officer Rasmussen."

He looked right at me and showed his dimples that were a lot like mine only larger and I looked right back at him, right into his green eyes. Two peas in a pod. Suddenly it all made sense. Why he had always looked at me the way he had. He'd been missing me. That was hard for me to take in because it meant so many things at the same time.

He rinsed his coffee cup out in the sink and dried it off with a red terry-cloth towel that looked brand-new from aisle two at the Five and Dime. "You two can just call me Dave, okay?"

Troo said in a voice I had never heard her use before, a voice so cold that it gave my goose bumps goose bumps, "Shouldn't Sally call you *Daddy*?"

It got so quiet then that all you could hear was the ticking of the kitchen clock that hung on the wall behind the stove and looked like a black cat.

Rasmussen said, "Your sister can call me Dave. I think that would be fine for now, don't you, Sally?"

I just nodded because I was imagining how it would be to call Rasmussen Daddy. I never called Hall Daddy. I just called him Hall. And sometimes when he couldn't hear me, a couple of other names that I would have to confess since he was going to be in jail for a long time now. I probably would never, ever do that, call Rasmussen Daddy. Maybe after a while I would call him Mr. Dave. Because Daddy was still my Sky King no matter what anybody said, and I would never, ever let bygones be bygones.

"I have to head over to the station now." Rasmussen noticed that I was staring at the gun on his hip. I'd never seen one up close like that. "The first rule in this house, girls. You stay away from this." He patted the holster and then plopped his police hat on top of his head. "I've been meaning to tell you, Troo, I mean . . . ah . . . Margaret, you don't have to worry anymore about Greasy Al, I mean . . . Albert Molinari. I've taken care of that subject." And like he'd turned a page in a book, he said real happy like, "It's a beautiful day. Why don't you two head over to the playground? And if you could later, take Lizzie for a walk. Her leash is hanging in the back hall."

I looked up at him and his tallness. And then I looked down at my fly-like-the-wind long legs. I looked at his green eyes again. I'm sorry to have to say this, but I thought it all felt sort of good because right then, for the first time in my life, I finally looked like somebody. So because of that, and because he was being very nice, making us waffles and crispy bacon and saying he'd take us to the fair, I said, "See you later, Mr. Dave."

I could tell he liked that by the look on his face. "See you later, Sally." He started to leave the bright kitchen but then said very seriously, "You keep in mind what happened to Sara and Junie. I know how you two like Sampson, but I don't want you going over to the zoo or anywhere else in the park for a while. Not until we catch this guy. Okay?"

I said, "Okay." But Troo didn't.

"If you need anything when I am at work, you can call me. The number is over there next to the phone. And also Ethel will help you out." He looked back at me real quick and watercolor pink came into his cheeks when the screen door slammed shut.

Troo was sitting with her elbows on the table, her hands underneath her chin. "So Daddy really said that? You're sure?"

"I'm sure."

"That it wasn't my fault, the crash? You swear?"

"I swear." I made the sign of the cross over my heart. "Want some Ovaltine?"

Rasmussen had pointed out where he kept the Ovaltine in the cupboard. Ethel musta told him how much me and Troo went nuts for it.

She set her face down on the yellow kitchen table and said with some wonder, "So I can quit feeling that it was all my fault that I killed Daddy?"

"Yup." I opened the new refrigerator that was a lot larger than our old one and packed with fruit and cold cuts and Graf's cherry soda. Brimming up like the food could just jump out at you. I had never seen a refrigerator so full up. I reached in for the milk bottle and smelled it. "You didn't kill Daddy. You had an accident and that is two completely different things."

"But what about Uncle Paulie? I made his brain damaged and he doesn't forgive me," Troo said with a heavy heart. "That's why he keeps saying peek-a-boo all the time."

I didn't know what to say because that *was* what happened

to Uncle Paulie. And he always *did* say peek-a-boo, which made me realize now why Troo didn't like him. "Well, maybe you could . . ."

Ethel yelled over from Mrs. Galecki's backyard, "O'Malley sisters?"

Thank goodness, because I couldn't think of one darn thing to say that would make Troo feel better about weird Uncle Paulie and his damaged brain.

"You decent?" Ethel laughed, and came through the screen door.

"Mornin'," I said. It was so great that Ethel was now our next-door neighbor. She gave us each a hug and said she was glad to see us looking so nice and clean because as everyone knows cleanliness is next to godliness. I didn't know where Rasmussen kept the glasses so Ethel showed me and then took three out of the cupboard. I mixed us up three servings of Ovaltine and set them down on the table. Ethel was dressed in the white housecoat that she always wore when she was on duty at Mrs. Galecki's. She also had on a couple of the lanyards that Troo and me had made her, which was one of the many reasons I loved Ethel. She was sensitive like me to people's feelings and she knew seeing those lanyards would make us feel better because really, we had a big, se-cret, shocking day yesterday, moving into Rasmussen's and all. Ethel only knew the half of it, so while she braided my hair I told her the other half. Everything. About Daddy's forgiving Mother and what'd happened in the car crash with Troo and how Rasmussen was my father.

When I was done, Ethel said, "My gracious, y'all have had quite the summer."

I woulda bet my best steely boulder that Ethel had known all along that Rasmussen was my daddy because I had turned around to check her eyebrows and they hadn't gone up at all when I'd told her that part, which was what her eyebrows always did when she was surprised. After all, Miss Ethel Jenkins from Calhoun County, Mississippi, was the smartest woman I knew, and once you saw me and Mr. Dave together you'd probably know right away that we were related, if you paid attention to the details and were looking for that sort of thing.

Ethel leaned over the table toward Troo and said, "You know, Miss Troo, you just gotta let that go with your daddy's accident. Chil'ren, they don't know what the heck they's doin' so it don't count what they do in God's eyes like a bad thing 'til they get much, much older and they *know* when they's doin' a bad thing. And I know that Mr. Rasmussen, he can't replace your other daddy, but . . ." Ethel took a sip of her Ovaltine and it left a mustache on her lip that she licked off with her startling pink tongue. "If I know anything at all about Miss Sally, it's that she's very good at sharin'."

Troo looked over at me and I nodded so she'd know what Ethel said was right. I *was* good at sharing and would be happy to share Mr. Dave with Troo equal equal. After all, Troo had shared Sky King with me. Not knowing. But she did. I think even if she had known, she would've. Maybe not right at first, because that was something Trooper could use some work on, but she would eventually. I think.

And since she, like me, thought Ethel was the smartest person we knew, Troo asked her the same thing she asked me earlier, which was exactly what I was hoping she'd do. "But what about Uncle Paulie? I made him into a brain-damaged person and now he just builds Popsicle stick houses and can't be a carpenter like he was."

"Paulie a carpenter? Wherever did you get that idea from?" Ethel said, frowning. "Your uncle Paulie weren't no carpenter. Paulie was a bookie."

I was the one who told Troo that Uncle Paulie was a carpenter because I could have sworn I heard Mr. Jerbak call him a carpenter before the crash, when Uncle Paulie was gonna give me a ride home back to the farm after a visit at Granny's. We'd stopped up at Jerbak's Beer 'n Bowl on the way because he said he had some business to attend to. When we walked into the dark room that smelled of Vitalis and beer and chocolate chip cookies, from behind the bar Mr. Jerbak hollered, "Hey, lookee who's here. If it ain't Paulie the carpenter. The guy who nails more broads than Jesus nailed boards." And all the men at the bar laughed and laughed and I had three kiddie cocktails while some of the men gave Uncle Paulie their money. So maybe Ethel was mixed up.

"Do you know what that is? A bookie?" Ethel asked.

Hadn't Eddie gotten his Chevy car from a bookie who couldn't pay his dues?

Troo and me said together, "No."

"A bookie is somebody who takes bets for other people," Ethel said.

Troo asked, "Bets on what?"

"Well, it really don't matter no more, does it? But that was what your uncle Paulie were. A bookie."

Ethel took another long drink from her sweaty lavender metal glass and then set it back down on the kitchen table.

"I'll tell you one thing, Miss Troo, something I really noticed about your uncle after that crash. I knew him pretty good before that crash because I was keepin' company with a gentleman around that time who had a fondness for the ponies."

A fondness for the ponies? Like me?

Ethel got up and walked her empty glass to the sink. "You know I'm sad to tell you this, but your uncle Paulie, he weren't so nice in them days. In fact, some folks thought Paulie Riley was the baddest man around. So maybe in a way you did yourself and your family a favor, Miss Troo. Come to think of it, Paulie, too." Ethel pulled open the refrigerator and took something out. "Anybody yearnin' for a radish sandwich?" That was what Ethel always had during the summer for a snack. God only knows why. But her wavin' that bunch of radishes around, it made me have a memory that just came to me out of nowhere, just blew through my head like a hot wind.

On the afternoon of the crash, Mother and Uncle Paulie were standing on the porch at the farm. I was getting a drink out of the hose and cleaning off some of the little radishes I'd just picked from the garden, tending to it the way Daddy had told me to so he wouldn't be disappointed in me anymore when he came back from the game. I was feeling real, real bad about saying those mean things to him. I swore to myself I'd make it up to him. Later on I'd give him a rub on his tan neck. He especially liked that. Mother and Uncle Paulie didn't know I was out there. I set the hose down and snuck a little closer because Mother had a funny look on her face. Daddy and Troo were sitting in the car in the driveway, facing away from the house listening to some loud cha-cha music on the radio. I froze myself so I could hear what Uncle Paulie was saying to Mother. His voice was like how Butchy sounded when you tried to take away his bone.

Uncle Paulie was real close up to her, his chest pressing against hers. "Got myself into a little trouble and I need some dough. Break open the cookie jar, little Miss Stuck-Up, or I'm gonna tell your husband about you know who." Then Uncle Paulie touched her lips and ran his finger across them. Mother hauled back and slapped Uncle Paulie across the face, knocking the cigarette right out of his mouth. Then Uncle Paulie left through the screen door, but not before he smiled and said, "You're gonna wish you hadn't done that, Helen."

Mother stood there on that porch staring after Uncle Paulie until he got into the car. Then she ran into the house, and through her bedroom window I heard her crying. I got so scared. I needed to tell Daddy to come back . . . that Uncle Paulie had made Mother cry . . . that I was sorry I said I hated him and wished for another daddy. It couldn't wait. I dropped the hose and ran down the driveway after them, but all that was left was the dust of the car where it had pulled out onto the road in a hurry.

It was funny how those radishes made me remember that, but sometimes baseball and hot dogs with mustard and relish also made me have rememberings of Daddy, so maybe it was the same sort of thing. But for sure I knew now that Ethel was telling the honest-to-God truth about my uncle being a bad, bad man. I said to her, "I think Uncle Paulie might be the molester who murdered Junie and Sara."

Ethel made her eyes go so big that the brown part looked like a fly on a plate of mashed potatoes. "Paulie a murderer and molester? Oh, Miss Sally, you have got to get that imagination under control. Why, Paulie could never do nothin' like that. He can barely get hisself dressed." She looked over at Troo and said, "Now he coulda done somethin' like that in the old days, cuz in the old days that man was nastier than chicken poop on a pump handle. I could tell you some stories that would make your hair stand straight up. Back then, Paulie was always drinkin' up at Jerbak's and takin' bets and most of all—womanizin'." Ethel shook her head like she was so disgusted. "I'm gonna tell you something now that maybe I shouldn't but I think I'm goin' to anyway, for Miss Troo's sake." She lowered her voice and said, "But you gotta swear that you don' ever tell nobody. Spit and shake." Ethel spit into her hand and we did the same and shook on it. "Paulie got hisself arrested that summer for breakin' the legs of a man who wouldn't pay him his bettin' money and then takin' advantage of that man's wife. He was gonna have to go to jail for a very long time for doin' that. But after that car crash with your daddy . . . your mother, she got Officer Rasmussen to make that work out all right by asking him to give that man and his wife some money so they'd drop them charges against your uncle."

The O'Malley sisters' mouths fell right open.

Ethel shook her head back and forth and made her *aaah-hhaaa* sound. "God the Father sure do work in mysterious ways."

We just sat there and thought about that together until Ethel said, "Why ever did you think Paulie was the murderer and molester, Miss Sally?"

I told her about the first time I got chased down the alley, the night Fast Susie told me and Troo that Frankenstein story. And how I hid under the Kenfields' bushes and when I was there I saw those pink-and-green argyle socks. And how I found those same pink-and-green argyles soaking in the cold water in Granny's sink.

Then it was Ethel's turn to hang her mouth open. "Why in Sam Hill didn't you tell nobody about gettin' chased down the alley like that?"

"Because back then I thought it was Rasmussen and I didn't think anybody would believe me because of my imagination being overactive."

"Oh Lordy, Lordy, Lordy, I'll tell Dave about this when he comes home from work, though I'm not sure what good it'll do now." Ethel checked her watch. "Mrs. Galecki, she's gonna be wakin' up soon from her mornin' nap. I gotta go give her the new medicine to keep her calm. Been a little somethin' somethin' going on with Mr. Gary that I'll tell you about later at lunch." Ethel walked toward the screen door, saying, "You two go off now to the playground and come back around when you hear the twelve o'clock church bells and I'll have some of them peanut butter and marshmallow sandwiches waitin' for you."

Troo went after Ethel and put her head on her giant bosoms. Troo wanted to say thanks for telling her about Uncle Paulie, because now she just noticed she hardly didn't feel that bad anymore. She didn't say that, but I knew that's what Troo would say some other time, when it wasn't so hard for her. Mental telepathy.

When Troo let go of her, Ethel stared us each straight in the eyes and said a little scarily, " 'Member your promise, you two," and let the screen door slam behind her.

"You know, Ethel is right. God," Troo came back and said. "Our Father really does work in mysterious ways."

And all I could think to say as I was standing in our new kitchen with a chocolate-chip-cookie-smelling breeze coming through the checkered yellow curtains and Junie Piaskowski's picture hanging on the dining room wall, that clock counting the minutes slow and steady with pussycat feet, "Yes, He does. Yes, He does."

CHAPTER THIRTY-TWO

W e didn't live across from the playground anymore so to get over there Troo and me had to
cut through the Fazios' backyard. Laying on the
grass on a white blanket, listening to rock 'n' roll music, was
Fast Susie. She had on her pink polka-dot swimsuit with the
pleated skirt, a matching glass of pink lemonade next to her.

"Hi," I said, coming up next to her. I couldn't believe she
was working on her tan some more. She was past Egyptian
dark and almost the same color as Ray Buck.

Fast Susie shaded her eyes and looked up at us. "O'Malley
sisters? That you? Where the hell you been?" She laughed
like whatever she was about to tell us really fractured her.
"Heard the word?"

Troo was so happy to see her that she smiled so big, you
could practically see it coming out the back of her head. Fast
Susie was Troo's idol.

Fast Susie grinned like the cat in *Alice in Wonderland* and
said, "Reese Latour is goin' into the army."

"Really?!" I yelled. I just hated Reese Latour and I felt so
happy for Artie since Reese couldn't run around the neighborhood anymore yelling harelip, harelip, harelip. And Reese
couldn't call Wendy the idiot anymore. Or stare at Troo

with those eyes that gave me heebie-jeebies while he rubbed the front of his pants. No doubt about it. Reese going into the army was fantastic news! Almost too good to be true.

I said, "You absolutely sure?"

Fast Susie made her eyebrows go up and down like Groucho's. "You bet your life, little lady."

Whatever thing with garlic Nana Fazio was making for supper tonight, the deliciousness of it was coming out the back window, and Elvis was singing about "A Big Hunk o' Love" on the radio when Fast Susie said, "I heard Tony and Jane talkin' about it." Those were Fast Susie's parents. Sometimes though she called them the ape-man and Jane and I didn't blame her because Mr. Fazio was almost as hairy as Sampson. I am not kidding. Mr. Fazio worked selling silverware. That's what Willie O'Hara had heard. That Mr. Fazio worked for somebody called Frankie the Knife.

"Remember when Wendy fell down the Spencers' cellar steps?" Fast Susie asked.

Troo said, "Yeahhhhh . . ."

"And remember how everybody thought she just had one of her silly wanderings?"

I said, "Nooo . . ." I never believed that for one second.

"Reese did it." Fast Susie popped up, which made me and Troo jump, which was exactly what she was trying to make us do.

"Reese pushed Wendy down the Spencers' cellar steps?" I asked her.

"Yup. And Wendy finally told on him."

I thought back to that day when Wendy and me were sitting on the Kenfields' porch swing and I asked her if Rasmussen had done it to her and then her mother with the opera lungs called her and she ran home. Why didn't she tell me then that it was Reese?

"Reese is saying Wendy made it all up, of course." Fast Susie squirted some baby oil into her hand and smoothed it on her legs. She had told Troo and me at the beginning of summer that she was thinking of starting to shave, which I thought would be a very good idea since her legs took after Tony the ape-man. "He's telling everybody that Wendy is just a dumb idiot and that if anyone believes her, they're an idiot, too."

"Oh my God, sweet Jesus, Mary and Joseph," I said. Reese Latour had been the murderer and molester all the time. I just couldn't believe that. Why hadn't I been paying attention to details?

"When he found out what Reese had done to Wendy, Mr. Latour beat the living shit out of him with a strap. I'm surprised you didn't hear him yellin' over at your house." Fast Susie was getting a lot of good feelings out of telling us this news. She hated Reese even more than the rest of us did. Who wouldn't?

Troo snorted, "Good riddance to bad rubbish."

"And guess who else is going away for a little trip?" Fast Susie showed her eyeteeth. "Greasy Al."

Troo started hopping around. "Really? Really? Greasy Al is going into the army, too?"

"No, they wouldn't take him into the army because of his gimpy polio leg," Fast Susie said, taking a sip of her lemonade. "He's going to reform school up north."

So that's what Rasmussen meant when he said he had taken care of that subject.

Greasy Al's departure didn't really register in my mind just then because I was still so shocked about what Fast Susie had told us about Reese. He'd been the one who chased me down the alley that night, and when he couldn't get me he musta turned back toward home, and Wendy was doing one of her wanderings and he found her and tried to murder and molest his own sister. She probably got away because Wendy was *really* strong and that was another one of those things that God gave people when He took something else away. I once saw Wendy Latour pick up Artie when she got mad at him one day and throw him about six feet in the air. That's how strong Wendy was. And some of those hugs she gave me, holey moley.

But wait a minute.

If Reese was the murderer and molester, how come he wasn't getting electrocuted and was just getting sent to the army? That didn't seem right. "What about Sara and Junie?" I asked Fast Susie.

"What about 'em?" She was smoothing baby oil all over her arms, her hair standing up like a black forest.

"Don't you think it was Reese that murdered them?" I asked.

Troo said, "Yeah, that's what I told you before!" She looked so proud of herself. "That Reese Latour is the murderer and molester." She was right. She'd told me in the hospital lobby with her ventriloquism lips.

Fast Susie said, "Naw, I don't think it was Reese. If it was, Officer Rasmussen woulda come by and taken Reese off in handcuffs, and I been lyin' here all morning and woulda seen him come by."

I still thought Troo was right. It was Reese. And when Mr. Dave came home tonight from the police station, I would tell him that. He probably hadn't thought it through all the way because of his excitement about me being his new daughter and everything.

"Troo," I said, crossing over into the Latours' yard, "I'll be right back. I'm gonna go over and check on Wendy."

"I'm goin' over to the playground and celebrate Greasy Al going to reform school. Come over there when you're done, Thally O'Malley." Troo could do an imitation of Wendy that was so close I had to smile. Even though it wasn't very nice of her, it was still a good imitation.

When I was almost to the Latours' front door, Fast Susie called over to me, "You know what, O'Malley?" I turned back. "You're a nice kid. A square, but a nice kid." And then she turned her radio up so she could sing along to "Splish Splash, I Was Taking a Bath."

That was a nice thing for Fast Susie to say. I was feeling pretty nice. Very happy that Reese would no longer be able to murder or molest anybody ever again. Especially me. And maybe up north Greasy Al would get reformed, and when he came home he would not be such a bully. And Mother hadn't died and Mr. Dave's house was much more wonderful than our old one. Nell and Eddie were getting married. And Ethel was going to be my next-door neighbor with visits from Mr. Gary every summer. I even felt better about Uncle Paulie being brain damaged because according to Ethel he was a real pain in the patootie before the crash.

So I felt . . . I didn't know how to describe it exactly.

Maybe . . . light? A lot lighter than I had for a long time. Like sunshine could get into me now.

Feeling that way, I made the worst mistake ever. I stopped paying attention to the details. And by the time I remembered what Daddy'd warned me about, it was too late.

CHAPTER THIRTY-THREE

After Wendy's mother came to the door and told me she wasn't home, I started to look for her, and then I saw her over on the swings at the playground. She was having one of her nude wanderings and was swinging so high that I could hear the chains snapping from across the street. By the time I got over there, Bobby, the playground counselor, was screaming, "Stop that, you're gonna go over the top!"

Wendy was smiling and not listening to Bobby, but when she saw me she yelled, "Thally O'Malley, look me. Wendy bird."

Bobby said, "What a moron," and walked off.

Gee, what was wrong with Bobby? It wasn't at all like him to say something so mean. Maybe he was feeling out of sorts. This kind of bad summer heat could do that to a person. I wanted to chase after him and say, "Wendy is not a moron, she's just celebrating because Reese has been mean to her all her life and now he is going to the Big House once Mr. Dave grills him tonight." But I didn't say that because Bobby was not one of us. When the playground closed down next month, he would be gone back to his college and wouldn't be coming back again until next summer. So it really wasn't any of Bobby's beeswax. It was Vliet Street beeswax.

"Wendy Latour, stop swinging and I'll give you a candy bar," I shouted.

That got her attention, because Wendy loved candy more than sticks of butter or old hot dogs on the ground. Wendy *adored* candy. Troo came over and watched Wendy slowing down. "She's just the happiest girl in the world, isn't she?" she said in a sad, admiring way.

"Everything is going to work out okay, Trooper, you'll see," I said.

When Wendy came to a stop, I gave her the Three Musketeers bar I had in my pocket and then watched her while she sat there enjoying it, naked on the swing.

"O'Malleys," somebody hollered behind me. I turned to see Mary Lane making her way across the playground. She was looking unbelievably skinny. With her big black hightops and white socks, she looked like an exclamation point! Troo and me hadn't seen her since the Fourth, so when she came up next to me I was so happy to see her that I almost gave her a hug, but I didn't because Mary Lane was wiry and would beat the hell out of you. The only person I'd ever seen beat Mary Lane in a fight was Troo, and that was only because Troo was fighting Irish.

"What ya been doin'?" I asked, not sniffing Mary Lane's usual stale potato chip smell but something a lot stronger.

"Been secretly helpin' my dad with the animal feeding because one of those goddamn flamingos bit him in the hand." Mary Lane spat on the ground. "Goddamn it to hell, I hate those birds. They look so pretty but then when you get to know them they have the worst personalities. Kind of like somebody else around here." She was watching Bobby turning rope for some little girls jumping double Dutch. Mary Lane despised Bobby.

I looked back at Wendy, who had stuffed the Three Musketeers, that whole bar, in her mouth, and I realized that even though she was a Mongoloid, her bosoms had begun to grow. And since she was naked I could also see that she had some hair down below, and that was a very odd thing to me. Wendy's body was growing up without her.

I yelled over to Artie Latour, who was playing tetherball on the other end of the playground. "Artiiieee . . ." He didn't hear me, of course, because of his ear that Reese had hit so hard, but then he just happened to look our way when he was changing sides and he came running.

"Time to go home to Ma, Wendy." As Artie helped his sister off the swing, he looked over at Troo and smiled. He still had the hots for her.

Troo said, "We heard about Reese going away."

Artie's smile smeared across his face like the chocolate did on Wendy's. "Yeah, that's something, ain't it?"

The three of us watched as he led his naked-as-a-jaybird sister toward home. Halfway across the street, Wendy got loose from Artie's hand and ran back and grabbed me into one of her large hugs. When I could breathe again, I said to her, "So it was Reese that pushed you down the Spencers' steps?"

Wendy let go of me, looked me right in the eye and did something I didn't know that a Mongoloid could do, something I'd never seen her do before. Wendy Latour gave me a huge wink! And in that moment, I knew for positive that

Wendy had just *fallen* down the Spencers' steps during one of her wanderings. She hadn't been *pushed*. She'd just told her ma that made-up story about Reese so he would get blamed. Oh, Wendy! You stinker! I looked at her closely again just to make sure it wasn't my imagination. She smiled and took off back toward her Artie. That girl had rescued her beloved brother from the always-evil Reese. I wondered if Artie knew that. I knew that. No matter what. That was not a flight of my imagination. That wink had said it all. And Wendy's sly smile was like the amen on the end of a prayer.

Sorta.

Because then I realized that if Reese hadn't pushed Wendy down the Spencers' cellar steps, then he probably wasn't the one who'd chased me down the alley that same night or grabbed at me in the Fazios' backyard. There couldn't be two loonies running around, could there? Naw. Troo had been wrong. Reese Latour wasn't the murderer and molester after all. I didn't want to wreck her afternoon. I didn't want to tell her she was mistaken. She already had too much else on her mind what with Mr. Dave being her new father. I'd wait to tell her when the timing was right.

After Troo and Mary Lane and me got onto the swings, Mary Lane said, "Did you hear about Father Jim and Mr. Gary Galecki?"

I wished we were all going up and down at the same time but we weren't. I was in the middle and Troo was on my right and Mary Lane was on my left and we were all pumping like crazy but at different times, so I had to wait until our swings crossed to say, "What about Father Jim and Mr. Gary?"

Mary Lane said, passing by me, "They are light in the loafers together."

"*What?*" Troo yelled across from me. "*What did you just say?*"

Mary Lane was the biggest, fattest liar. She could only go so long without tellin' one, like she just had to do it or she would burst into flames, which probably woulda been okay with her. Next thing she'd say was that Mr. Gary kidnapped Father Jim and they were going to go make pot holders with Germans next to a big lake with slimy trout up in Rhinelander.

"Father Jim and Gary Galecki run off together to Rhine . . . I mean, California, to get married," Mary Lane yelled back to Troo. "I heard Ethel tellin' Mr. Fitzpatrick at the drugstore this morning." Mary Lane put on an Ethel voice and waggled a finger like Ethel did. " 'I had my 'spicions 'bout Mr. Gary bein' a little too dear to his mother, if you get my understandin'. Now everybody's gonna know. That boy is a royal queen.' " Mary Lane looked at me and made a funny face, like what the hell is that supposed to mean? "Father Jim left a note in the sacristy saying he was sorry but he couldn't help himself and that he knew it was a mortal sin but he was in love and runnin' off with Gary Galecki to California."

Sweet Jesus, Mary and Joseph! Was that what Ethel'd meant when she said there'd been a little somethin' somethin' with Mr. Gary? I almost ran over to Mrs. Galecki's to ask her, to see if Mary Lane was lying. But then Mary Lane said, "And you know what else?"

She'd stopped swinging and so did me and Troo because Mary Lane was telling us some fantastic stuff and we wanted to pay very close attention.

"What else?" Troo asked.

"Big-shot Bobby is up to something," Mary Lane said.

Her hatred for Bobby had been going on for the last two summers. Bobby started it all one day when she was hanging upside down on the monkey bars and he said to her in a jokey kind of way, "Look at Mary Lane hangin' around her home away from home." And then he set a banana down on the ground and walked away scratching under his arms. Okay, I'm sorry to have to say this, but Mary Lane truly did look like a chimp with her skinny little body and long arms and spread-out nose, but Bobby shouldn't have told her that. He musta been outta sorts that day, too.

I asked, "What do you mean Bobby is up to something?" just to be polite, because after all Mary Lane was our best friend. I was pretty sure that this was gonna be another one of her whoppers.

Mary Lane said, "I was peepin' on him when he was in the shed yesterday and he was going through this Kroger bag."

"So?" Troo said.

"He was touchin' himself."

My head whipped toward Mary Lane. "What do you mean?"

"You know what I mean. Like Reese Latour is always doin'." Mary Lane put her hand down to the front of her shorts.

Troo was leaning way back in the swing, her hair almost draggin' on the ground. "What was in the bag?" I could tell Troo didn't believe her and was just humoring her.

Across the playground, Bobby must've felt me staring at him because he looked over at me.

Mary Lane said, "He was takin' stuff out of the bag and

puttin' it on the wooden table in there and lookin' at it like it was something special."

"What was in the bag?" I asked her again.

Bobby had set the jump rope down and was walking toward us.

"You know the shed window is kinda dirty so it was hard to see real clear, but I'm sure there was a shoe."

"What kind of shoe?" I was getting a very bad feeling.

"A tennis shoe."

I shot out of that swing and knelt down in front of Mary Lane and said, "No kiddin'. You sure about that?"

She nodded. "Now shut your trap about it, he's comin' this way."

I shoulda run over to Mr. Dave's house right then and called him on his telephone at the police station and told him I knew who the murderer and molester was. But then again, I'd just about had it with everybody telling me that I had to get my imagination under control and maybe so did Mary Lane. Everybody calling her liar liar pants on fire. But I had to also face facts that Mary Lane could be telling one of her whopper weenie lies. There was just no way of knowing for sure.

I got back into my swing to think it through. Bobby'd stopped walking toward us and was getting a drink at the bubbler. I felt guilty about suspecting him. He was a good egg even if he was a little out of sorts today. He was usually such a terrific friend to all of us and always dressed clean and nice. Mary Lane had to be making it up.

"Are you really, really sure about this?" I asked her again. I'd started to doubt her even more because she had just told us that story about Father Jim and Mr. Gary, and that was such an out-and-out lie. Father Jim and Gary Galecki? Light in their loafers? But then I remembered Father Jim's fluffy white dress with the petticoats and high heels. And Mr. Gary's smooth skin and high voice. According to Willie O'Hara, that was how you could tell if someone was light in their loafers. Because his mother knew a lot of loafer-light people who seemed to be on the artistic side. Smooth skin, high voice, and then Willie made his wrist floppy and said, "And that's what they do with their hands. And oh yeah, they really like flowers." Flowers? Mr. Gary *loved* flowers. So did Father Jim! He'd planted over ten purple snowball bushes in the rectory backyard. Oh boy. I had to talk to Ethel.

"You're not making this one up, are you, about Bobby?" I asked Mary Lane again, keeping my eye on Bobby, who was up on the balls of his feet, bouncing along toward us with his electric energy.

"No," she said. "And I didn't make that up about Father Jim and Gary Galecki either. Go over to Ethel's and see."

So maybe Mary Lane was lying, and maybe she wasn't. Bobby was about a hundred feet away and taking giant steps toward us.

It was just too hard to believe that Bobby with hair that went in tight curls on his head like a soprano choirboy would have a Kroger bag with Sara Heinemann's tennis shoe in it. Nobody would believe us. I wouldn't. And for sure Mr. Dave wouldn't. And I really wanted to get off on the right foot with him and not get him sad that he let Troo and me move in with him, or maybe he would change his mind and then what would we do? Mother would be so mad.

"What's buzzin', cuzzin? Anybody up for a game of tetherball?" Bobby asked when he got to us. "Or maybe you wanna head over to the monkey bars?" He smirked at Mary Lane.

Troo said, "Ah . . . thanks. But we were just talkin' about headin' over to the zoo."

Bobby was so handsome. So *ooh la la*, Troo said. He looked at the three of us one at a time in a strange kind of way, and then said, "Maybe when you get back?"

"That sounds great," I said.

"Okay," he said, backing up, "catch you later."

"Boy, I hate him," Mary Lane said once he was out of earshot. "He reminds me of a boa constrictor, all cold and slithery. Did you know that over in Africa boas grow so big that one of those things can swallow a child whole?"

I sighed and started doubting her all over again, about what she'd said about Bobby and Mr. Gary and Father Jim. "That's not true."

"Is too."

"Is not."

The three of us got up off the swings and started walking toward the end of the playground through the waves of shimmery heat that were like in that French Foreign Legion movie we saw over at the Uptown.

"Is too."

"Is not."

I spent the way over to the park feelin' like we shouldn't be doing this. Mr. Dave had warned us at breakfast about staying away from the zoo, but boy, I sure was missing Sampson and had a desperate, desperate need to see him. Troo kicked a rock all the way over so I could tell she was thinking. Mary Lane kept running off and peeping into people's yards, reporting back nothin' too exciting except for the peeing boy statue she saw over at the Raymonds'.

We stopped at a couple of the other cages on the way to Sampson's. The lion's fur was all falling out and he looked like he had ringworm or something. And the elephants didn't move at all and looked kinda fake. The hippos were underwater and I couldn't blame them because if it got much hotter, I could fry an egg on my face.

After we climbed up into our tree across from Sampson's cage, I felt so relieved to see the King that I almost started to cry. He was laying on his back singing, but he turned toward me when I called his name and in his eyes I could tell that he'd missed me as much as I missed him, like anybody would miss a long-lost relative. And then he went back to sucking on his toes. That made me laugh, seeing Sampson like that, not a care in the world. It made everything that was worrying me—Bobby rubbin' himself in the shed and Mr. Gary and Father Jim being light in their loafers together and how Mr. Dave and Troo were getting along worse than the Battling Bickersons—just sorta fly out of my head.

Until Troo lit up a cigarette and blew out one of those French smoke rings and said, "Girls . . . I got me a plan."

CHAPTER THIRTY-FOUR

t was warm that night. The heat wasn't giving up like it did sometimes after the streetlights went on. And the air around me smelled like just-cut grass and the macaroni and cheese Mr. Dave had made us for supper with a slice of Ethel's black-bottomed pie for dessert.

Mary Lane and Troo and me were sitting on top of the monkey bars closest to the shed, watching Bobby play checkers with Mimi Latour over on the benches, and going over Troo's genius plan one more time.

Everybody knew there was a padlock on the shed door, but it had a chain that was loose and you could pull it apart pretty far. Not real far, a kid couldn't sneak in between the chain and the door or anything. Not a regular kid. But a kid like Mary Lane, the skinniest kid in the whole world, she was pretty sure she could get in there, and once she did she was gonna get her hands on that Kroger bag and take it to the cops.

"You ready?" Mary Lane asked as she swung down off the monkey bars.

This was one of the reasons Troo and me loved Mary Lane, because she was always ready for anything. Like ringing doorbells and running away, or kicking car tires up at

Fillard's Service Station and then laying down on the ground and moaning like she had got run over. And one time she even said she was a crippled child and went door to door collecting pennies that she used to buy herself licorice. She was a wild little monkey that Mary Lane! Especially when it came to peeping.

"I'm ready," I said. But I wasn't. I felt scared the same way I did after I climbed those steps to the high dive over at the swimming pool, walking slowly across that rough board over to the edge. Then I'd just stand there, bouncing in the breeze, waiting for my courage to come push me off. I can't tell you how many times I backed down those steps, my head hangin' low and embarrassed.

But I wasn't gonna back down tonight. I could feel it. I wondered why that was. Maybe it had something to do with Mr. Dave being my father or Mother getting better or both those things getting put into one big bowl and mixed up together to make a batch of a different, braver Sally O'Malley. Was that how growing up worked?

Across the street, the big lights were on at the playground. The ones they put on when there was a softball game being played by the men in the neighborhood. Tonight it was the Feelin' Good Cookie Factory against the policemen. Mr. Dave was up there. He was playing third base. All the men were yelling baseball words at each other. *C'mon, Gil, just a little hit. Pitch, you got about as much control as two rabbits on a first date. Hey, ump, if you're just gonna watch, buy a ticket.* And a lot of hootin' and hollerin' from the benches. When the wind changed directions, I was sure that the cookie factory team would win. The smell of those chocolate chip cookies would give those factory men strength.

I jumped down from the bars and looked over at Mr. Dave in his baseball uniform with the red stripes and thought I'd just run over to third base real quick and tell him about Mary Lane seeing that Kroger grocery bag in the shed.

Troo did some of the mental telepathy on me and said snippy-like, "Forget it, I don't care if he is your daddy, he's not gonna believe you and he's gonna get mad that you bothered him while he's playing ball."

"Who's your daddy?" Mary Lane asked.

Troo said matter-of-factly, "Rasmussen is her daddy."

Mary Lane nodded like Ethel did sometimes, all low and wise. "Yeah, I knew that."

"You did not, Mary Lane. That is your biggest lie ever," I said.

"Did too know that. For Chrissakes, Sally, who are you? Helen Keller? Look how much you two look alike."

I looked over at the softball field. Mary Lane was right. Mr. Dave was crouched over at third, smacking his hand into his glove. He'd told me and Troo that we could come over and watch the game but *not* to leave the playground under any circumstances. Eddie Callahan was playing for the cookie factory because his dad used to work up there before he got all caught up in that cookie press, so Nell was sitting in the bleachers, waving at Eddie every two minutes. I wished Mother could be here to see Mr. Dave. He looked so handsome with his honey-colored skin, his hair almost as white as mine now with just the right amount of muscles, the kind that didn't look like he wanted to punch you, but that he'd be handy if you needed him to lift furniture. It would make Mother feel a lot healthier just looking at him. I bet they ended up getting married and then they would go on a honeymoon to someplace they both would really like, maybe someplace glamorous like Miami Beach, Florida, and when they came back they—

Mary Lane shoved me and said, "Quit your dreamin' . . . it's time to do a peepin'." She laughed like one of those chimps that lived out on the Monkey Island. "She's a poet but doesn't know it but her feet show it. They're long fellows. *He he he*." She didn't seem scared at all. In fact, I hadn't seen Mary Lane this happy since she accidentally lit that huge fire up on North Avenue last summer.

"Troo," I said, "make sure Bobby stays on that bench, and if he doesn't, yell something like, 'Oh hi, Bobby, wanna play tetherball' very loud, okay?"

Troo was staring at Bobby real concentrated with her tongue between her lips. "I got him in my sights." She had her Davy Crockett coonskin cap on, and her wiggly red hair that had lightened in the summer sun to a not quite ripe strawberry color was halfway down her back. "What about Barb?"

I said, "She's not workin' tonight. I asked."

I turned to Mary Lane to say let's go but she was already heading toward the shed. I looked over at Mr. Dave one more time and I thought how proud of me he was gonna be if Bobby turned out to be the murderer and molester, and if he wasn't . . . no harm, no foul.

Mary Lane disappeared around the corner of the school. I looked back once more at Bobby, who was now leaning over the checkerboard toward Mimi Latour. He had his hands laying on top of hers.

"Sally," Troo whispered loudly to get my attention.

I looked over at her. She gave me double thumbs-up.

I did the same back to her and then I slipped around the corner. My poor heart. It wasn't so much beating in my chest as panting like it had Old Yeller rabies. It was pretty dark back there because there weren't any lights except for a small one over the door of the shed and that one was flickering. While I let my eyes adjust to the dark, I set my face against the brick of the school, hoping it'd be cool. But it wasn't. It was warm and rough and smelled like sidewalk.

"Mary Lane?" I called out.

She whispered loudly over to my left, from behind a tree, "C'mon, we don't have a lotta time. It's the eighth inning." She ran toward the shed door and waved me over.

There was a light on inside and a streak of it came through the shed and laid there like a piece of broken glass on the grass. Mary Lane pointed at the door. The plan was for me to pull it open as far as I could because I was so strong from all my gardening. I got my hands around the edge and yanked. Mary Lane was standing sideways to the door. She slipped most of her body through, but then stopped and said, "More, you gotta pull it open more, Sally. I can't get my head in." I closed my eyes so I could concentrate and tried to pull even harder, with every ounce of strength I had, telling myself if I could do this, I would be named Queen of the Playground. I tugged and grunted and it musta worked, because when I opened my eyes Mary Lane said, "I knew this skinniness would come in handy one day," as she disappeared inside the shed.

No other human being on Earth could've done it.

And then I listened for Troo, but I didn't hear anything at all, no warning, no talking. Nothing. I watched Mary Lane through the slit in the shed door as she walked past the big metal container they kept the red balls in and past a bunch of bats and gloves. She hurried over to the long wooden worktable where they probably fixed stuff that broke on the playground and where she said she saw Bobby open up that Kroger bag. She looked in a cupboard and behind these shovels. She pulled the top off a green metal box that had some paint cans in it. Mary Lane turned toward me and hunched her shoulders up to her ears and then let them down. She couldn't find the bag. Maybe Bobby had figured out she'd peeped on him and had gotten rid of it. Or maybe Mary Lane *had* been telling one of her big fat whoppers.

I stuck my arm through the slit in the door and pointed over to a corner she hadn't checked. "Over there."

Mary Lane walked over and picked something up in her hand. It was just a rusted old swing chain. She turned back again and made a face at me like, now what? I pointed at the red balls container. I just had a feeling. A picture of Bobby always bouncing one of those red balls came into my mind. "Dig into the ball barrel. Way down."

A cheer went up from the baseball game. Two . . . four . . . six . . . eight . . . who do we appreciate! The game was over. The playground was closing. Bobby'd be here any minute to switch the big lights off. I called through the door, "Hurry up." Mary Lane stuck her skinny arms down into the ball barrel as far as she could and was rooting around, and then finally she brought her arm back up. In her hand was a Kroger bag, folded at the top. She grinned and started walking back to me. She was almost home free when I heard the whistling.

I could feel his breath on my neck. How'd he get past Troo?

"Lookin' for me, Sally?" Bobby asked real friendly. He placed his hands on my shoulders and turned me around to face him. "Cuz I've been looking for you." I looked down and he didn't have those white tennis shoes on anymore. He had on black shoes, those spongy kind. And pink-and-green argyles. Mary Lane had not been telling one of her fibs.

Bobby Brophy was the murderer and molester.

He had the keys for the shed padlock in his hand. If I didn't warn her, Mary Lane was gonna get caught by Bobby. So I imagined, just imagined that Bobby was the guy I'd always thought he was. My friend. My chess teacher. "Oh, Bobby," I said real loud, and laughed. "You scared me. I was just thinking I could get into the shed and get some lanyards for myself. I wanna make one for my mother because she's coming home from the hospital and I saw you were busy playing checkers with Mimi and . . . hey, how about a quick game of chess?"

Bobby ignored me and looked all around. "Where's your pal Mary Lane? I saw the two of you come over here. Where'd she go off to?" He peered into the shed and the light came across his face and lit him up like he was an angel. I held my breath and prayed Dear Mary Mother of God, help your namesake. It seemed like a long time until he pulled his head back away from the crack and asked again, "Where is she, Sally?"

"She's not here. She had to go home. She . . ."

Bobby grinned and took another step closer to me. "Gosh, that's too bad. I had something real special planned for her and now she's gonna miss out on all the fun."

"Bobby, I really gotta get going. Troo is waiting for me." I started to walk off. He grabbed me by my wrist. "Well, actually, Sally, she's not. Troo seems to have fallen off the monkey bars and is taking a little nap."

"Troo," I moaned, and tried to break free. He pulled me closer.

There was a little gap between Bobby's front teeth that I had never noticed before. He picked up my braid and ran the end of it across his lips. "I just love blondes. And those green eyes of yours. Delicious." He was making a funny noise in his throat, like the Kenfields' cat did when I rubbed her tummy. "We are going to have a very special night. I've been planning it all summer long. Are you ready?"

I tried to scream then, but all that came out was, "Ahhh." Just like in my dream when the Creature from the Black Lagoon caught me. Just a gagging sound that nobody could hear but me. And Bobby.

"So that's a yes?" he purred. He was running his fingers down my blouse toward my shorts. His breathing sounded like it did after we played tetherball. And then he wrapped his arms around me and I recognized the feeling coming off his body from that night in the Fazios' backyard when he'd come after me with the pillowcase on his face. The feeling that I thought was fear coming off him. It wasn't fear . . . I knew that then. Bobby felt excited. The way you do when you wanted something for a very long time and you finally got it.

He pulled me into his chest and held me and his warm breath on my neck smelled milky like a baby's. If you were in one of the houses across the street and you were watching us, you would think to yourself, what a nice counselor that Bobby Brophy was to care so much about those kids. He put his lips in my ear and his flickering tongue licked the insides and all I could think about was what Mary Lane said about boa constrictors that ate kids whole.

Out of the corner of my eye, I could see her climb out from under the gray shadow of that worktable, and then as quiet as a mouse she pushed open the dirty window that was just above it. Did she have the Kroger bag with her? If she didn't, and she ran over to find Mr. Dave and tell him that Bobby Brophy was the murderer and molester, he wouldn't believe lying Mary Lane.

Bobby stepped back and brought one of his hands up to the back of my neck and first tickled it and then squeezed. He stuck his other hand through the crack in the shed door, pulled at something, and the playground went dark. Then he yanked me toward the back of the school, where there was another way out. When I tried to tug back, he said in another kind of growling voice, "If you don't stop fighting me, I'll strangle you right here, right now, and then you know what I'll do?" He pulled me across Fiftieth Street and back behind the Grinders'. He had me up against their garage and was pushing against me with his body and something hard in his pants was pressing against my chest. "I'll go back for Troo."

I stopped struggling and fell against him. Then he said in this pretty-sounding voice, "I'm sorry to be in such a hurry tonight, Sally. Usually I like to take my brides out to this spot in the country so we can spend a little more time together, and then I bring 'em back to the lagoon after we've gotten to know each other a little better." He pulled me through another yard with a barking black dog struggling hard against a chain. Bobby kicked at its head. The dog yelped and then went quiet. "You know where we're going?

I'll give you three guesses." My legs were shaking so bad that I couldn't walk, and finally Bobby gave up on dragging me and picked me up in his arms. "We're going to one of your favorite places."

I could feel his muscles through his shirt when he half ran past Fitzpatrick's Drugstore. Through the dim window light I could see Henry at the counter reading. I tried to call, "Henry . . . help." Bobby put his hand that smelled like car oil over my mouth and in a raspy voice in between breaths he said, "You like that little Homo Henry, don't you?" He sounded like I had done something to hurt his feelings. "You don't like Henry more than you like Bobby, do you?" He was staring through the window at the boy I would never get to marry.

I whispered, "No, Bobby. No. I don't like Henry more than you. I like you the very best of all." I didn't know why I said that because saying it made me cry.

Bobby said kindly, "Oh, now, now, don't do that. We're gonna have so much fun and then when we're done you can be with your daddy. And I'll bring pink carnations to your funeral just like I did for Junie and Sara." He stroked my cheek and rubbed his nose against mine the way Daddy used to, humming along with the siren I heard. Was it coming for me?

"I know what you're thinking, sweetheart, but don't get your hopes up. Bobby is too smart for those cops. Take my word for it. Nobody knows." He seemed to get extra strong then, like a second wind. We were almost to the lagoon. "Oh, look, there it is. Our honeymoon spot." He ran across the street with me flopping in his arms. I could hear the siren getting closer and I prayed please please please let Mary

Lane have taken that Kroger bag and found Mr. Dave. If she hadn't, when he was through with me, Bobby could go back and get the Kroger bag and nobody would be the wiser. And when Mary Lane tried to tell people what happened, they'd just shake their heads and think she was telling another one of her whoppers. And Troo . . . what had he done to my Troo?

Bobby giggled when he set me down so gently on the grass under the trees right off the zoo entrance. Not far from the red rowboats, but away from the streetlights. I could smell wet dirt and hear the lagoon water lapping up onto the muddy rocks, and not far off, music and a girl laughing. Bobby pulled his shirt off over his head and then began pulling at his leather belt, grunting when it gave him some trouble. When he looked down at the buckle to get it untangled, I heard Daddy's voice in my head . . . *Now, Sal, now. Fly like the wind.* I jumped up fast and scrambled over the fence and ran down the path that led to the zoo before he had time to grab me. Behind me, Bobby's feet rattled in the chain-link fence and he was singing, "Red light, green light, hope to see the ghost tonight." His laugh sounded high-pitched, like an air-raid siren.

I couldn't keep up that running. I was so tired and my chest was fiery hot so I had to slow down, and I knew when I did, Bobby would catch up to me. So I veered off the path toward the animal cages. He didn't know the zoo like I did because I heard him trip on the old sewer handle that stuck out of the asphalt in front of the bears' den and he screamed, "Fuck." But then right away I could hear his running footsteps and smell his stink when he said from the darkness close, real close, "Stop, or when I catch you, I will make you hurt like you never hurt in your life, you little bitch." His voice was deep and as harsh as anything I'd ever heard, and I knew in my heart that Bobby was the devil in the details. And that he'd been true to his word. Nobody knew. The siren had stopped.

But I didn't. I could hear and smell some of the animals stirring around in the dark. I ran past the lion cage and past my and Troo's favorite tree and jumped over the black iron fence in front of Sampson's enclosure. I knew they didn't put the animals away in their houses when it was this hot. He was there in the dark. Waiting for me. I hurried over the grass to the edge of the pit.

I could hear Bobby come up right behind me. When I turned to face him, he said, "Gotcha." When he leaped for me, the air came off his body like an airplane taking off, his arms the wings. I waited until the timing was right. And then, at the last second, I ducked and he flew over me, his chest shiny and sleek. It happened so slowly, like he was being held up against the sky by an invisible force. He smiled and reached out for me, and when he did, whatever was holding him up let go and he dropped into Sampson's pit with a beautiful, beautiful thud.

It was quiet for a while after that except for my breathing. Then rustling noises came from below and my King sang out in the voice of an angel . . . "Don't Get Around Much Anymore."

CHAPTER THIRTY-FIVE

They took us to the hospital that night. Troo had a bump on the side of her head the size of Iowa from when Bobby snuck up behind her and pulled her off the bars and made her unconscious. And her legs had scrapes on them from when he'd dragged her off behind those thorny bushes. I had some marks on my neck in the shape of Bobby's fingers and some cuts, but Dr. Sullivan said those would go away in time.

Mary Lane was the real hero of that night cuz she *had* taken the Kroger bag when she'd crawled through the shed window. Inside the bag was a pillowcase and Junie's medal and Sara's tennis shoe and bits of cut-off blond hair and some other things from some other girls that nobody knew about. Now the police had the proof that Bobby was the murderer and molester. I told her that I would make her as many peanut butter and marshmallow sandwiches as she would ever want to eat for the rest of her skinny life. She'd come along to the hospital just to be with us because she wanted to make sure we were okay. She even kicked Police Chief D'Amico in the leg when he tried to stop her. He ended up letting her ride over in his squad car, which wasn't as good as a fire engine, but it was close. In the emergency room when Dr. Sullivan was checking Troo and me over, he looked at Mary Lane, too, and said, "That child is severely undernourished."

When Mr. Lane came to take her home, Dr. Sullivan said something to him and Mr. Lane nodded back. But before she left, Mary Lane came to me and Troo (we were together on an emergency bed) and whispered, "Dr. Sullivan's breath smells like the lion cage." She inspected Troo's head and said, "Told you Bobby was a rotten egg. Maybe the next time you'll believe me when I tell ya something."

I thought I'd try real hard to do that . . . but I probably wouldn't. Lying was to Mary Lane what reading was to me. Just plain important. Maybe for both of us it was like what Mrs. Goldman had tried to tell me. A way to imagine away your life for a while so you could go to a place that was filled with *schnitzel.*

"Red light, green light tomorrow night?" Mary Lane said.

Troo and me said, "Of course."

Then the old nurse came down and took me and Troo up to Mother's room. Mostly I think Mr. Dave wanted us to go to the hospital so the O'Malley sisters could be with their mother because he wasn't very good yet at being a daddy. This does take some practice. So me and Troo laid down on either side of her bed, her arms around each of us. She was looking better than she had. Not quite so see-through.

Mother sighed one of her perfect sighs and said, "Well, I go away for a little while and sweet Jesus, Mary and Joseph, what have you O'Malley sisters gotten yourselves into?"

I told Mother all about Troo's plan to catch Bobby. She listened closely and every once in a while made a sharp gasp.

I wanted to say, "You know, Mother, the name game, maybe you are wrong about that. Because an Irish boy tried to murder and molest me and an English girl saved the day." But I didn't want her to feel bad so I didn't say that. But I thought it and I would remember it and would tell her when she was feeling better because that was extremely important information to have in life.

Then Troo piped in with, "After Mary Lane crawled out the window she found Rasmussen and showed him the Kroger bag, and that wasn't easy because it was so dark. And then she told him that Bobby had kidnapped Sally and how he'd pulled me off the monkey bars. And then the cops found me behind those bushes and woke me up with something that smelled real bad and I told them where to go and Rasmussen ran to his squad car and blared the siren and all the rest of them went to their regular cars with their baseball bats." She took a gulping breath. "He found Sally in front of Sampson's cage right where I told him she'd be."

Mother smiled at the sound of Sampson's name. She knew how I felt about him and why. It used to make her sort of mad, but that night she said, "Looks like the King was watching over you tonight, Baby."

I didn't tell her how I'd heard Daddy's voice telling me to fly like the wind. Thought I'd keep that between the two of us.

And then Nell came into the hospital room. And Eddie. And, of course, Mr. Dave. After Mother fell asleep and the old nurse told us to go, Mr. Dave took me and Troo back to our new house and ran some water for baths and put in some of that vanilla smelling Avon bubble bath. When Troo was in the tub singing "Ninety-nine Bottles of Beer on the Wall," Mr. Dave had me sit out on the back porch with him. We were next to each other on the top step. Our legs were touching. He smelled just like freshly squeezed orange juice. And that made me think of Mr. Gary and his orange tree that grew in his backyard in California.

I said, "Mary Lane told me that Father Jim and Mr. Gary are in love and ran away to California together to get married. Is that true?"

He didn't say anything for a minute. "Yeah . . . it is."

"Do you think that's okay?"

"Not sure. How 'bout you?"

I thought for a bit. "I think it's okay to be with somebody you love. Even if other people think it's not okay."

Mr. Dave musta gotten something in his eyes 'cause he took out his handkerchief and took some time to wipe 'em off. "You know, you were really brave today. But the next time you need somebody to believe you, come to me."

"But I wasn't brave," I said sadly. "I was scared to death."

"Brave doesn't mean you're not scared, Sally." He was stroking my braid. "Brave means you're scared and you do it anyway. Everybody gets scared."

"Do you?"

"I was scared for a long, long time," he said, squeezing my shoulder. "But I'm feeling a whole lot better now."

The crickets were going crazy, and next door Ethel was humming some low tune while she was doing the supper dishes. I hoped Mrs. Galecki thought it was okay about her boy being in love with Father Jim. I was pretty sure she would be. Mrs. Galecki loved her late-blooming Gary, and when you love somebody you're supposed to love them no matter what, right? Even if they are light in their loafers or what Ethel said—a royal queen.

"What's gonna happen to Bobby?" I asked.

Mr. Dave stared up to the sky for a bit and then said softly, "He's dead, Sal. We think the fall broke Bobby's neck." He looked down at me with our green eyes. "Sampson took Bobby up to the top of the cage and wouldn't let him go, like he was holding on to him for us. Mr. Lane had to shoot him with a sleeping dart so the ambulance drivers could get Bobby's body out of there."

Sampson. You are magnificent!

I didn't feel bad for Bobby at all. He got just what he had comin' to him. Maybe I felt a little bad for him because that would be the charitable thing to do, but then I remembered how he growled at me and how he murdered and molested Junie and Sara and what he'd done to Troo's head and I thought, aw, the heck with being charitable.

We sat there some more and didn't talk. Then Mr. Dave gently put his arm around me and pulled me closer to him. That was the first time he'd ever done that and it hardly felt weird at all.

Later, after I'd had my bath, Troo and me were spooned under the sheets that smelled sun sweet in our new bed with a wooden headboard and a white chenille spread. And across the room there was something I'd always wanted, and I wondered how Mr. Dave knew to get it for me. It was an aquarium that had a small chest of gold half buried in some shockingly pink gravel and loads of minnow-looking fish and a few called angelfish, which were my favorite. It was a lot like Dottie's aquarium, so Mr. Dave musta gone up to the Five and Dime.

I was rubbing Troo's back and staring at the tank and thinking about Dottie and how sad she must be without her mother and father. And how sad they were without her and why, just why did people do some of the things they did?

"This has really been a summer to remember, right, Sal?"

"Right, Troo."

"You know, Rasmussen's not even close to being as good as Daddy."

"I know."

"Not even close."

"Not even close."

Next door, Ethel had moved out to the screened-in porch with Ray Buck. They were listening to some of that jazzy music and every once in a while the two of them laughed and the sound of ice knocked around in their tall metal glasses.

Troo yawned and said, "Night, Sal."

"Night, Troo."

One of these summer nights, my sister had stopped sucking her fingers, but she still had her baby doll clutched in her hand. As Troo's sleeping breath filled the room, Annie and I watched as the fish swam back and forth through that glimmery aquarium water and over that little golden chest, not knowing at all what was inside. I dreamt that I discovered buried treasure that night.

CHAPTER THIRTY-SIX

After the newspapermen came and took our pictures and Dr. Sullivan got rid of Mary Lane's tapeworm, which it turned out was why she was so skinny (she wanted to tell us every icky detail until Troo and me couldn't stand it another minute), the rest of the summer days unwound just the way they had before we'd started locking our doors.

The Vliet Street kids went back to playing red light, green light, even Fast Susie Fazio, who'd decided she wasn't too old after all and told us a fantastic story on the O'Haras' steps about Barb the counselor and her brother Johnny, who she'd caught up in the attic playing "hide the salami."

We walked over to the lagoon a couple of times so Troo could hide under the weeping willow tree and I could do a little fishing. Troo wasn't smoking anymore. Mother had smelled it on her and told her if she ever caught her again she'd be smoking on another part of her body. Her *derriere*. While I fished, not far from the red rowboats, which the park said they weren't gonna have anymore after that summer because they were just too rotted, I thought of Sara and Junie. Especially Junie and how if she was still alive she'd be me and Troo's cousin and we didn't have any of those and now we never would.

Troo was still not adjusting so great to Mr. Dave even though they both loved that little dog Lizzie, which I found out had been named after me, Sally Elizabeth O'Malley. But you know what Mr. Dave did, even though Troo was giving him such a hard time? He went out to peeing Jerry Amberson's house and got Butchy back for her. And now Butchy had the hots for Lizzy.

Before I knew it, August was coming to a close. Before long Sister Imelda would be standing in front of our classroom with that ruler in her hand. So when I wasn't messin' around with Troo or Mary Lane or sittin' out in the backyard with Mother reading to her out of my *Secret Garden* book (which I would highly recommend to anyone) or helping Mr. Dave pull weeds and water, I finished off my essay.

"How I Spent My Charitable Summer"
by Sally Elizabeth O'Malley (Part 2)

There were a lot of charitable things going on this summer on Vliet Street. Mr. Dave took Troo and me to the state fair and we had the best time. The freak show was excellent this year with a woman who was 106 years old and a man that had no legs but could walk on his hands. Troo spent a lot of the night talking to the fat lady, who she learned was a really nice woman named Vera from Moline, Illinois, who said she was just born fat so she made being fat her job. Wasn't that the best occupation? Troo asked me later over cotton candy. So I think Troo has given up on being a carhop up at The Milky Way or a ventriloquist or Sal Mineo and now wants to be a fat lady when she grows up. Mr. Dave won both of us huge matching teddy bears by knocking over milk bottles. And we went on the roller coaster and the Whip and the Tilt-A-Whirl and my favorite, the horses on the merry-go-round. Mr. Dave bought Troo and me our own box of cream puffs that they made at the state fair and only the state fair and he bought another box for Ethel and Mrs. Galecki. And, of course, we got a cream puff for Mother, who did not end up dying after all. Which was very charitable of her. And me. (Because I really, really wanted to eat Mother's cream puff on the way home from the fair.)

Nell and Eddie are going to get married after she graduates from Yvonne's School of Beauty, and they have a surprise package being delivered who they are going to call Elvis if it's a boy and Peggy Sue if it's a girl.

I think Mother and Mr. Dave are also going to get married after they have a talk with the Pope, but they are not planning on having a baby. Mother has been home from the hospital for two weeks, resting in the special room Mr. Dave set up in our house for her. It is downstairs because she is still weak and has to rest and maybe she might never walk again, Dr. Sullivan says, because her legs got too shrunk up, but I don't believe him because he does not know how ornery Mother can be. Her room overlooks the yard that has lots of sun and flowers, especially red

Rejoice in Hope
Romans 12:12

A Mug n Muffin Tea Time
Saturday, April 2, 2022 at 10:30 am
$5 per person
Bonita Valley Baptist Church
4701 Sweetwater road
RSVP to Nina 714.251.4211

geraniums that Mr. Dave knew all along were Mother's favorite. Mr. Kenfield came over to visit Mother and brought over a paper sack full of candy bars and said we had to give one to Mother every day to fatten her back up since they had gone to high school together. They also had a long talk and I think it was about Dottie.

And one more thing that I did that was charitable this summer was I wrote a letter to Hall, who murdered Fritz Jerbak's father with a beer bottle.

DEAR HALL,

    SORRY TO HEAR THAT YOU ARE IN THE SLAMMER. COULD YOU PLEASE WRITE BACK AND TELL ME WHAT YOUR WHOLE NAME IS? TROO SAYS IT'S HALLITOSIS AND BET ME A CAT'S-EYE.

    THANK YOU,

    SALLY O'MALLEY

Mrs. Kambowski found out that Troo cheated on the Bookworm ladder but gave her the movie passes to the Uptown Theater anyway and said, *"C'est la vie."* I never did understand why. We snuck Mary Lane in through the Emergency Door. *The Tingler* was the scariest movie I'd ever seen, and in that part when the doctor, who was played by the very scary Vincent Price, told us that the Tingler had escaped in the movie theater, my seat started buzzing and I screamed so loud. Mary Lane didn't scream at all because she isn't a screaming kind of person. Troo didn't scream either, but she pinched my arm so hard it left a mark that I think might be permanent.

And, of course, we went to the zoo and visited Sampson and it was funny that I didn't hear him singing "Don't Get Around Much Anymore." Maybe he was just feeling better about everything because the zoo had gotten him a girlfriend, whose name was Lola, and it looked like they were getting married because they had something in common. They spent a lot of time picking things off each other.

Troo and me even started going back to the playground. Barb was the boss now and she mentioned Bobby a couple of times in conversation until Troo said to her in her lava mad voice, "Let sleeping dogs die." Barb never brought Bobby up again.

CHAPTER THIRTY-SEVEN

Soon the leaves would be turning and before we knew it we'd be drinking warm Ovaltine instead of cold. Ethel had taken us that morning to get new pairs of loafers up at Shuster's and then over to Kenfield's to the going-back-to-school aisle to get pencils and erasers and crayons. And then the three of us took some Coca-Cola over to Granny, who stuck shiny gold pennies into the crackling brown shoes and said, "A penny saved is a penny earned."

After lunch, Troo and me and Barb were sitting on a playground bench, enjoying the last day of vacation. Barb asked, "You girls ready for the block party tonight?"

Troo's tongue tip was sticking between her lips but she still said, "Yup." She tied her knot off down on the bottom of her lanyard and held it up to inspect it. It was white and gold. We were both making new lanyards for Mother so she could attach a whistle to it and call us whenever she needed us to bring her anything, since she couldn't walk too good with her shrunken-up legs.

"So . . . who you think's gonna be Queen of the Play-ground?" Barb asked, in a teasing way.

"Mr. Gary?" Troo said.

Barb laughed and laughed at that until Troo said, "Sally

is going to be Queen this year." Then she flashed Barb one of her danger looks and said, "She better be anyway. Or there will be hell to pay."

Both ends of Vliet Street were closed off with yellow blockades. And folding tables were stacked with food up and down the block. Mr. Gary had called Ethel all the way from California and told her to hire Johnny Fazio's band the Do Wops for the block party. Mr. Gary could afford to do that because, like Ethel said, "He may be light in his loafers, gals, but he ain't so light in his wallet." Then she leaned down to me and whispered, "Tol' ya that boy had some fanciful ideas."

So that night there were Christmas lights hanging from everybody's front porches and all of us were glad because now we could go back to the way we were before there was a murderer and molester, which was a big relief. Like when the war was over, Mr. Dave said. The night was bittersweet, he said.

The band had a little stage over on the baseball diamond and they were playing some good rock 'n' roll by Chuck Berry called "Johnny Be Good," which made all the girls swoon at Johnny Fazio. Mother came to watch for a while but she couldn't dance. Mr. Dave was taking good care of her, though. He'd bought her a nice pair of pink open-toed shoes she liked so much from Jim the brownnose salesman, who was the top dog of Shuster's Shoes now that Hall was in jail. And around Mother's finger was that ring I'd found down in the hidey-hole. That cookie wrapper ring. Mr. Dave had given it to Mother when they were engaged and she had kept it all those years.

I sat next to her on one of the wooden benches when

Mr. Dave went to get her a plate of food. "Are you happy now?" I asked her.

I didn't think she heard me at first so I was going to ask again but then she said, "Happy? Well, for a while there I didn't think I was going to get to see you and Troo grow up and . . ." She didn't give me one of those sad looks like she used to, but there was some sadness in her voice. "You've forgiven me, haven't you? Let bygones be bygones?"

"Yes," I said, even though it wasn't the complete truth. I had forgiven her. Mr. Dave, too. But I had one last thing to do before I could let bygones be bygones.

"That reminds me. I got a little early birthday present for you." Mother dug around in her skirt pocket and came out with Daddy's Timex. "He'd want you to have it."

She dropped it into the palm of my hand. It looked smaller than it used to.

"Go on, put it on," she said. "I had it sized for you. It'll grow with you."

I slid the stretchy silver band over my wrist and put it up to my ear and remembered how the sound of it had always made me feel safe when I'd rest my cheek against Daddy's hand.

Then Mr. Dave came back with plates full of food for both of us. He sat down on the other side of me and said, "Gosh, I'll be darned. I seem to have forgotten my watch. Anybody know what time it is?"

I held up my hand so he could see. Takes a licking and keeps on ticking, I thought.

And then we settled in and ate and watched everybody dancing their heads off. You should have seen Ethel and Ray Buck goin' at it. They were really something! Better even than Justine and Tony on *American Bandstand*, in my opinion. Ethel brought Mrs. Galecki in her wheelchair for a little while, even though everybody was talking behind their hands about how Mr. Gary had run off with Father Jim and how they were gonna go to hell, but I could tell that didn't bother Mrs. Galecki at all, or maybe it was the new medicine that made her smile so much.

That night Troo was well on her way for her new fat lady job, me too, that's how much food we ate. Nana Fazio's spaghetti and meatballs and Mrs. O'Hara's (who was about to become Mrs. Officer Riordan) corned beef and Mrs. Latour's slumgoodie. Nell had even made Mother's special tuna noodle casserole with the potato chips on top. (It was still kinda black, but a lot less black than the last time she'd made it.) Of course, Ethel brought her Mississippi blond brownies. And Mrs. Goldman brought us some beautiful tomatoes from her garden in a straw basket. Mrs. Kenfield came alone and empty-handed.

While everybody was dancing the Stroll, I was having some growing pains and felt a need to stretch my legs. It was dark by then and the crickets had started up and, I knew, so had the *creak creak creak* of the swing. I missed hearing it even though it had always made me feel lonely. I could hear Troo's "Chopsticks" laugh and Nana Fazio yelling something in Italian and everybody clapping along with the music as I stood in front of the Kenfields'. But when I looked up to the porch and saw him there, the bulk of him, I wondered what the devil had come over me. I turned to go back to the party, but Mr. Kenfield called out of the dark, "Come here, Sally."

I climbed the steps and just for a second I thought I'd take off, but then he patted the other side of the swing and so I sorta had to do it because I didn't want to be rude. But my heart, it started knocking against my ribs like it'd been locked out in a storm. I was afraid of Mr. Kenfield. And I could not ever remember him talking to me before. He probably was going to have a big talk with me about how me and Troo were always stealing stuff from his store or maybe he would even call Mr. Dave down from the party and tell him that he thought I should be sent to Juvenile Hall.

I sat down next to him and looked at his hands. His nails were bitten down to the half moons. "How come you aren't at the block party, Mr. Kenfield?"

He threw his cigarette into the bushes. "Don't feel much like celebrating."

"Is it because of Dottie?"

In the glow of his porch light I could see his face get real mad and it looked like he was about to yell something, but then he quieted down.

"You know," I said, resting my hand on top of his since it looked so forgotten about and coulda used a little Jergens lotion. "Like my mother always says, 'It's best to forgive and forget. Let bygones be bygones.'"

He said gruffly, "You're your mother's daughter, all right. The apple didn't fall far from that tree."

Mr. Kenfield reached deep down into his trouser's pocket and took something out. It was a picture of Dottie. You could tell he looked at it a lot because it was sort of worn down and grayish, like him. Dottie was sitting on this very same swing, smiling so big with her hands behind her head.

"You know who that is?" He pointed at the photograph.

I looked up into his face. There was a shadow across his eyes. "Yes."

"You know what she did?"

"Yes." She'd done the same thing Mother had. Fallen in love and had a baby with someone she wasn't supposed to.

"It's a mortal sin. Some things you can't forgive and forget."

"You're wrong about that, Mr. Kenfield. You should let Dottie and her little baby come home because I know how much you miss them. I don't think God would mind that at all."

He put his hands up to his face then so I wouldn't see, but I recognized that sound. Mrs. Goldman had been wrong. It hadn't been Mrs. Kenfield, crying every night in Dottie's room. It was her daddy. Who did not have a stiff upper lip after all.

I got up and left then. Because that sound, that weeping from the heart, I knew that sound. And I also knew there was nothing I could say that would make him feel better. Nothing else hurts worse in the world as much as tears for the missing.

"Test . . . test . . . one . . . two . . . three," Barb said up on the stage in front of the microphone. "Could I have your attention, please? It's the time you've all been waiting for. Test one . . . two . . . three." The microphone made a high screechy sound. Barb laughed when we put our hands over our ears. She was standing on the stage next to Johnny Fazio and you could see plain as the nose on your face that Johnny Fazio had the hots for her.

Barb announced, "It's time now to reveal the name of the girl who is this year's Queen of the Playground." She turned toward Johnny and said very seriously, "May I have a drum roll." She looked back at the crowd, holding the gorgeous rhinestone crown up to the stage lights. It was so beautiful that no words could describe it.

Troo picked up my hand and squeezed it. I knew it was me. Had to be. But just as Barb said, "The Queen of the Playground this year is . . . ," and looked over at me . . . I looked over at Wendy Latour. She was holding Artie's hand and smiling so purely. She was dressed in a pink party dress with lace on the neck and had some rouge on her cheeks and something shiny on her lips.

And for the second time that night, I didn't understand what came over me, but I jumped right on that stage and took the microphone out of Barb's hand and said into it, "The Queen of the Playground this year is . . . Wendy Latour."

When I thought later about why I did that, I figured it was because of that plastic Cracker Jack ring Wendy always wore on her wedding finger. She needed to be Queen more than I did. I knew I would go on in life and I would get married and have kids, maybe even marry a pharmacist someday. But for Wendy . . . well, at least she would always have that rhinestone crown.

When Artie brought her up to the stage to be crowned, Wendy gave me one of her *huge* hugs and then started throwing those Dinah Shore kisses at everyone. Just like a Queen should. Barb announced Teddy Mahlberg as the King and Wendy gave him a royal hug as well, which he took pretty well. Then everybody started going nuts with their hooting and hollering, but that was also because they were, a lot of them anyway, three sheets to the wind, and I had noticed that this generally improves people's moods.

All of us got a partner when Johnny Fazio sang the last song of the night called "That's Amore," which Nana Fazio told me was Italian for love and was certainly the right song to sing because there sure was a lot of love dancing going on. Including me and Henry Fitzpatrick, who gave me my first on the lips smooch after we got done with the box-step waltz. His lips tasted like black licorice, which I never liked, but the rest of it wasn't half bad.

Seeing us all there like that, I thought of how much my lush daddy would've loved the party. I wished he was there. If he was, I knew he woulda given me two thumbs up. And when I tried to say, "I'm sorry for saying what I said . . . ," he would just hug me close with his tan hairy arms and tell me he knew I hadn't meant those awful things I said on the day of the crash. And how proud he was of me for doing what he had asked me to do. Keep my promises. Tend my garden.

After the party was all over, the Vliet Street kids called to each other, "See ya tomorrow at school." I walked home by myself, gazing up at the great beyond, thinking about how love never really dies. It's always out there, leaving a twinkling trail to another place where you can go and rest when you need to forget that things really do happen when you least expect them. And sometimes, those things can change your life forever. But what Daddy hadn't gotten around to telling me, and what I figured out that night all by myself, was that no matter what horrible things happen . . . you have to go on with your life with all the stick-to-itiveness that you can muster up.

So with the fireflies flashing and the chocolate chip cookies smelling and the Moriaritys' dog barking two streets over,
I sat down on the O'Haras' front steps and looked up and said
in my most certain voice, "To the clear blue of the western
sky, it's me, Sal your gal, telling my Sky King, my magnificent Sky King . . . roger, wilco and out."

Photo by Richard W. Bublitz

Lesley Kagen is a writer, actress, voice-over talent, and restaurateur. The owner of Restaurant Hama, one of Milwaukee's top restaurants, Ms. Kagen lives with her husband and two children in Mequon, Wisconsin. Visit her Web site at www.lesleykagen.com.

WHISTLING IN THE DARK

lesley kagen

This Conversation Guide is intended to enrich the
individual reading experience, as well as encourage us
to explore these topics together—because books,
and life, are meant for sharing.

A CONVERSATION WITH LESLEY KAGEN

Q. Whistling in the Dark *is set in Milwaukee. Did you grow up there?*

A. Yup. I grew up on the west side in a neighborhood that had the same sort of feel Vliet Street does. Irish and German Catholic families jammed into duplexes. A cadre of kids playing kick the can or red light, green light when the streetlights came on. It was a wonderful setting for a childhood. As an adult, I've lived in New York, Los Angeles and Chicago, but I brought my children back to Milwaukee to raise them. I think it might've been an attempt on my part to recapture the flavors of my childhood. Especially that Bavarian cream–filled coffee cake.

Q. The book is set in the summer of 1959. I'm wondering about authenticity. May I ask how old you are?

A. I was ten in 1959. That makes me thirty-nine.

Q. Actually, that makes you fifty-seven.

A. Oh.

Q. Where did you get the idea for the book?

A. I think we all reach a point in our lives when our childhood memories become old friends we would just love to hang out with again. I don't think for a minute that I am the only woman on the planet who has become overwhelmed with the pace of life nowadays. I began to yearn for summers on the stoop. Cherry Popsicles. Secret hiding places. My sister snoring softly beside me. I needed to experience those feelings again.

Q. How much of this story is based on real-life experience?

A. Quite a bit. My father was killed in a car accident when I was four. Left penniless, my mother quickly remarried to a man who, while not a drunken sot, did share other personality traits with Hall. My mother almost died of a staph infection when I was ten, leaving us girls essentially on our own while she recovered in the hospital. I have two sisters. Sally is based on my younger sister, Ellie. Nell is modeled after my older sister, Ronney. And Troo and I have quite a bit in common.

Q. I was quite taken by the dichotomy of the time period. There was such innocence and yet . . .

A. Exactly. While talking to other women my age about their memories, so many of them remembered jumping double Dutch and Fabian and cloud watching and all those sorts of dreamy good times. But inevitably they'd pause, and shyly mention being flashed by their next-door neighbor. Or an older brother's nighttime visitations. Or an uncle who may have touched them in a certain way. So many of those traumas were swept under the fifties carpet. Children, especially girl children, have more value now. Thank God.

Q. *My heart went out to the girls' mother. She was a victim of the times as well.*

A. I don't know if that has changed all that much. I know many women still feel trapped in loveless marriages. They're simply too afraid to leave, unsure if they can provide for their children, for themselves.

Q. *Who is your favorite character in the novel?*

A. That's like asking who my favorite child is.

Q. *Okay, how about your least favorite character in the novel.*

A. That's like asking who my least favorite child is.

Q. *Give it a shot.*

A. I am quite fond of Sally. Her unflagging sweetness. Her deep-seated sense of responsibility. And her desperate need to protect Troo. I find these winning qualities. On the flip side, I like Hall the least. Of course, Bobby is de le, but Hall abandoned two small girls who needed tender loving care.

CONVERSATION GUIDE

Q. Ethel is a wonderful character. Why did you introduce a Southern Baptist woman into fifties Milwaukee?

A. Because she deserved to be there and wasn't. Not unlike today, Milwaukee in the fifties was a very segregated city. The only time I would see someone of color was on our way to the beach, when we drove through the Core. Until the summer I was thirteen, and my stepfather brought home an eighteen-year-old kid to mow the lawn. I was stunned. The enamel blackness of his skin, his bouncy natty hair. Teddy's mere presence in our backyard stirred me in a truly elemental way. That electric smile of his, the one that promised a girl could get into a little trouble if she wanted to? My oh my. What were you saying?

Q. Ethel?

A. Oh, yeah. I love Ethel. She has that no-nonsense, I'm gonna run you ragged, but only because I love you to death Southern sensibility about her. I adore that. Always have. I think it all goes back to my utter idolization of Gregory Peck as Atticus Finch in *To Kill a Mockingbird*. When your father dies when you are young, a girl looks for a replacement. He was mine.

Q. This is your first novel. What took you so long?

A. My award-winning fourth-grade poem, "I Am the Sun," is hanging in my daughter's room. I followed up that early success by writing a script for 77 *Sunset Strip* when I was eleven. I am still waiting for my royalties. I studied writing in college and wrote ad copy for years. After my daughter left for college, and my teenage son made it clear that he would rather stick a knife in his kidney than spend any more time with me than it took for the cheese to brown on his pizza, I made a dash for my computer. Mostly I played Solitaire for a month because the thought of setting forth down the novel road just about scared the bejesus out of me.

Q. In what way?

A. It's a little like that old Rooney-Garland line, "Let's put on a show!" It sounds fun, we've got a couple actors here, but wait just a cotton pickin' minute . . . how the heck do you go about something like that? I had no idea of the craft involved in writing a novel.

Q. How did you get around that?

A. I studied the works of other writers I admire to see how they constructed their stories. I analyzed movies. I also had the help of good early readers like my husband, Pete, who edited my everyday musings and said, "This is a nice story, dear. I like the characters. But when are they actually going to *do* something? They are spending quite a lot of time just, well, *feeling*." It was tough for me to learn how to integrate plot and character, humor and tragedy. To find that balance.

Q. Humor plays an important part in this story, which is primarily about loss. Why?

A. All of our lives are tough. We lose people, we lose love, we lose jobs, we lose our health. Humor is the only thing I know besides spirituality that helps transcend pain.

Q. Why did you choose to write the story from a ten-year-old's perspective?

A. I didn't really choose too much of anything. It's a funny thing, writing. For me it starts with the whispery voice of my main character, nudging me awake at night. Asking me to listen to a story.

Q. I know many authors outline their books before setting down to write. How about you?

A. (Laughing uncontrollably.) I'm lucky to get my grocery list straight. I just get up in the morning, drink four cups of tea, light a cigarette (I know, I know), and hope for the best. As I get to know the characters better, I'm able to apply an actual thought process. But when I start out, writing is completely about the characters.

Q. How did you feel when you completed the book?

A. Unbearably sad. I love those two little girls. I need

two fluffy dogs named Sally and Troo. That's how much I want to keep them close. To love them up.

Q. How did you feel when you found out that your story would be published?

A. It took me about a year to finish *Whistling in the Dark*. Three hundred and sixty-five morning mantras of . . . Lesley, you are a complete and utter moron. Shouldn't you be spending the morning doing something a bit more productive? Don't you have socks to sort? Writing is a solitary activity. There is no one in the next cubicle over, ready to tell you, good job! And no matter how many times my friends and family mentioned that they absolutely loved what I was coming up with, and how sure they were that I'd eventually get published . . . well, being the sunny, glass-half-fuller person that I am . . . let's just say I'm pretty relieved that someone other than my cousin Joyce in Sheboygan thinks I write okay.

Q. What's next?

A. I can't wait to meet readers via my Web site and bookstore appearances. I'm anxious to hear their impressions, their thoughts, their memories. I'm also quite busy running my sushi restaurant, getting my son, Riley, off to college in the fall, and my daughter, Casey, is getting married next summer. I'm still doing commercial voice-overs. And, of course, I'm pecking away on my next novel.

QUESTIONS
FOR DISCUSSION

1. Did the book transport you back to the fifties? Share some of your best or worst memories of that time. Or of your own childhood in the sixties, seventies or beyond.

2. Young women are treated differently now than they were back then. They're encouraged to have careers. To take care of themselves financially. To stand on their own two feet. Back in the fifties, a girl's primary goal was to find a man to take care of her. How do you think these changing mores have affected women? Are these changes all positive? If not, what are the negatives?

3. Sally and Troo forge a bond based on loss and guilt. Do you have any relationships/friendships like this?

4. Sally and Troo experienced a deep sense of abandonment after the death of their daddy. They manifested that sense of loss differently. How do you think the loss of a parent at any early stage of a child's life affects their emotional growth?

5. After her husband's death, Mother decided the only way to put food on the table was to marry Hall, a man she had little or no feelings for. What would you do if you found yourself in her position?

6. Sally is the product of an adulterous affair. Did you feel differently about her when this was revealed?

7. Mother hid her affair with Dave Rasmussen from her husband and children. Some women, after committing such an indiscretion, would confess and beg for forgiveness. What would you do?

8. Would you have a relationship with your sibling if they weren't your family?

9. The story touches upon teenage pregnancy when Sally discovers that her next-door neighbor, Dottie Kenfield, was sent away to have her baby. Nowadays young girls are allowed to continue high school and, in fact, many schools provide child care. Do you think this glamorizes teen pregnancy? Why do you think times have changed in regard to this once social taboo? What would you do if your teenage daughter became pregnant?

10. Troo appears to take Sally's "mothering" in stride. Why do you think that is?

11. Fear is a main theme of the book. Fear of our feelings. Fear of what other people think. Fear of the unknown. What are you afraid of?

12. When Sally finally accepts that Rasmussen is her birth father, she expresses a sense of relief that "she finally looks like someone." Yet, she must now come to terms again with the loss of her daddy. Much of life is a two-edged sword. Can you recall ever feeling this way?

13. Mr. Gary and Father Jim were gay. Did you find their relationship touching in any way?

14. Sally's devotion to Sampson was clearly based on the memories she had of her daddy. Did you find this disturbing in any way?

15. At the end of the book, Sally appears to have come to terms with her daddy's death. Have you ever lost someone very dear to you? How did you handle it?